Husband Wanted

Jae Henderson

Husband Wanted

Copyright © 2016 by Jean Henderson

The reproduction, transmission, or utilization of this work in whole or in part in any form by electronic, mechanical, or other means, now known or hereafter invented, including xerography, photocopying, and recording, or in any information storage or retrieval system is forbidden without written permission, excepting brief quotes used in reviews.

Printed in the United States

Put It In Writing
274 North Parkway
Memphis, TN 38105

This is a work of fiction. Any references or similarities to actual events, real people, living or dead, or to real locales are intended to give the story a sense of reality. Any similarity in names, characters, places, and incidents is entirely coincidental.

ISBN: 978-0-9969168-1-3

Printed in the United States.

Dedication

To every woman praying for a husband.

Acknowledgements

Thank you to the following:
Garbo Hearne
Esther Crain-Holden
Priscilla Johnson
Latrivia Welch
Jessica Wright Tilles
Kandace Tuggle
The Women of Zeta Phi Beta Sorority, Inc.
My Amazing Family & Friends
Readers, Book Clubs & Literary Professionals
Who Have Supported Me

Chapter One

The Purdue Girls

"I can't believe she did this!" Leslie screamed. "After all I did for her; she pulls this load of crap. How dare she put stipulations on how we can receive our inheritance! *And*, she's basing the conditions on whether or not we get married! Of all the manipulative things! She better be glad she waited until she was dead to do this because I would...*Ugh*!"

Sheila laughed. "Girl, shut up. You wouldn't do anything, but run your mouth like you're doing now. You could never stand up to Grandma Grace. I don't see why you're so upset. This is just like her. She had always tried to use her money to control us, and she always voiced her displeasure that none of us had a husband."

Leslie smirked. Her older cousin always did know how to get under her skin. She didn't ask for her opinion. "Yeah, you're right. She wasn't exactly happy that her only great-grandchild is illegitimate. How is the little bastard?" Leslie quipped, as she poured herself a glass of Cognac from the crystal vessel on the bar in their grandmother's study.

Sheila grimaced. So, her cousin wanted to throw jabs. It bothered her when anyone referred to her son, Xavier, as illegitimate, as if her baby was inferior to other children because she wasn't married to his father. Her son was the light of her life. He was handsome, smarter than most of the four-year-olds at his school, and was full of joy. He was her joy. The frown on her face quickly turned into a smile while thinking about him, but she wasn't going to let her little cousin get away with that remark.

Sheila stood up and got in Leslie's face. "Grandma Grace loved Xavier and he loved her. He cried for days when she died. At least I gave her something other than a headache. All you ever did was worry her with all your wild ways. Do you think she didn't know about all your drinking, drugging, and partying? She probably wants you to get a husband to slow your fast tail down. You need to repent of your sinful ways before it's too late. You know Jesus is coming back. No man knows the day or the hour, but whenever it is, you'll probably be somewhere with your legs in the air!"

Leslie grew quite uncomfortable. Sheila was invading her personal space. She was the smallest of the three, but she would not back down. Not this time. "Get outta my face!" Leslie screamed. "At least I am smart enough to use birth control when I get mine." She thought her older cousin was overly religious and boring. She was almost sure DaQuan was probably the only man Sheila had slept with in her thirty-three years on earth. Since she found Jesus, she always tried to act as if she were better than everybody else.

"You have to. If you get pregnant, you wouldn't have any idea who the father is," Sheila snapped.

Regina was lazily snacking and relaxing on the chaise lounge, pondering their present predicament. She was counting on that money to open her own clothing boutique and now she would have to put that on hold. Their screaming was derailing her thoughts and she had witnessed enough of their shouting matches to know things were going to get ugly if she didn't intervene. The last thing she wanted to do was spend her evening breaking up a fight. Grandma Grace had always been the peacekeeper and the disciplinarian in the house, but, unfortunately, she was no longer there. "Stop it, you two. Your bickering over open and closed legs won't change the fact that there is a lucrative fortune that each of us may never see if we don't get married to someone, we actually love, within nine months! That's fifteen million for each of us just for saying, 'I do.'"

Leslie wasn't done. "Why does it matter if we're in love? She's dead. It's not like she'll be there to see how miserable we are if we're not in love," she wailed before plopping down on an antique velvet couch. She'd loved that couch since she was a child. Something about the texture of the fabric beckoned her to touch it. She ran her hand over the smooth velvet and watched the hue of it change from dark to light.

"It's to make sure that we don't marry someone just to get the money," Regina clarified. "And, considering that if we stay married and together in the same home for at least five years we get more money; she probably wants to make sure that it's not a miserable five years. You know Grandma Grace always wanted us to find what she had with Big Daddy."

"That's true, but they don't make men like Big Daddy anymore. All men want to do, these days, is take off your panties, and if you're lucky, he's got something good for you after he does it," said Leslie. "I know Grandma Grace loved us and wanted us to have suitable mates, but she can't force it on us. She is *so* wrong for doing this to us, especially me. I lived here with her and took care of her until her dying day. I think I deserve something just for putting up with her royal highness. 'Leslie, will you get me a glass of tea? Leslie will you help me with my bath? Leslie, will you dim the lights; it's too bright in here. Leslie, fix me a sandwich.' And then, when I brought it, 'Oh, never mind. You took so long I'm not hungry anymore,'" she said, imitating their grandmother. "Do you know what she looked like naked? I do, and it wasn't a pretty sight. Gravity was pulling on her breasts. They hung so low they almost reached her vagina and her vagina looked like—"

"Enough! I'm eating," Regina said, popping a cheese ball into her mouth. Some of the crumbs got on her new cashmere sweater. She brushed them off onto the couch and a few landed on the plush carpet. She didn't care. The maid could clean it up later. "That was Grandma Grace's way of making sure you earned your keep. It's not like you bought groceries, paid rent, or one bill while you were here. Quit your griping. Freeloader."

Sheila snickered.

Leslie shot her sister an angry look. "Oh no, you didn't. I seem to remember you having to move back home because Antonio was beating your behind."

"That only happened once," Reginaa snapped. "We were having problems, and I moved out because I thought we needed a break. Why are you bringing up old stuff? We've moved past that."

"You needed a break from his fist. Tell that lie to someone who believes you. I don't see how you could stay with a man who put his hands on you. If a man ever touched me he'd be six feet under," said Leslie.

Regina held her tongue, but she wanted to scream, *Men touch you all the time, whore!* Her sister didn't understand what it was like to love a man as much as you loved breathing. Antonio wasn't perfect, but he was a good man at heart. They would be fine. Right now, he was feeling stressed. He was fired from his job and with no income the finance company repossessed his prized Corvette, but things were looking up. Antonio had an interview that day. She hoped he would get that job so they could get back to the way things used to be. Now, she had no worries. She knew as soon as she told him about her grandma's will, he would pop the question. The question she had been waiting to hear for the seven years they had been together. She would finally become Mrs. Antonio Dockers, and their relationship and money problems would be over. Two solutions in one. Sheila's voice interrupted her thoughts.

"But seriously, where are we supposed to find quality husbands in nine months? None of us have a man and it's not like we can just take an ad out in the paper or something."

"Excuse me, I have a man," Regina interjected.

"Correction, none of us have a *good* man that's worth marrying," said Leslie.

Now it was Regina's turn to shoot Leslie a dirty look. At least she had a man. Her sister seemed to be satisfied with screwing anything that moved, and her cousin thought her coochie was made for collecting cobwebs, while she waited on Jesus to send her a husband. Actually, Jesus would probably return before she got laid again. She was so self-righteous and uppity; no man in his right mind would want to deal with her. No wonder her baby daddy didn't want her. Regina had had enough.

"You know what? I'm leaving. This conversation doesn't pertain to me. You two heifers are the ones who have to find someone to marry your tired behinds. I have someone who can and will. So, I'll leave you two lonely birds to figure it out. I'm going home to cook dinner. That's what those of us who have someone to go home to do, you know."

"Stop being so sensitive," Leslie advised Regina.

"You stop hating on my man. I don't understand why you two dislike him so much, but the good thing is I no longer care." Those were her parting words before she, along with her bag of cheese puffs, exited the study.

"She's right, you know," Sheila added. "We are the ones with no prospects."

"Speak for yourself. I have several. I just have to decide which one is worthy of putting a ring on this hand. I think I'll start my elimination process tonight. Which one should I call?" Regina said, scrolling through her iPhone with a well-manicured finger. "Why don't you go home and pray about it? Maybe some fine missionary will ring your doorbell and change your life."

Sheila didn't appreciate her cousin making fun of her religion. God had been good to her. "Shut up. What Grandma Grace is doing isn't even biblical. The Bible says *'he that findeth a wife findeth a good thing'*. We're not supposed to be out scouring the earth for a man. She's messing up the natural order of things. Men are the hunters, and we are the prey. This is ridiculous!" Sheila walked over to the bar and poured herself a glass of Cognac. She wasn't really a drinker, but at times like this, she needed something to calm her nerves. She had never had Cognac before. *How am I supposed to find a husband?* she thought. *I haven't had a date in three years.* She took a swig of her drink and spat it out. To her, it was as bad as her grandmother's plan to make them find a husband.

Chapter Two

Leslie

Leslie was glad Regina and Sheila didn't stay long. These days, she didn't particularly enjoy their company. She felt like they were always judging her. Who decided everyone needed to work, and there was something wrong with having a good time? So what if that good time included alcohol, drugs, and sex. She wasn't hurting anyone. Also, Leslie didn't believe she needed a man. She surely didn't want or need a husband, and if she weren't broke, she would refuse to play Grandma Grace's little game. The millionaires had used her money to control her since she was a teenager. She couldn't get a car unless she went to the private high school her grandmother wanted her to attend. Leslie wanted to go to the predominately-Black public school for the creative arts, but *no,* she had to go to the white folk's school that did not have contemporary dance classes or painting, but she could have private lessons, if she wanted. After graduation, she wanted to attend Spelman College, but Grandma Grace made it clear her money would only pay for an Ivy League school like Harvard, Yale, or Stanford. Leslie couldn't understand how a Black woman became so anti-Black. She truly seemed to believe the white man's ice was colder. She also believed she had to have everything her way.

During Leslie's freshman year at Yale, she told her grandmother she wanted to major in art. Her grandmother told her she had to major in something dealing with business. That was the last straw for Leslie. She decided to rebel and escape her grandmother's iron rule by dropping out of college and moving to New York to pursue acting. People always said she brought the drama, so why not be paid to bring it on stage or on screen? She didn't talk to her grandmother for an entire year. However, moving to New York, with no job, turned out to be a fatal financial mistake. In the South, she had name recognition. She was Leslie Watson-Purdue, heir to the Purdue publishing dynasty. In New York, she was just another rich kid who was mad at her family. New York is not a city for someone of meager means. Although she managed to use her name to land an agent, no one was willing to give her a chance. Leslie must have gone on one hundred auditions and only landed one gig in a dog food commercial. Soon the few people she knew grew tired of her living in their spare bedrooms and not being able to contribute to the rent or the groceries. She eventually had to swallow her pride and call her grandmother. Grandma Grace refused to send her any money, but told her she could return home whenever she was tired of being a pauper. Leslie was home in less than a month. Grandma Grace never said, "I told you so," or threw her failure in her face, though. What she did was much worse. She looked at her day-in and day-out with a condescending glare, and gloated about how well Sheila and Regina were doing because they listened to her.

Leslie quickly grew tired of listening to Grandma Grace's demeaning comments about how if she had stayed in college she probably would have found a good man from a good family and could freeload off him instead of her, or, at the very least, landed a good job to help her set a foundation to self-sufficiency. That all stopped when Grandma Grace became sick. Diagnosed with terminal pancreatic cancer, she began deteriorating right in front of Leslie's eyes. The strong, proud woman quickly grew frail. Her money afforded her a lot of luxuries, but it couldn't save her from the devastation of the disease. She sought the opinion of several specialists, and each one provided a grim diagnosis. Grandma Grace tried several forms of treatment: drugs, aggressive chemo and holistic, but none of them seemed to work. She eventually grew so weak she was unable to feed herself. Her fierce edge became soft, and she clung to her granddaughters more than she ever had before. It was obvious she was grateful for the company. The servants were there and they took good care of Grandma Grace, but there's nothing like family. Leslie waited on her hand and foot some days, and she was quite in disbelief that she was now requiring her to do more work to get her inheritance.

"She told me she was going to take care of me in her will when she passed," Leslie said aloud to an empty room. As a child, her sister and cousin were often too busy to play with her, leaving her to entertain herself. She created imaginary playmates and developed a habit of talking to herself that she had yet to break.

"Is this what she considers taking care of me, making me get a husband?" Leslie exclaimed. "I have no desire to cook, clean, and be at the physical whims of someone else. The way my life goes now, I do what I want, when I want, and that's good enough for me! Well I'm not going to do it. I get by just fine without a husband. Besides, one man isn't enough for me. I'm like a coach with an all-star team. Men do it; why shouldn't women be allowed to get our needs met by more than one man? Even in the Bible days, men had more than one woman. They could have as many wives as their pockets could afford. King David had over one hundred wives. I wonder who decided polygamy was wrong. I only think it's wrong because it's sexist. Why can't women be allowed to have more than one husband? I'm a liberated woman! I don't see how my grandmother stayed with one man for over thirty years. Sounds boring, if you ask me."

The Purdue women had used their feminine wiles before to get what they wanted. What's wrong with doing it again? In their youth, all three girls learned the story of Great, Great Grandma Dovey. She was a beautiful slave who used what she had to get what she wanted. When her master, Mr. Cherry, died, he left her and her children a house and gave them their freedom. That was unheard of in those times. You left your favorite slave a small house on a small plot of land, a few mulatto kids, maybe a family heirloom, but *never* a great big house with acres of land. Sure, he had more than one house, but still one can only imagine how upset his wife and children were when they found out he left a piece of property to a slave along with giving her and her children their freedom. Grandma Dovey must have been working with something mighty good! Mr. Cherry's good friend, Mr. Proper, was the lawyer who drew up the paperwork and he made sure to follow the orders to the letter. Mr. Proper was a widower, with no children, and he knew a good thing when he saw it. So, he sweet-talked Grandma Dovey into taking up with him so he could move into the house and reap the benefits of her good fortune. Now, Grandma Dovey was no fool. She knew that racist white folks would be around soon enough to strip her and her children of their inheritance, and they would murder them or force them back into slavery. So, she took Mr. Proper up on his offer for her own protection, but she was so good to that man that he fell in love with her and would do just about anything she asked.

Grandma Dovey was a beautiful woman. Most people were surprised when they found out she was dark-skinned and so loved by white men. "The blacker the berry the sweeter the juice" rang true for her. It's not uncommon to hear stories about white men falling in love with the light-skinned house Negros, but Grandma Dovey's skin was the color of molasses and as smooth as freshly sanded mahogany wood. She had a figure like a Coke bottle, and she could sing better than the birds. Thanks to her master and Mr. Proper, she was living the good life. Mr. Proper treated her well until one of their children came out the color of night. Mr. Proper would have thought Grandma Dovey cheated on him if it weren't for the fact that the boy looked just like him, except he was dark-skinned.

They named the boy David. Grandma Dovey had six children: three by Mr. Cherry and three by Mr. Proper. They were all light-skinned, except David. The other five children chose to assimilate into white society, but David didn't want to assimilate. That was probably because he couldn't. When he left home, he became somewhat of a rebel and an opponent of slavery. He even started an anti-slavery newspaper called *Freedom*. He changed his last name to Purdue so his abolitionist activities wouldn't bring harm to his family.

Leslie remembered Grandma Grace telling her granddaughters that story as they sat at her feet by the fire on cold winter nights. She wanted each of them to know where they came from and that they had greatness and a spirit of entrepreneurship on their lives. David Purdue was Grandma Grace's grandfather. He turned that paper into a publishing empire. He published newspapers, books, and other literature. If it could be printed, he did it. With the help of one of his "passing" siblings, who handled sales and served as the face of the company, he was able to secure contracts from whites who had no idea their money was helping fund abolitionist work. When Great Granddaddy or David, Jr. took over, he changed the company to focus solely on textbooks, which turned out to be a gold mine of an idea. As long as there were schools, there would be a need for textbooks. When Grandma Grace came of age, she and her brother, David III, ran the company. When she fell in love with one of the printers, Henry Watson, the three of them ran the company together. Grandma Grace never took his last name. She wanted people to know she was a Purdue and she gave her children the hyphenated last name Watson-Purdue for the same reason. The publishing company thrived and grew into a multi-million dollar empire. David, Jr. had three children: Grace, David III, and an outside child named Teresa. Teresa was acknowledged, but when they were growing up, she wasn't allowed to come around. Grandma Grace's mother, Francis, forbade it. For years, Grandma Grace and Teresa acted more like distant cousins than sisters, but they seemed to form a bond after David III died of a heart attack about twenty years ago. Maybe it was because she was Grandma Grace's only surviving sibling and she thought she should take the time to get to know her. Losing David III was hard for Grandma

Grace, but she persevered. That was until she lost her two sons and their wives in a boating accident. She and Big Daddy took over the care of their three precious granddaughters.

The loss of their parents devastated Sheila, Regina, and Leslie, but with time and love, it didn't hurt so much. They adored their grandparents, especially Big Daddy. Unfortunately, their heartache wasn't over. One day while overseeing a construction project to expand the Purdue Publishing home office, an unsecured beam fell and hit him on the head. His doctors declared him brain dead, and he was on life support for six months before Grandma Grace made the decision to let him go. She said he wouldn't want to live that way. She had to do it, but it proved to be too much for Grandma Grace. She was never the same. She sold her publishing empire for sixty million dollars. Then, she resigned to charity work and raising her granddaughters. The light went out of the old woman's eyes. The laughter she once held diminished greatly. Her once large circle of friends grew very small and she began watching her granddaughters like a hawk. She became paranoid that she would lose them, too, in an unforeseen accident. They were escorted almost everywhere they went. They were forbidden to participate in any kind of sport and could never go anywhere near water unless it was a bathtub. The expansive house where they lived once had a pool. Leslie remembered playing in it as a small child. After Big Daddy died, Grandma Grace had it filled in and had a basketball court built. A court they were forbidden to use because Grandma Grace was afraid they would get hurt. The girls would watch the servants' children stay outside for hours playing underneath the hoop, but they could never join in.

Regina thought the house was eerily quiet without Grandma Grace and all the servants around. Her grandmother believed in keeping a full staff, but after her death, the girls could no longer afford to pay them and they all left. Everybody except the housekeeper, Ms. Pearl, and her husband, Frank, who was head groundskeeper. They lived in one of the guesthouses behind the big house and had no desire to uproot their life if they didn't have to. Ms. Pearl was sixty years old. She agreed to come into the house at least twice a week to clean the most used areas and cook. She said she couldn't bear to let Grandma Grace's house go to the dogs and she knew none of them would clean it properly. She was right, though. The old antebellum mansion was massive and drafty, and attracted dust like a magnet. There had been several renovations over the years, but they preserved the rich heritage of the home while adding a more modern flare. Ms. Pearl watched those girls grow up and took part in their rearing. She stayed and she cooked because she loved them and didn't want them to starve. As long as she was around, they could come home and get a good meal.

Leslie sat in the room her grandmother referred to as the parlor, contemplating her present dilemma. She had no desire to get married, but she needed that money. She probably needed it the most because she was the one who was unemployed and liked it that way. She had plenty of men in her life, but she never considered marrying any of them. To her, dating was a game similar to checkers or chess and men were her playing pieces. Grandma Grace grew tired of her refusal to work and cut her off financially a year ago. She had been relying on men and the Purdue name to continue to live her high society lifestyle. She was amazed what she could get when she told people she was the granddaughter of Henry Watson and Grace Purdue, the original owners of Purdue Publications. Although they no longer owned or ran the company, they still had hundreds of shares of stock and other investments that vetted them a nice income, not to mention the company sold for millions. The money was just sitting in an account, waiting on her and her sisters to do the taking. Once they were allowed to access it, they would never have to work again. The money would be released to them in increments, as they grew older. Why did her grandmother have to be so old fashioned? Women didn't need a husband anymore. With porn, sex toys, sex without commitment, women's liberation, and child support, a woman could get along fine without ever saying, "I do."

Leslie's phone vibrated. She picked it up off a nearby table and read a text from one of her friends, asking if she wanted to go to a party. Oh yeah! Partying was a crucial part of her weekly social activities. Maybe she would meet a rich man and she wouldn't need Grandma Grace's money, but what if she didn't? First, she needed some loving. She knew just who to call. Beau could swing by before she went out. Well, if marriage was the only way she was going to get her hands on that money then she had better get busy trying to find a husband. She went to her room and pulled out the most low-cut dress she owned. She needed her double-D breasts to be at their perkiest tonight and on display. They had a husband to attract.

Chapter Three

Regina

There comes a point in every woman's life when she just wants to be loved, never really considering who gives it or how it's given. She yearns to feel wanted. Regina's yearning became so strong she was willing to scrape the bottom of the proverbial barrel to have a warm body lying next to her in the morning. The problem was after a while it got pretty cold and dark at the bottom of the barrel and that warm body no longer seemed to emanate enough heat to keep the woman next to it feeling toasty.

Regina sat in her bedroom with the lights off, listening to Anita Baker while holding a cold compress to her swollen cheek and busted lip. Her conversation with Antonio wasn't the happy occasion she had hoped for. His interview didn't go well. According to him, the interviewer was a condescending jerk who challenged everything he said. Antonio knew she had been to the reading of her grandmother's will earlier that day. He asked when she was going to get her inheritance. When she replied that she didn't exactly know, he slapped her before she had a chance to explain about the stipulation that she get married. He thought she was lying to him. It stung like hell. She tried to fight back, flailing her arms as fast as she could, and managed to hit him in the nose. That's when he punched her in the mouth. She immediately tasted blood, ran to her room, and locked the door.

So blinded by love, Regina hadn't realized she didn't just scrape the bottom of the barrel, she allowed herself to become covered in the sludge that resided there and then laid down in it. That man had the keys to her apartment, her car, and her heart. He also had a violent temper. What he didn't have, though, was a job to help pay the bills, and he was taking it out on her.

This had to stop. She couldn't keep lying to people and covering her bruises with makeup. The last time Antonio struck her was because she asked where he was going in the middle of the night in *her* car. He told her it was none of her business, and when she continued to question him, he hit her, knocking her backward and over the top of the couch. Regina told him if he was going to see *her*, he couldn't take the car. Antonio's car, a black Corvette, had been repossessed a month earlier. Regina had no idea who Antonio was cheating with, but what she did know was this woman had the power to summon her man at will. She didn't really want to know more than that. It's been said that if you go looking for trouble you'll find it, and not to ask questions if you really don't want to know the answer. She already knew the answer to her question. Yes, her man was cheating. She didn't need or want specifics. What she needed was a faithful, loving boyfriend who treated her like the mocha queen she was.

The lyrics to one of her favorite songs by Anita Baker rang out over her stereo *No one in the world's gonna love me like you do, baby…*

That's what she used to believe. Antonio was supposed to be her happily ever after. Her fairytale prince, but instead he'd turned into the villain. Regina screamed. Then she broke down and cried, letting the salty tears run down her face and neck and into her cleavage until she had no more tears to cry. This wasn't supposed to be happening. On the outside, they appeared to be the perfect couple. They were both attractive, intelligent Harvard Business School graduates. That's where they met. She thought fondly of their time on campus, strolling arm-in-arm. They had such big plans for their careers and their family. Upon graduation, she worked a job for a few months, but then quit to take a non-traditional path and blend her knowledge of business with her love of fashion. She became a buyer for Belle's, an exclusive boutique. Initially, this was much to the displeasure of Grandma Grace, but once Regina showed her how she could use her high societal connections to make the place a success, the old woman gave Regina her blessing. She even offered to buy Regina her own boutique. Regina declined the offering, stating she wanted to learn the business from the ground up before investing in her own place. This earned Grandma Grace's respect and support. Her grandmother told the women she knew, and recommended they shop at Belle's. Sales at the boutique shot through the roof, but not just because of the new clientele, but because Regina had an amazing eye for fashion and predicting trends. It became known that if you wanted to be on the cutting edge of couture fashion, but still sophisticated, you shopped at Belle's. Regina didn't make much money, but she enjoyed her job. It combined her business intellect with an industry she loved.

Antonio, however, chose the road she shunned and worked as a junior executive at an investment company. Initially, he did very well, managing small portfolios of up-and-coming businessmen. Small businessmen who had a desire to plan for retirement early became his niche. He appeared to have a promising future with the company. Until the market crashed, and people began investing less in their portfolios and putting whatever income they could generate back into the company to save it. Antonio was downsized during company cutbacks. At first, he remained optimistic he would land another position easily. However, the market was tight, unemployment was rampant, and competition for the few available jobs was stiff. He went on several interviews, but none seemed to lead to a job offer. He was now going on almost a year of being unemployed and seemed to grow more violent each month. He was resentful of Regina and her success and her family. Knowing her grandmother didn't like him, he was convinced she had something to do with his inability to land a job. He also knew all she had to do was make a phone call and one of her longtime friends could give him a job. He once hinted at such and the old woman all but scoffed in his face, stating his inability to get a job was a reflection of his lack of skills and if he were good enough for her granddaughter, he would have already found a job. Grandma Grace's dislike for Antonio was not without merit. She once caught him making out with the daughter of one the maids when he had come with Regina to visit. She told Regina, but he had her so wrapped around his finger he was easily able to convince her that the old woman wasn't wearing her glasses and was mistaken in what she saw.

As far as he was concerned, he was good to Regina, and Grace Purdue had no reason to condemn him for kissing the help. Initially, he gave her everything she wanted, except for a ring. She was a happy woman and the envy of all her friends who wished they had a handsome, doting, Harvard graduate on their arm. More than one of her conniving socialite friends had tried to lure him away from Regina permanently, or just long enough to get him into their beds. However, he knew a good thing when he saw it. Regina was heir to a massive fortune, and as her husband, it would be his as well. He had no plans to leave her, but occasionally he did take a friend of hers up on their offer to bed him. Since he lost his job, those didn't come as frequently as before. Antonio could no longer afford his plush, downtown condo and moved in Regina's apartment—an apartment her grandmother paid for—near the expansive golf course where they hosted major tournaments each year. He lied and told her the move was because he was ready to take their relationship to the next level. He drove the BMW Grandma Grace gave her as a graduation present, like it was his.

Regina used to believe if Antonio could find a job things would go back the way they were, but now she wasn't so sure. His pride prevented him from accepting any job offer below six figures. Regina didn't understand why he didn't accept a position just to help them make ends meet until a better offer came along. Her salary wasn't enough to support two people who were accustomed to a lavish lifestyle. She sat in the room in the dark and prayed to God for strength. She didn't talk to Him as often as she should. Regina was raised in the church and knew how important a relationship with her Heavenly Father was, but Antonio wasn't big on religion. She had allowed him to persuade her she didn't need to go to church often and praying was a waste of time. He believed people made their own destiny and not some deity he couldn't see. Regina touched her lip and winched from the pain. The bleeding stopped about fifteen minutes ago, but the area was now swollen and throbbing. He had hit her as if he were fighting another man. She was afraid to stay in her own home.

Antonio knocked on the door. "Baby, look, I'm sorry. Open the door. I'm sorry."

Regina jumped. She shuddered to think what would happen if the flimsy lock on the door didn't remain secure. She wasn't able to get to her phone before locking herself in the room and had no way to call for help.

"Leave me alone, Antonio. I'm not your punching bag. I thought you were leaving. You should do that. Just go!" she screamed.

"Even when I try to make things right you won't let me, and you wonder why I'm mean to you. You are right. I should leave and I am. You don't know how lucky you are to have a man like me. No one else would put up with your selfishness and whining. I know you went to the reading of your Grandma's will and I know you got a lot of money coming. Here I am struggling and you choose to hold out on me. We will talk more about this when I return."

Regina knew his version of talking could involve more violence. Fear continued to grip her like the captured prey of a starving animal. Sweat rolled from her temples and she wasn't able to relax until she heard Antonio start up her car and leave. He was probably going to see *her* again, but at that moment, she didn't care. She was actually grateful that whomever she was had given him a reason to leave. Regina breathed a sigh of relief that he was gone, wishing he would never come back. She placed her head on a pillow, turned her quickly swelling face on the side that wasn't throbbing and closed her eyes. She knew she needed to get some ice to put on it, but she didn't want to move. Something had to change, but for now, she would settle for a little sleep. She was physically and emotionally exhausted. Tomorrow, she would figure out what to do next.

Chapter Four

Sheila

Sheila looked at her son as he came strolling through the door after one of his regularly scheduled weekend visits with his father. It was Monday. DeQuan took Xavier to school and picked him up instead of dropping him off on Sunday evening as he normally did. He could tell something was wrong, but respected her wishes and didn't pry when Sheila said she didn't want to talk about it. He didn't need to know about Grandma Grace's will and the problem it presented for her. She spent the afternoon relaxing and watching *Law and Order* reruns.

"How you doing, buddy?" she asked, giving Xavier a tight hug.

He warmly hugged his mother back. "Fine, except I got the shits."

Sheila stared at her four-year-old in disbelief. Did he say what she thought he said? Surely, her ears were deceiving her. "What did you say, baby?"

"I got the shits, Mommy. Daddy had to come get me from school early. I been on the commode all day. I messed up my clothes. They're in my backpack," he said, sliding his Spiderman backpack down his arms and pushing it toward his mother.

"Xavier! You know that is a bad word, and we do not use bad words in this house."

"Yes ma'am, but Nana uses it all the time. Is she going to go to hell?"

She decided to ignore his question. *We don't use commode, either*, she thought. He probably learned such an old-fashioned word from his paternal grandmother, Ms. Bobbie Rae. She was a sweet lady, but she was an uncanny combination of country and hood. She could kill a chicken, pluck the feathers, and fry it with some vegetables she grew in her own backyard. Then, she'd wash it all down with a forty-ounce of beer while smoking a pack of Kool menthol cigarettes.

Shelia sighed before taking the backpack from her son. She shuddered to think what awaited her inside, but saw no need to prolong the inevitable and pulled out a plastic grocery bag sitting on top of Xavier's schoolbooks and a lone Transformer toy she could have sworn she told him he could not take to his father's house. She untied the knot, peered inside, took a whiff of the contents, and quickly tied it back up. Not only did DeQuan and his family teach her son another bad word, but also they were trifling enough to send soiled clothes home to her instead of washing them. His father probably didn't even give the boy a bath before he gave him fresh clothes to put on.

Xavier stood in front of her, waiting for her to say something. "Stinks don't it? Can I have a cookie?" She bent and smelled her son's behind. Just as she thought, his behind held a faint smell of boo-boo. TRI-FA-LING! He probably just wiped his behind with tissue, changed his clothes, and sent him back out to play. "It's *may* I have a cookie, and no you may not. You need a bath. Go to your room and take off your clothes. I'll be up in a minute to run your bath water."

The little boy's face fell. The only thing he hated more than baths were naps. "Aw, man! Then can I, I mean, *may* I have a cookie?"

"I'll think about it. Now go!" Xavier ran up the stairs as fast as his little legs could carry him. He hoped his obedience would earn him a cookie.

Her son was the spitting image of his father and a constant reminder of a foolish mistake. This situation was yet another reason why two people needed to be equally yoked before they begin dating. Sheila was the perfect example of a good girl who fell in love with a bad boy. DeQuan looked so sexy when he pulled up next to her at the gas station in his white Lexus truck, trimmed in chrome, with the shiniest rims she had ever seen. After he got out that truck in a tight-fitting wife beater that accentuated every muscle in his chest and washboard stomach and offered to pump her gas, Sheila knew she wanted to get to know him better. His nicely trimmed goatee encircled deliciously delectable-looking lips and his butterscotch skin seemed to glow in the afternoon sun. He introduced himself as simply D.Q. and asked for her number. Sheila didn't hesitate to give it to him. They quickly became an item. The hood boy and the rich girl were inseparable for about three months. She willfully and gladly did things that good church girls like her didn't do. He introduced her to marijuana, liquor, and lots and lots of sex. She was a virgin when she met him and one evening, after drinking and smoking with his friends, she let him enter her sacred space and make her a woman. DeQuan had plenty of experience and knew exactly what to do to make her temporarily forget every moral she ever had and race back to him to give her amnesia again. Sheila tried her best to hide her new boyfriend and newfound pastime from her grandmother, but Grandma Grace was a wise woman. She knew when a young girl had become a woman and all the problems that could come with it. She forced Sheila to bring her man to the house and introduce him.

Grandma Grace interrogated DaQuan for an hour. She could tell he came from a good family that taught him responsibility and manners. He kind of reminded her of her late husband when they first met. Big Daddy was from the hood, too, but he soon learned the ways of high society so he could talk to the right people in the right way to expand her family's empire. DeQuan seemed to have a good heart and cared a great deal for her granddaughter, but the old woman also knew they were from different worlds. She tried to tell Sheila it wouldn't last, but the young woman wouldn't believe her. As far as Sheila was concerned, she was a grown woman and didn't need Grandma's Grace's permission or her blessing when it came to whom she should date. She continued to date DeQuan and pick up all kinds of bad habits while learning about a way of life she had never known and experienced. About six months into their relationship, Sheila realized her grandmother's words rang true. His muscular physique, bad boy swagger, and hood rich demeanor no longer enamored her. The sexual high he gave her had lost some of its luster as well. His body was gorgeous and the sex spectacular, but she needed more. The man didn't own one suit. She was sick of seeing him in jeans, wife beaters, and Timberland boots almost every day. She was horrified when she invited him to church one Sunday and he showed up half way through the service in a plain white T-shirt and jeans. She questioned him about it later and his response was, "Jesus said come as you are and this is me, baby. Take it or leave it." That was the first of many things he began to do that rubbed her the wrong way. She soon developed a disdain for Coronas, weed, and music by Biggie, Tupac, 50 Cent, and Lil Wayne. If she had to spend another weekend over his cousin, Pookey's, house playing spades, dominoes, and grilling chicken or frying fish she was going to scream. She tried to get DeQuan to broaden his horizons and invited him to the symphony, the opera, and a wine and cheese reception. He declined each offer. His last response was, "Just 'cause you like doing what white folks do don't mean I do. My boys told me you wasn't Black enough for me. You fine, sexy chocolate on the outside, but inside you vanilla pudding. Now, stop trying to turn me into a socialite when I'm more like Dolemite."

Sheila was appalled someone would question her ethnicity because she liked museums, classical music, and champagne that came with a cork instead of a screw off cap. It also bothered her that he refused to fly. So being with him eliminated any chance of international travel with the man she loved. He refused to face his fear and justified it by saying if God wanted him to fly he would have given him wings.

It was no surprise to anyone but her when the relationship ended. Actually, most people were surprised they lasted that long. Shelia knew it was for the best and didn't look back. DaQuan didn't try to contact her either. They both chalked it up to having fun while it lasted. Sheila knew they had made some wonderful memories that would last a lifetime. She thought she was rid of him for good until six weeks later when she realized she had missed her period. When Sheila told

DaQuan she was pregnant, he was excited about being a father and tried to get her to work things out. He even offered to do the honorable thing and marry her, but she knew that was a disaster in the making. Especially after he told her his dream wedding included groomsmen who wore Jordans and fitted baseball caps.

She told him they weren't right for each other, but she wanted him to be an active part of their son's life. DeQuan promised he would and he'd kept his promise. He accompanied her to every doctor's visit. He was there for Xavier's birth and paid his child support on time every month. Sheila didn't even ask him for it. He went down to family court and signed up to pay it himself. He said he never wanted her to be able to say that he didn't take care of his son. Their visitation agreement allowed him to get his son every other weekend and at least two major holidays a year. DaQuan was there to pick up Xavier like clockwork. He wasn't a bad father, but in Sheila's opinion, those visits often did more harm than good. DaQuan's lifestyle didn't blend with the life she was trying to provide for Xavier. Almost monthly, she found herself deprogramming him to counteract some inappropriate conduct he acquired. Last weekend, she had to explain why holding his penis all the time would not be tolerated, and this weekend it seemed she would have to make him understand why he wasn't allowed to say the S-word. She couldn't get him accepted into one of the prestigious private schools he would be interviewing with soon if he started grabbing his crotch and cursing during the interview. Sheila let out a sigh of exasperation before she put his soiled clothes in the washing machine, poured in some Liquid Tide, and let them soak for a few minutes before she turned it on. She then headed toward Xavier's room to put him in the tub. She was going to scrub his little behind real good before it started itching. He might even have to suck on a little soap to clean out his dirty mouth.

Grandma Grace warned her the day she brought DaQuan home to meet the family that he was all wrong for her. Her exact words were, "Sheila, I have nothing against the underprivileged, but that boy is common. There is nothing common about you. You'll grow bored of him soon. I just hope it's before any damage is done."

Whether it was wisdom or an old woman's premonition, Grandma Grace was right. When Sheila announced her pregnancy, her grandmother was kind enough not to say, "I told you so," but gave her a very disapproving look before asking if she wanted an abortion. Sheila told her no. She'd lain down in a bed with a man and she was woman enough to lay down in one and have his child. Sheila didn't consider her son damage, but her situation was challenging to say the least. She never wanted to be a single parent. Why did Grandma Grace have to be right all the time? If that weren't enough, she never missed an opportunity to tell her how much she needed to find a suitable father for Xavier.

"Children need two parents to provide the proper amount of guidance and balance in their lives. You really should go out more and meet someone," she would say.

Sheila didn't have time for dating, not when she was working hard to provide for her son. Unlike her siblings, she actually decided to go into the company business and headed the accounting department at Purdue Publishing. Before she sold the company, Grandma Grace wrote in a provision that any of her family members who desired to work there had to be given the opportunity to do so for at least the next three generations. Sheila didn't like the new owner's style of management and left two years ago to work as the chief financial officer of her best friend Vivian's company. The position was demanding, but rewarding.

Sheila ignored her grandmother's advice about dating, but she wouldn't ignore the ultimatum she placed in her will. No husband. No money. She and Xavier could live nicely off her inheritance. She didn't want to work hard her entire life. If it's a husband she had to have, then a husband she was going to get. She was going to pray extra hard for God to send her the husband she desired. Sheila also decided to call her godmother, Linda. She had been trying to fix her up for years. This seemed like the perfect opportunity to accept. As she walked up the stairs, she quoted one of her favorite scriptures in the Bible, Matthew 7: 7-8. *"Ask and it will be given to you; seek and you will find; knock and the door will be opened to you. [8] For everyone who asks receives; the one who seeks finds; and to the one who knocks, the door will be opened."*

Sheila scrubbed her son's boo-boo stained booty so hard he cried. To make him feel better, she gave him a cookie and some milk. After he was in bed and fast asleep, Sheila rubbed Xavier down in Holy oil and pled the Blood of Jesus over him. She could not have her son lured to the streets because his daddy had ties to it.

Chapter Five

Regina

The next morning, Regina awoke to the smell of bacon frying. She was hungry and the smell of her beloved strips of pork was too tempting for her to continue to stay in the bedroom with the door locked. She cautiously opened the door, tiptoed down the steps, and peered around the corner into the kitchen. Just as she suspected, Antonio was standing in front of the stove, cooking in a pair of silk boxers with lips all of them. Regina gave him those for Valentine's Day last year. Her boyfriend's physique wasn't as solid as it had been in college. He had actually developed a bit of a beer belly, but he still looked pretty good. Antonio stood over the stove singing at the top of his lungs. That was a sure sign he got some last night. When they first started dating, every morning after they made love, he got up and walked through the house getting ready for work, singing as if he were tone deaf. Regina stood there for a moment taking it all in.

He noticed her standing there and said, "Good morning, beautiful." Who was he kidding? She rubbed her face in the spot where his blow landed last night. It was no longer throbbing, but still swollen and it hurt. She could feel the scab that had formed in the corner of her mouth where it bled and she had a splitting headache. Antonio walked toward her with a smile on his face, as if nothing were wrong. He bent his head slightly to give her a kiss on the cheek, but Regina turned her head and stepped to the side.

"I want you to leave," she said.

"Huh? You're kidding, right? How long have we been together? You know you don't want me to leave. You love me, *guuuurl*, and I know I love you. We just had a fight. We'll be fine. Let me fix you a plate. I know you're hungry."

He walked over to the counter, picked up a plate, and returned to the stove and began spooning a heaping of cheese grits. He added two pieces of bacon and scrambled eggs, and held it in her direction.

"Come eat. You'll feel better. I made your favorites: cheese grits and bacon."

Regina was starving, but she wasn't going to let her growling stomach prevent her from doing what she knew she needed to do. She moved toward the end of the counter where they kept the kitchen knives. She didn't want to hurt him, but she would if she had to.

"I used to love you. I've had enough of your disrespecting me in my own home, and I want you to leave. I'm not your punching bag, your dorm mother, or your sometimes girlfriend. I need you to get out of my home and out of my life. I've wasted seven years of my life waiting for you to marry me."

"Baby, I know I haven't been the easiest person to live with, but being unemployed is really stressful for a man. It's my job to provide and it hurts like hell that I'm not in a position to do so. I messed up last night. Please forgive me. Here I am cooking you breakfast in your favorite boxer shorts and that's the way you act. I'm sorry I hit you. I was wrong for that. Let Big Poppa make it up to you with some early morning lovin'."

"If you put that thing in me after you put it in her, I'll cut it off. It's also your job to protect me and all you've done lately is cause me pain. I know you were with someone else last night," Regina growled.

"What? Girl, you crazy. It belongs to you and only you. Come here, Gina Baby. Let me show you.

"Who are you kidding, Antonio? I know you like a book. You always sing after getting laid."

"You don't know what you're talking about, Gina. I'm singing because—"

As Regina readied herself to hear another one of his lies, Antonio's cell phone rang. He eagerly welcomed the distraction and instead of finishing his statement, he answered the phone.

"What up, Percy!" There was a pause while he listened. "You did? That's great. Give me thirty minutes to shower and dress and then come pick me up. Thanks, man. I won't forget you."

He hung up and turned his attention back toward Regina. "Gina Baby, that was Percy. He's been telling his boss about me and he wants to meet me. They may have a position for me. You better be glad I don't have time to argue with you over nonsense. I have to get ready. I am really sorry for last night. Why don't you keep the car today? Take yourself shopping or something."

Antonio kissed Regina softly on her bruised cheek as he passed her, heading toward the steps. "I love you, Regina. I'm gonna get this job and we're gonna work this out like we always do. You're my ride or die chick. I know you won't leave me. We belong together. Enjoy the breakfast I cooked. "

He ran up the stairs, his long legs taking them two at a time. That hadn't gone the way she planned, but

Regina was grateful he was leaving without a fight. Although, it bothered her that he dismissed her request so easily, as if she were kidding about him leaving. Regina sat down on one of the stools next to the island and began to eat. If he thought he could get back in her good graces with a kiss and some cheese grits he was sadly mistaken, but why let food bought with her hard-earned money go to waste? She took one bite of the bacon and spit it out. It was burned. She gulped down some orange juice to get the taste out of her mouth before tasting the grits. At least he got that right.

Antonio was back downstairs in thirty minutes, as promised. He didn't say a word to her as he shoveled some breakfast into his mouth until Percy pulled up in front of their apartment building and blew his horn. Before heading toward the door, he stopped next to where Gina sat finishing up her second helping of grits. She looked straight ahead in an effort to pretend he wasn't there.

"Gina, I have a good feeling about this. We'll be back on top before you know it. When I get home, we're going to talk about what happened with your inheritance. I know that old bat left you some money. I'll probably hang out with Percy for a while before I come back. Try to have a good day." He sat her keys down on the counter as if he were doing her a favor.

Regina didn't say a word as she watched Antonio grab his suit coat and brown leather satchel and run out the door. Immediately after he left, she called Leslie.

"Les, can you come over to the apartment and help me pack? I'm leaving Antonio and I'm serious this time, but I've got to get all of my stuff out of the house before he comes back."

Leslie had a full night of sexing and partying and was in no mood to pack and move boxes. She was not leaving her bed. Besides, give it a week, some sweet talk and Regina would be back home and all their hard work would be for nothing.

"What? You are letting that man run you out of your own apartment? Are you crazy! Put his behind out! Just change the locks."

"Trust me. This is much better. In a month, it won't be my apartment because I didn't renew the lease. So, it doesn't matter whether I leave or he leaves. Now, will you get over here and help me pack, *please*. I'll pay you three hundred dollars."

The offer of money rocked Leslie out of her sleep. "Okay. I'm coming, but if he shows up while I'm there I'm not responsible for my actions. You know I can't stand his arrogant behind."

"No worries. I don't expect him to come back until this evening. He's with Percy. You and Percy are cool, so please tell him to text you when he's about to drop him back home."

After she hung up, Regina called her job, told them she was sick, and wouldn't be in. She called her friends, Audrey and Karen, and asked them to help her to which they readily agreed. Both of them secretly wanted Antonio for themselves and helping her move would get them one-step closer to their goal. It was going to take more than her and Leslie to move an entire apartment in a few hours. Everything in it belonged to her, with the exception of Antonio's clothes and the sixty-inch flat-screen TV he watched for hours while ignoring her. She called and arranged to rent a moving truck for the day. Regina didn't know where this newfound feeling of empowerment came from, but she was going to use it before it left her.

Everyone arrived as promised. Regina delegated tasks and the team went to work. She got a couple men who lived in the complex to help with the heavy lifting. By three in the afternoon, the entire house was packed and in the truck. Regina was saying goodbye to her life with the man she loved. She examined the apartment one more time to make sure she didn't forget anything. She left Antonio's clothes, shoes, and accessories in a pile in the middle of the floor. As she walked through the living room, she glanced at his TV and the small stand it sat on. She could remember countless days when Antonio sat in front of that thing instead of taking her out or holding a conversation with her when she needed his attention. She passed by it, stopped in her tracks, turned around, and looked at it again. She peered at the screen. Her reflection in it was dark, but she could still see her bruised cheek and swollen lip. Regina backed up, ran toward the TV, and kicked it as hard as she could. It fell off the stand and onto the floor. It now had a large crack across the screen. A sinister smile graced Regina's lips as she exited the house.

Her sister and friends were standing outside waiting for her. She gave each of them a hug, told them "thank you" before climbing into the truck, and starting the engine. *I can't believe I allowed a man to string me along for seven years*, thought Regina. *Now I'm going to find someone who loves me to help me get my inheritance. He'll never see a dime of my money. He doesn't deserve it or me.*

She turned the truck onto the street and headed to the storage unit she rented online to house her things until she figured out where she would be staying next.

For the time being, her grandmother's house would have to do.

Chapter Six

Leslie

Leslie wasn't happy her sister was moving back home, but Grandmother Grace left the house to all of them, so it wasn't as if she could tell her no. It was a massive structure on twenty-two acres, with four guesthouses previously used for staff, a basketball/tennis court, an eight-car garage, and a barn for animals they didn't own. Therefore, they really didn't have to be anywhere around each other if they didn't want to be. Leslie loved her sister, but she got on her nerves with her naivety and her incessant talking. She also tended to be a little clingy when she and Antonio were apart. She was grateful her sister liked the rooms on the east wing opposed to the west wing where her room was located.

She was also grateful for the three hundred dollars Regina had given her, but that wouldn't last long. Leslie took out a piece of paper from her desk drawer and began to make a list of the men in her life. This would help her decide which one could possibly be marriage material. She affectionately called them her All Star Team. She would start with her favorite and end with her least favorite. She wasn't sleeping with them all, just most of them. She didn't really see anything wrong with what she was doing. As far as she was concerned, she was doing what she needed to do to survive. Some men wouldn't give her a dime if she wasn't giving up the goodies.

The first name she wrote down was Simon. Everyone wanted to see her with him. He was rich, handsome, and successful. Their fathers had been the best of friends. She spent countless days at his house as a child until her parents were killed. She was eight at the time. Her grandmother didn't approve of little girls playing with little boys, so they lost touch for a while, but reconnected when they ended up going to the same high school. Simon was busy building his empire, and marriage was the last thing on his mind. Besides, he was boring. He thought stock market fluctuation and watching golf was fun. They complemented one another well, though. It was necessary for her to be seen if she wanted people to continue to give her things and do her favors based solely on who she was. They often attended society events together: charity balls, high-profile weddings, and elite dinner parties. They had an arrangement of sorts. If people thought he were with someone, they saw no need to always try to fix him up with their daughters, nieces, or cousins. After all, he was considered one of the most eligible bachelors in town. It worked for Leslie because he wasn't pushy or needy and he didn't monopolize her time. She didn't have to sleep with him unless she felt like it. Like her, he had plenty of options. It really was a no pressure situation. He would actually make a great husband if he weren't so in love with his work. Sometimes Simon worked eighty hours a week. Several times, she had to make an appointment to see him. Other times, she took matters into her own hands and showed up at his office wearing nothing but a trench coat. She laughed, thinking about the look on his face the first time she did that. He turned beet red and called his receptionist to tell her to cancel all his appointments for the next two hours. He was also a good lover. He was definitely her top candidate.

Then, there was Cult. He was the oldest of all the men she dated. She was only twenty-four and he had to be at least forty. He could easily pass for early thirties. He was sexy and mysterious. He had a body that rivaled most NFL players and a face that made most women melt. He was a native of Barbados and his accent drove her wild. She met him one day while standing in Starbucks ordering a latte. By the end of the week, things were hot enough between them to brew coffee. She only saw him once or twice a month. He did private security and his job required him to travel often. He could be husband material, but Leslie didn't know him very well. However, she did know that he was highly intelligent, world traveled, and an excellent lover. She loved hearing his tales of Italy, Spain, France, and Africa. He was constantly feeding her brain with interesting facts about almost everything. She truly found him fascinating and she wouldn't mind having more with him if he were open to it, but they'd have to do more than have earth-moving sex to make that happen. The way he commanded her body was almost hypnotic. She never missed their appointments because if she did, she probably would have to wait an entire month to see him again. She almost missed Grandma Grace's funeral trying to get a piece of him. Cult would certainly look good next to her and he would be able to keep her attention for years. He even gave her a little "pocket money," as she called it, without her having to ask. Leslie doodled on her pad: *Mr. and Mrs.*....then it dawned on her; she didn't even know his last name and his real name certainly wasn't

Cult. She made a mental note to get his legal name the next time they were together.

Next was Percy. Leslie met him through her sister. He was one of Antonio's flunkies. He was the definition of a nerd. Yet, he gave her something no one else could. He fed her inner geek. Ever since she was a child, technology fascinated her. She was actually quite good in math and science. Engineering was initially her major in college, but when she found out how demanding the classes were, she decided to switch to art. Being buried in a book did not vibe well with parties, alcohol, and sex. She could have easily passed her classes if she had actually gone to class. Her mind was like a sponge. She retained knowledge without even trying. Percy was an engineer for Si-Cor, the leading company in medical technology. He worked in the artificial limb department. Each day, he worked at making electronic limbs that functioned almost as well as the ones people are born with. His job could be stressful. He destressed by buying and creating gadgets. She spent hours at his place talking tech talk and playing with whatever new toy he had, from the prototypes for the new iPhone and iPad—he had been on Apple's consumer testing team for years—to the newest video games.

Percy was sweet, but she couldn't be serious about him. She wasn't physically attracted to him. He was actually kind of gross. His year-round allergies made him a mucus factory. He was always blowing his nose and snorting hard in an effort to clear his nasal passages. His face was full of red pimples and his hair was greasy. That wasn't something she wanted to wake up to every morning. He was extremely fond of her, but she refused to give even him a kiss on the cheek. What if one of those zits decided to pop as she pressed her lips against his face? It made her want to gag just thinking about it. She considered him a trusted friend and nothing more. He was also good for a couple thousand dollars every now and then. He made a truckload of money at Si-Cor.

Leslie chewed on the end of her pen and wrote down the name T-Money. He was her bad boy and her drug dealer. She wasn't heavy into drugs, though. She was more of a recreational user, but it never hurt to know where to get the best product. She met him at a party at Simon's house a couple years ago. He took her into one of the bedrooms and gave her a couple lines of coke "on the house." She went home with him that night, and they had been hooking up at least once a month since. She knew he had other women, but he had money and whenever they were out, he spoiled her with lavish gifts. He asked her to be his girl a couple times, but she always declined. They were from two different words. She was the socialite heir to a multi-million dollar empire. She couldn't show up to country clubs, art shows, and the Kentucky Derby with someone who everyone knew was a drug dealer. He supplied most of her friends. She had heard about T-Money's hard side; he wasn't above killing people either, but when he was with her, he was a big ol' teddy bear. He was kind and attentive. He really seemed to want to make her happy. The sex wasn't that great, but his care for her made up for it. He wasn't a bad guy, but she could never date him seriously. She saw what dating a dude from the hood did for Sheila. Her need for a husband was making her reconsider, though. If she married him, he wouldn't need to continue selling drugs because they'd be rich. She wrote "potential" by his name and circled it.

Last, there was Beau. She should have never slept with him. The first time she had an excuse. She was drunk and high, but she didn't know why she kept doing it. Maybe it was because their love was forbidden because he had a well-known girlfriend. The thrill of sneaking around excited her. She wanted to stop. She needed to stop, but sex with him was unlike anything she'd ever experienced. He seemed to know every position on the Karma Sutra chart. He loved foreplay and role-play. He liked toys and porn they used as how-to manuals for new things to try. She'd never been with a man whose sex drive and freakiness matched her own. He didn't judge her for it either. He just wanted to experience new things with her. She tried to stop, but every time she said it was over, he found a way to reel her back into his bed. She knew she was wrong and if anyone found out, the backlash would be catastrophic. She didn't even bother to put his name on the list because he wasn't an option.

Chapter Seven

Sheila

Sheila walked through the unlocked door and headed into the kitchen where she knew her godmother would be. "When I told you I wanted a husband I thought you would know that I didn't mean somebody else's husband," she said, before setting her purse on the island in the middle of the kitchen.

Linda didn't even look up from the peppers and onion she was chopping with a large knife. She hated small knives, even if she were doing a small job. There was something empowering about wielding a big knife.

"He's separated and filing for divorce soon. Lots of women date men while they are in the in-between phase. Given your situation, I didn't think that would be a problem for you. Time is of the essence," said Linda. "By the way, I hate when you just walk in my house. At least knock first. I could have thought you were an intruder and stabbed you."

"Then stop leaving your doors unlocked. How is he separated when he and his wife are still living in the same house? And given my situation, I need someone who's not going to ask me to wait for their divorce to become finalized. Polygamy is illegal."

"Not in the mountains of Utah, I think. Although, you have a point and I didn't know they were still living together. You need to stop being so picky, Sheila. You're in your thirties now."

"You talk like that's old, Linda."

Linda continued chopping. "No. It's not old, but you're not the young hot chick in the club anymore."

"I never was into clubs, and what is that supposed to mean?"

Linda put down her knife. "It means that your choices aren't as great as they once were. The older you get the more men we lose to marriage, incarceration, homosexuality, and the grave. A man that's almost divorced isn't a bad option. I've worked with Greg for almost five years. He's a good brother."

"If he's so good, then why is he getting a divorce?"

Linda picked up her knife and started chopping again. "That's not fair. You know as well as I do that sometimes things don't work out. He and his wife were young when they married. They grew apart, and he's trying to move on." She finished chopping, scooped up the onions and bell peppers in her hands and tossed them in a skillet with olive oil that had been heating on the stove. She then began stirring them around with a wooden spoon. When she was done, she put a top on the skillet to let them simmer a little bit.

"If that's the case, he needs to move out. It doesn't sound like he's moving on to me. He most definitely won't be moving on with me."

Linda stared at Sheila.

"Don't look at me like that."

"Like what?"

"With that what-in-the-world-am-I-gonna-do-with-this-child look like my mother used to give me.

"What do you expect me to do? Why do you have to be so stubborn, just like your mother?"

Sheila's mother, Gladys, had been Linda's friend and she swore when she died she would still be there for her child. Sheila was so much like Gladys in features and behavior.

"He's separating himself emotionally? Did you have a good time?"

Sheila thought back on her evening and softened a little bit. "Yeah, I did. I'll admit that he does seem nice. He was attractive, intelligent and had a good sense of humor. However, I have no desire to date a man who is still married. Technically, that's adultery. How do I know he's not still sleeping with her? That is his wife."

"It's only adultery if you sleep with him. I'm sure he and his wife behave like roommates. He assured me it's over between them. He even told me that he didn't have a problem with you being celibate. How many men do you know that are okay with not getting any?" She turned around and added ground turkey to the onions and bell peppers in the skillet.

Sheila slapped the marble countertop. "Oh, that proves it. He's okay with it because he's still sleeping with his wife."

Linda spun around and raised her eyebrow at Sheila. "How do you know that? Did you ask him?"

"I sure did!"

Linda laughed. "Shut up! No you didn't! What did he say?"

"He didn't say. He looked away and changed the subject. Avoidance usually means 'yes'. Do me a favor, Linda. The next time you have the urge to hook me up, don't."

"Sheila, I was only trying to help. Besides, you called me. You're a great girl and you deserve to be with a great guy. I can't understand why you are still single. You're the total package. What are you doing wrong?"

"Stir your turkey before it burns," said Sheila. "What am I doing wrong? Linda, did you really say that to me? Now there's something wrong with me? Well, call me crazy for wanting an honest man who loves me more than he loves his car, knows how to treat a lady and doesn't need five of them in order to be happy. Not everyone lucked up on their dream guy in college like you!"

"Look, I'm sorry. That was the wrong choice of words. I didn't mean that there was something wrong with you, but maybe there is something wrong with your methods. Traditionally, dating doesn't seem to be going your way and you haven't dated much. You've had three boyfriends your entire life and one of those was in high school, so he technically doesn't count. Maybe you should try one of those online dating services or perhaps take out an ad on Craig's list or in the newspaper."

Sheila scoffed, "You can't be serious. I'm not so desperate that I am going to publicize my singleness for the entire world to see."

"Well, have you heard from Desmond?"

"Linda, stop!" Desmond was her boyfriend in college and they broke up over twelve years ago. "Why do you always mention him?"

"Because the two of you seemed so perfect for each other and I never understood why you two broke up. The only reason you even gave DaQuan a chance is because you were still broken up over Desmond."

"That's not true. Linda, I have to go now. I'll be praying for you."

"Baby, I'm sorry. There's no need for you to leave. I could use the company. Preston is out of town on business. I didn't mean to upset you."

"I'm not upset, Linda, but I have to go now. I need to pick up Xavier."

Sheila picked up her purse and walked out the house, making sure she locked the door as she exited. Having her mother's friend as her confidant was frustrating at times. Because she used to wipe her butt as a baby, she believed she could say and do anything she wanted. When her parents died, Linda fought hard to make sure she stayed connected to her. She didn't care how much money the Purdue's had, they weren't about to shut her out of her life. She made sure Sheila spent some holidays and weekends with her and her mother's side of the family and she was better for it. She had someone to turn to when Grandma Grace got out of hand with her iron fist, but not even Linda could help her get that money without finding a man.

She maneuvered her car in the direction of her boss's home. There was at least one man who was always happy to have her around and his name was Xavier.

Sheila's boss, Vivian, was her son's godmother. She agreed to keep him while she went on her date. Vivian seemed to have the dream life. She was beautiful, with a nice position as the owner and chief executive officer of her own accounting firm. She had a handsome husband and two adorable, intelligent, well-mannered children: her fourteen-year-old son, Aiden, and John's ten-year-old daughter, Eve.

Sheila parked her Volvo on the street, walked up to the house, and was just about to knock when the door swung open. Vivian stood there with her finger pressed to her lips to indicate she wanted Sheila to be quiet. She motioned for her to come in the house and pointed toward the den. Sheila peered in and saw Vivian's husband, John, and the three children curled up on the couch fast asleep. John cradled Xavier in his arms. It was such an adorable sight to behold that Sheila took out her cell phone and took a picture.

Vivian motioned for her to come into the kitchen. She wanted to hear how the date went. She took two flutes from the cabinet, poured them both a glass of Chardonnay, and said, "Well."

"Crash and burn. You know I don't drink."

"If it was that bad then you need that drink. What did he do?"

"He didn't do anything wrong. He is handsome, smart, articulate, witty and *married*," said Sheila, emphasizing the last word before taking a sip of wine.

"Oh my."

"He said he's separated, but they still live in the same house. How are you separated, but still living together? He claims it's for their three children. I don't understand. The whole thing made me uncomfortable, so I told him I thought it was best that we didn't see each other until his divorce is final."

"That seems to be the in thing these days, to have a girlfriend while getting divorced. It never ceases to amaze me. I've even heard of men proposing to another woman while they're still married. It's an insult, if you ask me, because if he gets killed before they get divorced the wife is still entitled to everything. The girlfriend would be left out in the cold."

"I hear you. I don't think I'm up for dating. For one, I don't have time. With my job, Xavier, and church, almost every minute of my day is accounted for."

"Yes, you do have a very demanding profession." Vivian smirked.

"You should know, boss." Sheila laughed.

"Hey, you were the one who said you wanted more responsibility so you could get a bigger check. I gave you what you asked for."

"I know and I'm not complaining. I needed the money. I want Xavier to always be able to attend the best private schools and those cost money."

"You're preaching to the choir, sister. I have two tuition payments in the living room slobbering on my couch, but let me let you in on a little secret. I really didn't meet John at a museum like I told everyone. Well I did, but it was after I had been chatting with him online for over a month."

"Really? You used a dating site? You don't look like the type."

"I sure did, and what type is that? I was trying to make my mark in the business world, working lots of hours, working on my MBA and, like you, raising a child by myself. When did I have time to date?"

"I don't think I could do that. That's too weird for me. Besides, what if someone I know sees my profile? I am a Purdue. No offense, but that seems a little desperate for me. I prefer something a little more discreet."

"None taken. Honey, I was desperate. I was desperate for a companion. I was desperate for someone to help me with the upkeep of this beautiful, but old, house that needed a lot of work, and I was desperate for someone to have sex with on a regular basis. Since I didn't even have a piece of a man, I wasn't getting any. I also needed a father to replace my child's absentee one. I've never been into casual sex and online dating isn't for everyone, but here's another option for you. How about a dating service? You could use a professional matchmaker. They screen all of your potential dates for compatibility before you meet them. All you have to do is agree to meet Mr. Wonderful."

Sheila thought about it for a moment. "That sounds discreet. I might be willing to try that. Do you have someone in mind?"

"As a matter of fact, I do. John and I met with him last week at an art show and tried to discuss his becoming a client of John's. However, he already had an accountant he's happy with. He claims that his success rate is 80%, which isn't bad, if you ask me. His brochure says that he's responsible for over 100 weddings. I have his card in my purse. I'll go get it."

Sheila sipped her wine, while Vivian was gone. She returned a few minutes later with the card and handed it to her.

"Logical Love, Inc. Maximillan Beauregard, professional matchmaker," Sheila read aloud. "Hmmm, I don't know. I just always envisioned bumping into my Mr. Right while I was at the grocery store, the dentist, or maybe church."

"Have you even come close to getting a date at any of those places?"

Sheila giggled. "Nope."

"Then you better find an alternate plan for getting a husband because that one isn't working, my friend. Call Max. You have nothing to lose and everything to gain."

"I'll pray about it tonight and see what the Lord says," said Sheila.

"You do that," said Vivian. "And tell the Lord I said hello."

Chapter Eight

Regina

Regina looked at her phone. It was Antonio...*again*. He had called at least twenty-five times in the last two days. She thanked God her aunt put a security gate around the property with twenty-four-hour monitoring, so there was no way he could bother her while she was at home. She was enjoying her time away from him. She even took a couple days off from the boutique in case he decided to show up there, which he did. The owner's daughter, Olivia, told her he had stopped by twice already. When he asked how long she would be gone, the owner told him they did not give out that type of information for vacationing employees. He would have to get that information directly from her and he needn't return if he wasn't going to make a purchase. What Olivia didn't tell her was that she followed him outside to the parking lot and got his phone number.

Regina occupied her time working on fashion designs in her sketchbook, but she couldn't hide out forever. She would eventually have to face him. She could only imagine the look on his face when he came in the apartment and realized there was nothing there. She even made sure the apartment manager came by the next day to tell him he had a month to move out because she didn't renew the lease. With his credit, there was no way he could get an apartment in that complex. Antonio was living off his credit cards and he was behind on his payments. They both initially thought his unemployment would be temporary and he'd be able to pay them off easily as soon as he landed a job.

Regina's phone chimed to let her know he had left another message. She stopped listening to them after the fifth one. She didn't miss him and she didn't want him back. At least that's what she told herself. He was free to be with his chick on the side now. It was time for him to accept her decision and move on. Being without Antonio left her with a problem, though. How was she going to get married? Antonio was her only prospect.

Regina popped some popcorn in her mouth with one hand and used the other hand to continue drawing. She would worry about finding a man tomorrow. Tonight, she'd focus on her first love, which was fashion.

Chapter Nine

Antonio

Antonio's inability to get in touch with Regina was driving him crazy. He got Percy to take him by her job, but she wasn't there. Her boss and that thirsty co-worker of hers, Olivia, wouldn't give him any information. He knew she was lying when she said she didn't know when she'd be back. He knew it was useless going by the house. He wouldn't be able to get past the gate. Olivia asked for his number and told him as soon as she heard something she would give him call. He gave it to her, but he could tell she wanted it for other reasons. He wasn't even surprised when she sent him a picture of her breasts later that night and asked if he wanted some company to make him feel better. Antonio texted his address. He couldn't come to her since he didn't have a car, but she didn't know that. She barely even knew him. She only saw him when he came to pick Regina up from work in her car. It never ceased to amaze him how little effort it took to bed some women.

Olivia arrived in less than an hour in a skintight dress and no underwear. She was shocked when she walked into the apartment and it contained no furniture but she didn't comment. He led her to the kitchen and offered her a glass of Pinot Grigio, which she accepted. Antonio wasted no time at all. He knew what she came for and saw no reason to prolong her being there with small talk. Within fifteen minutes, he had her on the kitchen counter screaming his name. He didn't like Olivia. She wasn't even cute. She was just something to help him release the frustration he felt toward Regina's leaving. Not only did she leave, but she also took everything with her. Yes, it was her apartment and she was perfectly within her rights to do so, but coming home to nothing, but your personal items and a broken television, had a debilitating effect on a man's ego. He also wasn't offered a job after the interview Percy arranged for him. He was told that Si-Core would keep his resume on file and call him if a position opened.

Antonio worked Olivia over like a madman and then told her she needed to leave because he had to get up early in the morning. To keep her from getting an attitude, he promised he would call her the next day. If he played his cards right, Olivia would tell him everything he wanted to know about Regina's whereabouts and probably more.

Chapter Ten

Leslie

Leslie decided it was time to start seeing which man on her All Star Team was worthy of her hand in marriage. Cult wouldn't be back from one of his business trips for a couple days, so Simon would be first. It was 7:00 pm and she knew most of the staff in his downtown office would be gone, but he would still be at work. It wasn't uncommon for him to stay until nine or ten. She spoke to the security guard to confirm he was there and then walked to his office. Simon was standing behind a glass desk looking sexy as usual. He wore a tan business suit that day with a white shirt but by evening, he had shed his jacket, loosened his tie and his sleeves were rolled up. It was obvious he was hard at work. She almost hated to interrupt. Simon was going over some financial reports. He smiled when he saw her and gave her a warm, tight hug followed by a kiss on the cheek. Leslie was going to be straight up with Simon. She took a seat in one of the chairs in front of his desk and told him what she needed, why she needed it and hoped he would agree to help. He continued to stand. She probably could fall in love with Simon, if she tried.

His lackluster response wasn't what she expected. "What do I get out of this?"

"What do you mean? You get a beautiful woman on your arm and unlimited access to this pudding pop you love so much. Think of all the fun we could have jet-setting around the globe. Every time we go out, people say what a nice couple we make. We're good together, Simon."

Simon ran his hand through his brown curly hair. He thought Leslie was beautiful and sexy, but physically was the only way she stimulated him. "Yes, I admit that we make a handsome pair, but you forget that I'm a businessman and my family is rich. I already have money. I'm also capable of getting plenty of other attractive women to escort around on my arm. That just comes with the territory of the life I live. It's not anything I need or enjoy. At this stage in my life, if it doesn't make dollars it doesn't make sense. I want half."

"What? Half of what?"

"Your inheritance. As your husband, I want half of whatever you get and I want it in writing."

Regina propped her hands on her curvaceous hips. "No way. That's my money. That's my family's money. I'd be a fool to give you half. All you're going to do is divorce me later."

"No, if I have to stay married to your spoiled, selfish, untalented behind I want half. Since I've known you, you haven't been good for anything other than partying and sex. You can't even hold a decent conversation."

Leslie turned beet red and her body became heated. She had been bedding him for years and had no idea he thought so little of her. She was smart and she knew that years of dumbing herself down so as not to intimidate her dates was coming back to haunt her. That didn't give him the right to be mean to her, though. "I thought you were my friend."

"I am your friend and that's the only reason I didn't cut you loose years ago. You're also a quick and easy lay and you don't get easily attached. All I have to do to get you to go away is give you a few dollars. A man with my schedule has no room for attachments."

Leslie knew, at that moment, Simon was no longer a viable option for a husband. He was all business. Being married to him would be pure torture. She didn't even care that he had just insulted her repeatedly.

"Thank you for your time, Simon, but I'd like to rescind my offer."

Simon went back to looking at his papers. "Fine with me. It's not like I need your money. My family is worth almost as much as yours." He looked up and smiled at her.

"Stop lying. Grandma Grace told me years ago that your family was drowning in debt because of your father's bad business decisions. If it wasn't for your family's trust fund set up by your grandparents, you would have nothing."

The smile on Simon's face disappeared. "I don't know what you're talking about."

"Sure you don't." Regina smirked. "The reason you work so hard is because you know your parents can't leave you anything. It hurts, doesn't it? Knowing your parents are surviving off your inheritance. Money that should have been saved for you and your little brother. They care more about their precious reputation than they do about making sure their children are well off. So you've got to make your company successful before everyone finds out the truth....your family is on its way to the poor house. I've known for years, but never told a soul. You want to know why? Because I *was* your friend and I know how much pride you and your family have.

"You're so stupid. Instead of trying to negotiate for my money, you should have offered me a part of your company. I would have felt compelled to help you because not only would you have been my husband, but I also would have wanted to see the company grow and prosper because it would also be my company. If you married me, you would never be in the poor house. If I were you, I'd work on my negotiating skills. A good businessman knows when a great offer is on the table. You just missed out on an offer that could have solved all your problems. Goodbye, Simon. This is the last you'll see of me."

Simon stood there silently in embarrassment. Leslie knew all along his family was no longer a part of the millionaire club, but never brought it up or threw it in his face. All those times they attended social functions together and she stood by his side as he told others about his family's wealth, she knew he was lying. She smiled while he told stories about the expensive trips they never took and the multiple houses they no longer owned. Leslie was a better person than he thought. He still didn't think she was very talented. It was probably best they go their separate ways. He listened as the click of her heels on the hardwood floors indicated her exit. He didn't need her money. He could make it on his own. He had to.

As she boarded the elevator, Regina laughed. Simon was a fool and thankfully, he wasn't her last option. She was looking forward to seeing if Cult had any potential.

Chapter Eleven

Sheila

Sheila sat nervously in the restaurant, waiting for her date to arrive. She couldn't bring herself to call a professional matchmaker. It seemed so desperate. For now, she would keep doing it her way. Against her better judgement, she let her godmother set her up on another date. This one was a chiropractor, with his own practice. Having a man who could literally crack her back didn't seem like a bad idea. Sheila agreed to meet him for dinner after work at one of her favorite restaurants, Mae Lillie's.

Sheila entered, announced her arrival to the hostess, who told her she would seat her shortly. She saw a few people she knew and entered the dining area to speak to them. Before she made it back to the hostess stand, two parties invited her to join them. She politely declined, informing them she was waiting on someone. Once her table was ready, she followed the hostess to it and sat down. Her date was already twenty minutes late. She was a stickler for being prompt. For her, time was money and if a person disrespected her time, they were disrespecting her as a person. After thirty minutes, she called him. Her call went straight to voicemail. She hoped nothing tragic like an accident had happened while he was en route. After forty-five minutes, she gave up hope he was coming and ordered her food. Fifteen minutes later, she received a text that read: Sorry, not going to make it. Had an emergency.

The nerve of that man! He didn't even have the decency to call and explain to her what happened. There probably was no emergency. This was beyond rude. How dare he assume she had nothing better to do than sit in a restaurant by herself for over an hour. She was sure she looked sad and lonely. The two parties that asked her to join them kept eyeing her as if she had lied to them. She hadn't been stood up since college. This was embarrassing. She finally had to admit she needed help from someone other than her godmother, who obviously didn't know how to pick a good man.

Sheila fished the business card for the matchmaker out of her purse and dialed the number. A man with a smooth, calming voice answered the phone. "Max Beauregard, Professional Matchmaker, at your service."

"Mr. Beauregard, my name is Sheila and I need a husband."

He chuckled. "Thanks, but I'm not looking for a wife."

Sheila felt embarrassed all over again. "Excuse my haste. I want you to help me find a date that will hopefully lead to a relationship and marriage. Can you help me?"

"Perhaps. I like to meet with individuals before I accept someone as a new client."

"I can respect that. Are you free this evening?"

"I also like when people want to get right down to business. As a matter of fact, I am."

"Delightful. Why don't you meet me for drinks and dessert at Mae Lillie's? Do you know where that is?"

"As a matter of fact, I do. It's one of my favorite places and I don't live far from there. I'll see you soon."

Thirty minutes later, the most gorgeous man Sheila had ever seen walked through the door. She hoped he had a single twin brother since he said he wasn't available.

Chapter Twelve

Regina

Regina was missing Antonio like crazy. She knew leaving him was the right thing to do, but after being with him that long, it's hard to imagine her life without him. She returned to work and tried to keep busy so she wouldn't pick up the phone and call him. She was doing a pretty good job. Over the past two days, she had cleaned and organized the back storage area and put almost all the new merchandise on the floor. She was in the middle of putting some new accessories in the jewelry case when she heard Olivia buzz someone into the store. Since they carried several high-end items, the owner preferred not to allow people to walk in the store at will.

Regina had to catch her breath when she looked up and missed him dearly. There stood her ex-boyfriend in all his God-given glory. She hadn't seen him in days and he looked good! She bit her bottom lip and tried not to stare as he strolled through the boutique. He wore a pair of jeans and a black, button down shirt, with black and brown leather loafers. Their eyes met. She looked away. She wanted to put those accessories down and go undo each one of those buttons while planting soft kisses on his chest. Regina mentally chastised herself for having such thoughts. She had to be strong. She wasn't going to make it that easy for him to get her back. If she went back to him, it would be after he begged and groveled for her to do so.

"I warned you that if you kept harassing me I was going to call the police," said Regina. "Olivia, please hand me the phone."

"No need for that," Antonio said coolly. "I'm not here to see you." He moved past her. "Olivia, are you ready for our date?" He leaned over the checkout counter where she was standing and kissed her seductively on the lips. Before backing away, he took Olivia's bottom lip in his mouth and sucked it slowly.

Once he released it, she let out a breathless, "Yes, baby."

Olivia looked at Regina, with guilt written all over her face. "I just need to get my purse."

Regina was speechless. Her mouth fell open and it stayed that way while she watched Olivia scurry to the back to get her purse and then scurry toward the door with her ex-boyfriend's arm around her waist.

"I probably won't be back anytime soon," Olivia cooed. "Lock up for me, will you? For what it's worth, I'm sorry, but some men are too good to pass up."

Before he exited, Antonio turned around. "Close your mouth, darling, before a fly finds its way in, and don't forget to lock up."

Regina picked up one of the plastic hangers lying near her and broke it in half. The nerve of them! Was it that easy to disregard her feelings? Olivia wasn't even Antonio's type. She was tired of people thinking they could mistreat her and get away with it. She expected this from Antonio, but not from Olivia. She was supposed to be her friend. She wondered how long this had been going on. Was this a new fling or had they been seeing each other behind her back all along? Was she the mystery woman he tried to convince her didn't exist? Olivia was going to pay for this betrayal. They were both going to pay.

Chapter Thirteen

Leslie

Leslie sat across from Cult at his favorite restaurant, Jack's Chicken and Rib Shack. They had just finished eating a wing and riblet platter, with coleslaw and fries, and now she expected to drive to a hotel room for sex as they normally did. Tonight, she had something else up her sleeve. When they arrived at their suite at the Madison Hotel, Cult went to the minibar to make them some drinks. She went to the bedroom and stripped down to her hot pink bra and thong set. She lay across the bed in a seductive position and waited. Within five minutes, Cult entered with drinks in hand.

He licked his thick lips. "Very nice, Bonita." He spoke fluent Spanish and once told her that bonita meant pretty. She loved to hear Cult talk. His thick Barbadian accent oozed sexiness. It was an added bonus that he had the perfect body to complement it.

"I'm glad you like it." She threw her legs in the air and brought them down slowly one at a time.

Cult sat the drinks down near the bed and removed his shirt and pants. He wasn't wearing any underwear. He looked magnificent! He leaned in to her, but instead of offering her mouth to him for the sensual kiss that would begin their night of ecstasy, Leslie began talking.

"Cult, can I ask you a question?"

"Of course, Bonita," he said, as his mouth hovered over hers.

"What's your real name?"

He laughed and took a step back. I've known you for at least a year and you've never taken any interest in knowing my birth name. Why now?"

"That's just it. I know you, but I don't *really* know you and I want to. So what's your name?"

"My name is Jackson Hewitt," he joked.

Leslie moved to the head of the king-sized bed, picked up one of the large pillows, hurled it at him, and missed. "Cult, I'm serious!"

Cult didn't get naked to have a conversation about his name. Leslie needed to stop wasting his time. "Darling, everyone in my line of work uses an alias. Real names could get me, or the people I love, killed."

"Oh yeah, I forgot you're a top secret spy," Leslie said sarcastically.

"No, but I do top secret missions. You should feel honored that I told you that much. I tell most people I install security systems. Now seriously, what's this all about? I've never seen you so somber. It's usually all fun and games in the sack."

She moved toward him. Then, she reached up and put her arms around his neck. "I've been thinking about my future, and I think I'm ready to settle down. You seem like a great guy. At least from what I know about you and I was wondering if maybe we could have something more."

Cult removed her arms from around him. "I knew this was going to happen. I'm surprised you waited this long. Bonita, I think you're beautiful, but I'm not someone you want to settle down with. My job causes me to travel frequently. I don't want kids and I have a serious problem with monogamy."

Leslie pouted. "So you're saying you haven't developed any feelings for me."

"Bonita, I like you. I truly do, but love, marriage, and family aren't something that I want. If that's something you want then I'm not the guy for you. And just as you said, I don't really know you. I know every curve of this lovely body of yours. I know how to make you scream to the high heavens with pleasure, but I have no idea what your favorite color is and, frankly, I don't care."

His words stung even though they were true. Cult was saying all the wrong things in all the right ways. His accent turned her on as only he could.

She removed her bra and began circling her nipples with her index fingers. Cult licked his lips, again.

"What if I told you that any man who marries me would instantly become rich? Would that change your mind?" she cooed.

He leaned toward her as if he were about to kiss her. Leslie knew that would get him. Every man loved money. She planned to make love to him so good he'd give her his name, address, and social security number. Instead of takin her mouth in his, Cult said, "I'm already rich and if you have to flaunt your money at a man to get him to marry you there is something very wrong with you. Put your clothes on. I'm afraid our time together has come to an end. You need to go home."

Regina sat straight up in the bed. "What? You're putting me out? All I did was ask a question?"

"Yes, but it's for your own good. I wish you the best of luck on your quest to find a husband, but it won't be me. I'm going to leave and go to the store. Don't be here when I get back. Better yet, I'm not coming back." Cult put his shirt, pants, and shoes back on.

This couldn't be happening. She wasn't used to not being able to get whatever she wanted from a man. Regina looked at him with puppy dog eyes. "It's that easy for you to walk out on me after everything we've shared."

"Bonita, all we've shared are dinners, drinks, and orgasms. I can get those anywhere. I've never taken you to my home, around my friends or family. I don't even call to check on you or just to say hello when I'm not in town other than to let you know when I'll be able to sex you up again. I take you to hole in the wall restaurants and then a nice hotel to work off our meal. What makes you think I would want anything more with you than this? Here's a bit of advice. If you really want to get a man to marry you, try using your mind, not your body, or your money to lure him in. Beauty fades and money can buy a lot of things, but loyalty isn't one of them. A no good man will spend every dime you have and then leave you for another woman. Lucky for you, I have a conscience 'cause believe me, Bonita, I'm no good. Goodbye, Bonita." He bent down, picked Leslie's dress off the floor where she left it, handed it to her and then reached into his pocket and handed her a one-hundred-dollar bill. "This should be enough for the cab ride home," he said and left.

Leslie didn't know what to do. This was not how the evening was supposed to go. She briefly wondered if she should just lay there in case he decided to return. She decided it didn't make sense for her to do so. Why stay where she's not wanted? Within fifteen minutes, she was dressed and ready to walk out of Cult's life forever. She had slept with him too many times to count and he had never made her feel like this. She felt used, insignificant, and unwanted. She briefly thought about the words she heard Regina say years ago when she started sleeping with men with no commitment. *"When you act like just a vagina, men won't hesitate to treat you that way."*

What did she want with a man that old, anyway? That's two names she could strike off her list. She opened the door to the hotel room and then closed it. If he wasn't coming back there really was no need for her to leave right away. She drank the two drinks Cult fixed for them before calling room service and ordering a five-hundred-dollar bottle of Champagne and the most expensive steak they had, along with the lobster. She was still full from the wings and ribs she ate earlier, but that didn't matter. She also planned to find out how many pay-per-view movies she could order at one time. Cult was going to pay for this one…with his wallet, if nothing else.

Chapter Fourteen

Sheila

Maximillian Beauregard stared intently at the dark-haired beauty sitting across from him. He would have no problem getting someone to go out with her based on looks alone. However, he needed to know if there were more than sparkling white teeth and nice tits to her.

"This is what I call an informal interview," he said.

"I'm being interviewed? But, I'm the client. Aren't you supposed to be interviewing potential mates?"

"I haven't agreed to help you, yet. I run a very specialized service Ms..."

"Watson-Purdue. Okay. This is all new to me."

"Pardon me, Ms. Purdue, but I have to make sure I am able to assist you before I can agree to assist you. The bachelors you mention are also my clients and I have to protect their interests as much as I protect yours...if I agree to take you on."

"Fair enough. What do you want to know?"

Max opened the black portfolio he had been carrying when he first arrived. "Before I tell you what I can do for you, let me tell you what I can't do. I am not a sex service. I specialize in helping people find a life partner. If you are looking for casual sex, kinky sex or an outlet for a fantasy or fetish, you have come to the wrong place. I do not do celebrity hookups. Yes, I have celebrity clients, but I have never selected someone for them solely based on the fact that they are a celebrity. Actually, celebrities have come to me because they are tired of people trying to date them because they are looking to marry well. I cannot get you ready for a mate. Either you are ready or you aren't. If you aren't, I suggest you don't waste your money. I don't come cheap. Now, I can provide you with tips on grooming, fashion, and how to present yourself as a viable option for a man who is looking for a wife, but the rest is up to you. I accept credit cards, cashier's checks, and money orders. Personal checks are not allowed."

Sheila held up her hand. "Stop right there. What kind of people have you been dealing with? Please don't act as if you are doing me any favors. I realize I called you, but just as you have to decide if you want to take me on as a client, I have to decide if I want to be your client. So far, I'm not impressed. Are you always so straight to the business? This is my personal life we're discussing here."

Max smiled and sat back in his chair. "I understand, Ms. Watson-Purdue, but this is also my livelihood and reputation. I assure you that I will give you the best service possible because I want you to find love and to recommend my services to others, but please realize that although I may be a modern day cupid, at the end of the day it's all business to me."

Sheila waved the waiter over and said, "Please bring me the check." She then turned her attention back to Max. "I don't think this is going to work. I need someone with a little bit more concern and compassion for his clients. I've dated the wrong man before and I have no intentions of doing it again. If I were to utilize your services, I would be placing the well-being of my heart and my life in your hands. Not just my life, but also the life of my four-year-old son. So it's not *just* business, as you say, and I choose not to do business with anyone who thinks it is. Now, if you'll excuse me, I need to get back to my child. It's a school night and I have to get him ready for bed."

Max opened his mouth to speak, but Sheila raised her hand again, silencing him. "This informal interview is over." She decided not to wait for the waiter and fished a fifty-dollar-bill out of her purse to cover the tab and the tip. She scooted her chair back from the table and left, wondering if the night could possibly get any worse.

Chapter Fifteen

Antonio

Antonio didn't really want to see Olivia again, but that was the only way he was going to be able to get back at Regina for leaving him. No one walked out on Antonio. Sure, they'd broken up before, but she had always left the lines of communication open. This was the first time she'd refused to talk to him or see him and he didn't like it. He hoped she'd be so determined to keep Olivia from having him that she'd come back to him. That's what happened in college when he dated one of her sorority sisters after they had broken up. Regina saw them at a basketball game that evening and before the next morning, she was knocking on his dorm room door, crying her eyes out and begging him to take her back because she loved him and couldn't bear to watch him with another woman. After Olivia shared when Regina would return to work, he borrowed Percy's car and arranged to take her out.

"I'm so happy you asked me out. I've been wanting you since the day I met you. All Regina ever talked about was Tonio this and Tonio that. She made you sound like some type of saint, but after that night at your house, I see why she was so sprung. I was hoping I didn't ruin things by giving up the goodies too soon," said Olivia.

Antonio found the very sound of her voice annoying, but Olivia wouldn't be around for long. As soon as he and Regina got back together, he'd get rid of her. Not only was her voice annoying, it never stopped. She just talked and talked and talked. He was sure she didn't get enough attention as a child. He was barely listening to anything she had to say. What was she talking about anyway? He looked over at her in the passenger seat and shook his head. Olivia looked ridiculous in a dress two sizes too small and made for a teenager. Her hair wasn't done and neither were her nails. Her mother ran a boutique so she should have learned something about style and fashion. Evidently, she hadn't been paying attention. When he saw what she was wearing, he abandoned his plan to take her to a nice restaurant and took her to some dive on the Southside of town where there would be plenty of other women dressed inappropriately. He told her he had a taste for some ribs and he knew the perfect place to go for the best ribs in town. Fortunately, for him, Olivia didn't care where they went as long as she was with him.

"I especially didn't think you would let her go after you found out about her inheritance," said Olivia.

After hearing that one word, Olivia had his complete, undivided attention. How did she know about Regina's inheritance and he didn't? Antonio turned down the radio. Some rap song by Nelly was playing on the old school hip-hop station, but that was of no importance at the moment. He didn't want to let on that he didn't know anything about it, so he said, "Money means nothing when you are unhappy. I can make that on my own. I'd much rather be with you than her any day."

"That's sweet. Knowing that you turned your back on fifteen million to be with me is quite a boost to my ego."

Antonio started coughing. *DID SHE SAY $15 MILLION!*

Olivia patted him on his back. "Are you all right? Do you need something to drink? I've got a flask in my purse."

"I'm fine," he said, regaining his composure. "She probably won't get her hands on that money anytime soon. The way Grandma Grace wanted those girls to earn their keep, I'm sure it came with some stipulation that they couldn't have it until they were thirty-five or something?"

"Actually, no. All they have to do is get married within nine months. It seems all the old lady wanted was to make sure they all got a man, but don't you worry, I'm gonna make you so happy you'll feel like the richest man in the world." Olivia began playing in his hair. He hated when unattractive women touched his hair.

Antonio had to get rid of Olivia, and get Regina back *fast*, but he needed to pump some more information out of her first. "You are absolutely stunning. How about we get our food to go and go back to your place so you can give me some more "happiness," as you call it?"

Olivia started grinning. "Sounds like a plan to me."

*****

Antonio dropped Olivia off at the boutique three hours later. It was after six, so it was closed, along with several of the other shops in the elite shopping district. During their time together, she told him everything he needed to know and several things he didn't. He also learned the girl ate like a pig at a trough. She still had barbecue sauce around her mouth and on her fingers. This was their first and last date. He found Oliva repulsive and she was no longer useful to him. He exited his side of the car to walk around and open the door for her so she could get out and be on her way. Before he could get to her, Olivia looked out of the passenger side window and let out a blood-curdling scream. He ran to see what was wrong, but stopped in his tracks when he saw her brand new Acura truck. All four tires were flattened; the windows were busted out, and carved into the paint in big letters were the words: I QUIT and HE'S ALL YOURS!

Chapter Sixteen

Regina

Regina drove home with a smile on her face. As soon as she found a man to marry, she was going to open her own boutique, steal all of La Maison's clients, and put them out of business. Before she left, she made herself a copy of their customer's contact information. She also neglected to turn on the alarm and left the front and back doors open. She hoped someone would come by, realize the doors were open, and rob the place blind. Better yet, she needed to make sure it happened. She pulled out her cell phone to call Sheila's baby daddy. DaQuan was from the streets and he knew people who were selling stolen goods all the time. All she had to do was let him know what she had done and she was sure he would send some people over to clean the place out. Olivia was the manager and her mother would be absolutely furious with her.

She was so excited about the havoc she was about to enact that she dropped her cell phone down by her feet. Regina tried to reach down quickly to retrieve it, but when she did, she neglected to see the traffic light had turned red. She drove straight through the intersection and was almost hit by a Jeep. She then realized another car was coming toward her and swerved to avoid impact, but ran off the road and struck a pole with the front of her car. The air bag deployed, striking her squarely in the face and chest. Bystanders and other motorists ran to her car to see if she was okay. Regina wasn't moving.

After a few seconds, Regina regained consciousness. When she realized what had happened, she began to cry. She had no auto insurance. She forgot to pay it last month and received a cancellation notice a week ago. Luckily, the other cars hadn't suffered any damage. But, what was she going to do about hers? An ambulance was called, but she wasn't quite sure if she should let them take her to the hospital. With no car and no job, how was she going to pay for it and whatever costs her health insurance didn't cover? She knew she should probably go to the Emergency Room because her chest hurt badly where she and the airbag collided.

Regina couldn't believe she was worried about money. This was ridiculous. She was a Purdue. Her family was worth millions and here she was behaving as if she were penniless. She needed to call someone, but whom? Sheila, Leslie, Antonio? No, she didn't want to be bothered with any of them. She could call Audrey or Karen, but she didn't want their help either. She sat in her car, talking to the police officer who had arrived. The medics followed shortly and asked her several questions to determine her well-being. She answered all of them correctly and against their advice, she declined the ride to the hospital. Besides her chest, the only thing hurting was her pride. She was sure she would feel the aches and pains tomorrow. She talked to the police until the details of their report had been satisfied and received a ticket for running a red light, failure to maintain control of her vehicle and for having no insurance. She would have to appear in court next month to provide proof of insurance. When the wrecker showed up to take her car she asked him if he could give her and her car a ride home.

"No can do lady," said the driver. "This car has to go to wreck yard. Your insurance adjuster can come look at it there or you can pay to have it towed wherever you like," he said.

"I don't have an adjuster because I don't have insurance. I also don't have a job so I can't afford to move it anywhere," she told him. Regina began to cry. God was punishing her for being bad. People like Antonio did bad things all the time and got away with it, but not her. The first time she did something bad she ended up totaling her car and stranded by the side of the road.

The man took pity on her and said, "I tell you what. I got a buddy with an auto repair shop. It's against policy, but how about I take your car there instead of the wreck yard? Maybe he can help you fix it and that way you won't have to pay those wreck yard storage fees. Let me finish putting it on the tow truck. You go hop in the cab."

"Thank you, sir. Thank you so much," she screamed and gave him a hug even though his coveralls appeared to be covered in grease.

Chapter Seventeen

Sheila

Sheila was tired. She knew that finding a husband wasn't going to be a walk in the park, but she didn't expect it to be pure hell either. She was happy to be home, though. Her son brought her so much joy. Leslie agreed to babysit for a fee and left as soon as she came home and gave her the money. She gave Xavier a bath and read him a bedtime story. He was asleep by the third page. She took a shower, crawled into her own bed and pulled out the romance novel she had been reading. The women in those books always seemed to have no problem attracting men. Maybe she could learn a few tips from them.

Her phone rang. She didn't recognize the number, but answered anyway. Hopefully, it wasn't a telemarketer.

"May I speak with Ms. Watson-Purdue?" It was an unfamiliar male voice.

"This is she."

"This is Max Beauregard. I wanted to call and apologize for my behavior earlier. You are absolutely right. I've been doing this so long that I forgot that some clients need me to be a little softer in my approach. Most of the women I encounter are so desperate to find a mate that they don't care what I say or how I say it as long as I get them a man."

"I'm not desperate for a husband, Mr. Beauregard, nor do I need one. I want one," said Sheila coolly. She was waiting for him to say something else stupid so she could light into him. On the drive home, she thought of witty things she should have said when they were together at the restaurant.

"I understand that. If you're still interested, I would like to represent you. You seem like a lovely woman and it would be my pleasure to help you find a man who knows how to appreciate you and give you the love you deserve."

That wasn't what Sheila was expecting him to say, but she was unsure if she wanted to continue interacting with him. "I dunno. I'm kind of rethinking this whole matchmaker thing," she said.

"Please allow me to redeem myself. Your initial consultation is on me. What I'll do is present you with three eligible bachelors and if none of them tickle your fancy, as they say, you don't have to pay me a dime."

Sheila smiled. Max was actually offering his services at a significant discount! She was almost sure he only represented rich, spoiled men who thought they were God's gift to women and thought they could have any woman they wanted. But what if he happened to have the man of her dreams tucked away in that database of his? She really didn't have anything to lose and a husband to gain. "I guess I can't beat that deal, Mr. Beauregard."

"Please, call me Max."

This man's voice is almost as sexy as he is, thought Shelia. "Well, Max, you've got a deal."

"Great! Now if you've got a few minutes, I still need to ask you a few questions to help me gauge what kind of man would work best for you."

"Yes, I have time. Ask away." Sheila settled comfortably in her bed and proceeded to complete the preliminary process for finding her Mr. Righteous.

Chapter Eighteen

Regina

Chance Chambers didn't know what to think of the tear-stained young lady his friend brought to his shop, along with a car with the front end smashed in. She was pretty, but she looked scared. He offered Regina a cup of coffee, which she accepted. He sat down with her in his office and listened, as she poured out her heart about the day's activities. Her no good ex-boyfriend, her boss's horrible daughter, who was now messing with the no good ex-boyfriend, and how her plan for revenge ended with her totaling her car that she had no funds to fix. He usually had no sympathy for women who liked to destroy private property because they got their feelings hurt, but for some reason he felt sorry for her. He also thought she was doggone cute.

Chance had an idea. "Well, your car can be fixed, but it's not going to be cheap. Since you don't have any money, and I can't do it for free, perhaps we can help each other out. My front office manager just got another job and quit. She didn't even give me two weeks' notice because they offered to pay her twice what she makes here and needed her to start immediately. Since you seem to be recently unemployed, how about you come work for me and we can come up with some payment arrangements. I even have a car with insurance you can use until this one is fixed. It's nothing fancy. It'll get you from point A to point B. A being home and B being to work every day."

Regina looked at the greasy man standing in front of her. His coveralls were a far cry from the couture fashions at the boutique, but seeing that she had no job, no car, and no insurance to fix her car, she saw no other choice than to accept his offer. This was what her Ivy League education had earned her, a job as a high-level secretary in an auto body shop. She nodded and accepted his offer. Chance had her fill out the necessary employment documents and sign a contract for the use of the car. Afterward, he gave her a tour of the business and a summary of what she would be doing. Two hours later, she pulled up near her home in a black 1998 Acura RL.

"What does he want?" she muttered to herself, after spotting Antonio parked on the side of the road in a car she didn't recognize, near the front gate of her home, waiting for her. She decided to go around to the back. She just happened to have the key to the entrance that was locked with a heavy padlock. Good thing she wasn't in her car because Antonio had no idea that was her, as she drove right past him.

Chapter Nineteen

Leslie

Leslie sat at her computer chatting with some guy she met on a dating site. His screenname was Southern Gentleman69. He seemed nice, but a little too eager to meet her. She still had a couple members from her All Star Team to evaluate, but in the event neither of them worked out, she wanted to have a few other options lined up. A dating site seemed to be her best opportunity to do so. She was about to respond to his question about what she was looking for when her phone chimed, indicating an incoming text message. A large smile crossed her lips when she realized it was her forbidden lover.

Beau: Can I see you tonight?
Leslie: We need to stop.
Beau: I know, but just one last time. Nobody does it like you. I miss you baby.
Leslie: I miss you too but what we're doing is wrong
Beau: Baby Pleeeeaaaaase.
Leslie: I love it when you beg. meet me at the rendezvous point.
Beau: I'll be there shortly.

The rendezvous point was the barn located in the back of the house. They never had any animals so no one went there except her. In high school, her grandfather converted into an extra garage and art studio for her. She'd painted some beautiful watercolors there in her youth, but when Big Daddy died, she lost her desire to paint. Nobody took an interest in her art, but him. Instead of using the secluded location to create masterpieces, she began using the barn as a place to meet her lovers undetected. Leslie loved her little hideaway. The loft housed her desk and a twin bed. It was cozy and quiet and to be a barn, it stayed surprisingly warm. All she had to do was plug in a little space heater and, within thirty minutes, the place was a comfortable temperature.

Beau texted her when he was close. She unlocked the back gate. He pulled the car behind some bushes so no one would see it. They walked hand-in-hand to the barn. Since neither Simon nor Cult had slept with Leslie, she had some sexual tension she needed to release and welcomed his attention. The least Cult could have done was given her some loving one last time before he kicked her to the curb. It was painful to realize she was nothing more than a sperm release for a man. They'd spent countless evenings pleasuring one another and he didn't even pause to think about it before telling her it was over. Yeah, Beau was exactly what she needed.

He continued to hold her hand as he escorted her up the stairs that led to their place of passion. "Baby, I've been so stressed lately. Nothing in my life is going the way I planned. Your touch always makes me feel better."

"This is the last time," said Leslie.

"Okay. I love you."

"No, you don't. You love the sex."

"I do. We are cut from the same cloth. I just met her first and we've got history. I can't change that."

"You are breaking our rule."

"You're right. These moments are about us."

Leslie and Beau had one rule. Neither of them could mention another lover. She didn't want to hear about his girlfriend and he definitely didn't want to hear about the multiple dudes whose beds she occupied. They both knew what they were doing was wrong and it made it a little bit easier for Leslie to digest if they didn't talk about it. She didn't even use the same name for him everyone else used. She called him Beau so she could have a small piece of him to herself that no one else had.

Once they reached the top of the stairs, they kissed hungrily before heading toward the bed in the corner of the room. Leslie sat on the edge of the bed and Beau began removing her blouse. "Wait! One thing," she said, before slapping him with all her might.

She hit him so hard his head spun to the side. Beau grabbed his face. It stung badly, but he didn't retaliate. His need for her body was greater than his desire to show her why she shouldn't ever put her hands on him. "What was that for?"

"You know exactly what it was for. I hate that I love you. You don't deserve either of us. This is truly the last time."

"Now look whose breaking our rule. If it's truly the last time, then let's make it unforgettable, and you're right. I was wrong. I deserved that and a lot worse. I look forward to being punished repeatedly. You are so beautiful. I really do love you, baby. You're my soul mate."

No man had ever told Leslie he loved her. It was all about the sex. It was nice to hear and she really thought a small part of him meant it, but she knew he loved the number one woman in his life more. He could never be hers and honestly, she didn't want him. They were just so much alike and it was nice to be able to talk to a kindred spirit. Beau took off every item of clothing she wore and softly laid Leslie on the bed. He then began placing kisses on her neck and anywhere else he desired. She was petite, but voluptuous and he loved to explore her body. Once they had their fill of one another, Leslie laid her head on Beau's chest, right on top of a tattoo he had of his girlfriend's name. When they were together, she often closed her eyes so she wouldn't see it. Sometimes she even asked him to leave on his T-shirt. If they ever got caught, all hell would break loose, but right now, at that moment, while listening to the beat of his heart and being held warmly in his arms, she didn't care.

Chapter Twenty

Regina

Regina looked out of her bedroom window and saw the light on at the top of the barn. Her sister was at it again. Leslie had been sneaking boys in there since she was a teen. She wondered why she was still using the barn now that Grandma Grace was dead. She could have easily brought him in the house. She always enjoyed looking at her sister's eye candy. She had great taste. She once met Cult when she and Antonio were out to eat. He was so ruggedly handsome and sexy, she was at a loss for words. The only thing she could audibly release from her mouth was a weak, "Hey." She wondered if he was who she was with now. At least someone was getting their needs met. As mad as she was at Antonio, she had to admit she still loved the guy. What happened to them? They used to be so good together.

She wondered what he was doing. *Probably screwing Olivia,* she thought. She hit her pillow, reached over on the nightstand, turned out her antique lamp, and tried to go to sleep. She didn't need to show up for her new job with bags under her eyes.

*****

The morning sun shone brightly on Chance and Regina as they stood behind the mansion examining the Acura.

"Seems like you left the headlights on." said Chance. Regina looked down at her shoes. "What do you mean? They don't shut off by themselves?" She spoke meekly and her demeanor reminded Chance of a kid who was called on by the teacher to answer a question and didn't know the answer.

"Older model cars don't have automatic shut off, miss. I'll give you a boost."

This certainly wasn't a good way to impress her new boss. That morning, she couldn't start the car. She called Chance and he came right over. He worked on the car and he knew there was nothing wrong with it. He figured whatever was wrong was done by her hands and he was right. At least it was something minor.

Chance pulled his jumper cables from the back of his old Ford truck and had the engine purring in no time. As he put them back up, he looked around at the massive house and the sprawling acres it sat on.

"You live here?"

Regina knew he was wondering why she couldn't pay for the repairs on her car if she could afford to live someplace like this.

"I live in the servant's quarters with my grandmother. She's the housekeeper," she lied.

"Oh," was all Chance said.

Regina hoped her lie would satisfy his curiosity. It wouldn't take much to punch holes in it. All he had to do was Google her and he would find out she was heir to a fortune, but it was a fortune she couldn't get her hands on.

"Well it should drive fine now. *And,* we should both be heading over to the shop because I'm usually there by now and you, young lady, are late for your first day of work. Try to remember to shut the lights off from now on."

"Yes, sir. Thanks, Chance."

No need to call me 'sir' and you're welcome, Regina. Just remember to cut the lights off next time."

"Oh, I will. Sorry you had to come all the way out here."

"No problem. Drive safe."

Chance didn't know quite what to think of Regina. She was lovely, but a little naïve. He could tell she didn't have much life experience. She appeared a bit sheltered. He wondered if her grandmother was strict on her growing up. He had to admit he found her attractive and he wasn't quite sure having her around every day would be a good thing. His eyes washed over her slowly and took in every inch of her in the orange jumper she chose to wear with black, six-inch stilettoes. He knew she wouldn't last long working in those. He also noticed she had a bruise on her arm. It looked old so he knew it wasn't from the accident yesterday. She was a bit over-dressed for an auto garage, but she looked nice. He didn't want to mention it now because Regina might try to change and then she would be even later. He also liked the way the jumper hugged her Coke bottle shape. He did feel the need to give her one piece of advice.

"You probably want to bring a pair of comfortable shoes with you. Office managers tend to do a lot of running from the office to the garage at my business."

"No worries, I already have a pair of slides in the car." She smiled.

"Good." Chance had no idea what slides were, but they probably didn't look as good on her as those heels.

It was going to be nice having an attractive woman in the office. He just hoped he could stay focused.

Chapter Twenty-One

Antonio

"So you think you can just have sex with me and then act like you don't know me? I've been calling and texting you all day. It's a shame I have to call you from another number to get you to answer," said Olivia. "I'm going to tell Regina what we did, and I'm going to tell her that I told you about her inheritance! Then, I'm going to have her arrested for damaging my truck. I thought you liked me. You won't get away with this, Antonio! I don't deserve to be treated like this. I have feelings."

Antonio held the phone away from his ear, while Olivia screamed. If it was one thing Antonio hated, it was a whining woman and Olivia did it all the time and didn't even realize it. She was worse than Regina.

"I never told you that I wanted a future with you and you should never make assumptions about a man's feelings. Besides, you won't mention a word of this to Regina or you'll be sorry. Sorrier that you've ever been in your life."

"What are you going to do? You can't hurt me. Regina and I are no longer friends, so you can't hold that over my head," she squealed.

"No. I've got something much better. I've got a video of you with your legs wide open and screaming my name at the top of your lungs. What do you think all those dignified high society women you and your mother need to earn a living would say? I bet they would stop shopping at the boutique rather than be affiliated with the likes of you," Antonio taunted. "The best part of the video is where you banged your head against the cabinets a few times. Does it still hurt?"

Olivia didn't believe him. "You're bluffing."

"Baby, I don't like gambling because I don't care for the odds and bluffing isn't my style. I always put my money on a sure thing. Stay by your phone." Antonio ended the call and sent her a snippet of the video he recorded without her knowledge the night she came over to his apartment.

Olivia texted him: You win. I won't say a word just keep that video on the low. I'll even pay you for it if you promise to give me the only copy. How much do you want?

Antonio texted back: It's not for sale. Keep your mouth shut and you'll never have to worry about a soul ever seeing it. You better not do anything to Regina either or you'll pay dearly! Understood?

Olivia: Understood. Can I see you again? I really enjoyed you.

Antonio: We'll see.

Antonio prided himself on being a pimp with a capitol P. He honed his pimp game in college under the tutelage of his frat brothers: Rock Steady and B Smoove. They taught him the three things every pimp had to be able to do: make love to a woman's body, make love to a woman's mind, and intimidate her, if necessary. Master those three things and a man was guaranteed control of any woman. That way, if he lost his grip on her mind, her heart and body would make her want to stay. If he lost control of her heart and body, fear for her life or something else would help him keep control. He hadn't been faithful to Regina the entire time they'd been together. Regina was so meek all he had to do was slap her a couple times and she got in line. At least that's what he thought until she left him. Most women he ran into were a little more headstrong and needed more than a good backhand to keep them in line. Also, some leverage was needed. He began taping his sexual excursions in college. Whenever one of his chicks on the side threatened to tell Regina about him creeping, he just let them know that if they did he would leak the tape he recorded of them grinding horizontally, vertically or any other uncompromising position. Once, he even recorded a tryst with one of his graduate student professors. Needless to say, he got an A in her class and he didn't even go to class.

Regina was supposed to be his meal ticket so he did whatever he had to do to keep her in the dark about his wandering ways. His original plan was to marry her and get her to get him a cushy job with Purdue Publishing, but then he found out her grandmother sold it and gave up all her decision-making powers. There was no hurry to marry her then, but he knew he would have to continue to date her until he could figure out how to make sure the union worked in his favor. Regina majored in finance, like him, and she was actually pretty good at it. She was quite the mathematician. When she graduated, her grandmother pulled some strings to get her a position as a manager at Smith Global Investments. She was on the fast track to easy money street, but instead of keeping the job and earning her six-figure salary, she chose a career in fashion and was barely making one-fourth of what she had made before. He almost blew a gasket when she came home and told him the news. Then a month later, he was downsized. That's when the abuse began. He never meant to put his hands on Regina, but after he lost his job, the mere sight of her made him sick. His entire life he had to work for everything he had. He studied hard in school and upon graduation landed a job as a junior associate at an investment firm. He worked hard for them and made them a lot of money, but none of that mattered when the company didn't make as much as they projected and had to let some people go. Ms. High Society was born with a silver spoon in her mouth, and although her grandmother refused to give her large sums of money, she used her influence to make sure Regina was always sitting pretty with a good job with a lucrative salary and benefits, and what did Regina do? She walked away from it all to pursue some unprofitable designer dream. The thought of the money she walked away from made him so angry that he hit her. It was then he realized that he no longer loved her. He would never hit a woman he loved. Antonio wondered if he ever did, but whether he loved her was irrelevant at this point. He was going to marry her and her millions.

He had planned to leave her. Without a high-paying position and no means of getting to her grandmother's money, Antonio was going to break up with her as soon as he found a job. That's why he began getting so sloppy with his cheating. He didn't care anymore. He wanted to seem like a jerk to soften the blow when he left. Although, now that her grandmother was dead and she was about to inherit millions, he saw no need to leave her. All he had to do was give her what she wanted—a ring—to get his piece of that Purdue prize money. He knew just how to invest it to make himself a lot of money and after they were filthy rich, he was going to divorce Regina and make her pay him alimony. He knew she would never make him sign a prenup. Regina was sweet, but she was too sweet. A woman like that could never hold his attention. She was also a prude in bed. He liked his women uninhibited and every time he tried to do something freaky with Regina, she froze up and didn't want to do it anymore. There was no way he was subjecting himself to that. So he cheated and he would probably continue to cheat and that was just the way it was.

Antonio still hadn't figured out where Regina was staying. He drove past Sheila's last night and her car wasn't there. He went to her grandmothers and the only car he saw was some old Acura. He figured it had to be the housekeeper's because neither Regina nor Leslie would be caught dead in a car like that. Although, she could be parking in the garage, but he better make sure she's there before trying to enter the Purdue property. He had to find her and convince her to take him back, in spite of all his sins.

Chapter Twenty-Two

Sheila

Sheila sat at home awaiting the arrival of the wardrobe stylist Max said he was going to send over to help her pick out some outfits for her potential dates. It was one of the specialty services he offered. He wanted each of his clients to make a good first impression. Sheila had to admit her wardrobe could use a little sprucing up. She did as instructed and laid out five outfits she thought would look good on a first date, complete with accessories. They were all strewn about her living room, along the couch, love seat, and chaise. She thought her ensembles looked nice, but she was looking forward to seeing what the stylist could do to enhance them.

Her doorbell rang and Sheila moved hastily to let in a woman known simply as "Diva." She Googled her earlier and found a few videos online of her work. She had styled several local and national celebrities. Diva was excellent and knew how to get her clients runway ready. Although Sheila wouldn't be gracing any catwalks, it wouldn't hurt to look fabulous for a date.

When she opened her front door, she was surprised to see Max Beauregard. He looked quite handsome in brown slacks, with a cream-colored shirt and brown loafers. He also carried a man purse. Sheila wasn't too keen on man purses. They looked too feminine for her taste. DaQuan would never carry a man purse. What was

Max doing at her house, anyway? Where was Diva? She tried to mask her disappointment.

"Hello, Max. I wasn't expecting you this evening."

"Hello to you, too, Sheila. I didn't expect to be here either, but Diva got called to LA on business and cancelled on me. She won't be back for at least a week and I couldn't find another stylist on such short notice, so I came to assist you.

Sheila laughed. "What do you know about women's fashion?"

"I'll have you know that my mother was, and still is, a seamstress and a darn good one. She creates women and men's clothing for some of the most high profile professionals in the city. She taught me everything she knows about sewing and designing. I could make a dress out of your curtains if I wanted to. Do you mind if I come in? It's a bit chilly out here."

"Oh, yes. Please excuse my manners." Sheila stepped to the side and let him in. "There's no need to go all *Gone with the Wind* on me and make dresses out of curtains. If you say you can style me then I believe you. I placed the ensembles you asked me to create in the living room. Follow me."

Max followed her into the living room while scanning the décor of her home. It was modest, but well done. Sheila preferred classic looks that stood the test of time opposed to trendy ones. Many of the items came from her grandmother's stately mansion. She had more than enough furniture and when Sheila bought her house, she allowed her to select several pieces from her private collection.

"You have a lovely home," he said.

"Thank you."

Max entered the living room, abruptly stopped, and placed his hand on his chest as if he were clutching his pearls. "Oh, my. Sheila, darling, these outfits look like they belong on a fifty-year-old woman. With that body and those legs, why aren't you showing them off? No offense, but these will not do. Take me to your bedroom."

"Excuse me!"

Max laughed. "I'd like to go to your bedroom to see the rest of your wardrobe, if you don't mind."

Sheila grew uncomfortable. "Is that necessary?"

"Isn't that where you keep your clothes?"

"Yes. But..." she looked down at the floor. "I haven't had a man in my bedroom in quite some time."

Max put his fingers underneath her chin, lifted her face, and looked her squarely in the eyes. "That's not a bad thing. The Bible says a virtuous woman is more precious than rubies. You look like a woman whose worth waiting for. I'm here to work. I promise to be the perfect gentleman."

Sheila blushed and started walking toward the stairs. "Okay, right this way."

Thirty minutes later, her closet looked like a tornado had blown through it. Max pulled several articles of clothing out and laid them across any piece of furniture he could find. Every time he found something he really liked, he yelled, "Eureka!" and added them to his piles.

While he worked, he gave Sheila the assignment of writing down several words that described how she wanted to be perceived. She sat on the floor and scribbled on a notepad the words: important, desirable, and unforgettable. She didn't hear Max when he approached her and looked over her shoulder.

"Hmmm. Those are interesting choices. This Nubian Queen seems like she could use a boost to her confidence. You have some self-esteem issues, don't you?"

"Is it that obvious?" she asked softly.

Max placed his arms around her and hugged her from behind. "I can tell when it comes to business you are fierce, but when it comes to your appearance you aren't. Why is that? Honey, you are beautiful and you don't even know it. I'd describe you as an absolute diamond in the rough. I just have to polish you up and make you shine."

Sheila was caught off guard by the hug. She was even more surprised by how much she liked it. She wiggled out of it and stood up. "I have two younger cousins who are drop dead gorgeous. They're tiny little things and standing next to them, I look like an Amazon. We were raised together and were being compared to one another all the time. They were graceful, and I was awkward. Their hair was wavy and mine was nappy. I was a late bloomer and shy. When I finally did hit puberty, the breasts came with acne and an unproportioned body. I finally grew into everything by the time I was twenty-one. Although the outside looks all right now, I guess the damage to my insides have been harder to fix."

Max looked at her tenderly. It reminded her of her grandfather. He told her often that she was as lovely as the sunset. "That absolutely will not do. I hate to see a beautiful woman who lacks confidence. Consider me your fairy godfather because everything on this list I am going to deliver."

Shelia gave him a skeptical look.

"Oh yes, you just watch me work. I can do magic, baby. First, I'm going to do some hocus pocus ala kazaam on these old lady clothes of yours. All those curves and you're trying to hide them. What's wrong witchu?" he said, imitating a popular song by Erica Campbell of the popular gospel duo Mary Mary.

Sheila laughed, but stopped when she heard her doorbell ring. She looked at her watch. She had completely lost track of time. That was DaQuan dropping off Xavier. She wondered what bad habits her son had picked up this weekend. She went downstairs to let them in, opened to door and gasped. DaQuan was wearing a suit! She had never seen him in one. She didn't even think he owned one and he looked great in it. It was the popular close fit kind and it hugged his chiseled muscular body like an Isotoner glove. He smiled at her and her insides melted, which unsettled her. She was supposed to be over him. She became even gooier on the inside when she saw her sleepy child next to him in a suit as well. DaQuan picked him up. Xavier resembled his father quite a bit, but he had her chocolate complexion and long, thick eyelashes. He closed them as soon as he put his head on his father's shoulder.

"What's up, Sheila? Sorry I'm a little late. Tonight was my grandmother's ninetieth birthday party and X-man and I stayed longer than I anticipated. He had a good time playing with his cousins. He tired himself out. He should sleep good tonight." He walked past her. "I'll just take him up to his room and put him in the bed."

She suddenly remembered Max was upstairs. "No, that won't be necessary. I can take him."

She stepped forward to retrieve him, but DaQuan stepped back out of her reach. "Chill, Sheila. It's cool. I saw the car outside. I'm okay if you have company. I just want to tuck my son in. I don't care about your dude."

"I do have someone here, but it's not like that."

"Well if it's not like that, then it shouldn't be a problem for me to take him upstairs."

"I guess you're right."

DaQuan began climbing the steps and she followed. As soon as he reached the top, he almost bumped into Max.

"Oh hello," said Max. He was clutching one of Sheila's skirts in his hand.

"What's up, man? Don't mind me. I'm just putting my son in the bed."

They stood there eyeing each other for a moment before Max stepped to the side to let him by. DaQuan didn't move.

"Honey, you have been holding out on me. Where did you get these skirts and why were they buried in the back of the closet?" He held two fitted skirts in front of him. One was black and the other was hot pink.

"My cousins gave them to me for my birthday. They're not really my style and—"

DaQuan cleared his throat. Sheila got the hint. "Oh, I'm sorry. Max this is my son's father, DaQuan. DaQuan, Max is here helping me with my wardrobe. I have a few important meetings coming up and I wanted to make sure I looked the part."

"Aw okay. You one of them stylists, like the ones I see on TV. Cool beans. Well, I'll let you two talk skirts while I put my son in his room." He finished making his way down the hall to Xavier's room.

When he was out of earshot, Max said. "Oh honey, I never would have figured that you were into the hood types."

"Normally I'm not. It just happened and then I got pregnant."

"No need to explain to me. I think it was MC Lyte who said that every woman needs a rough neck in her life. I can see what you saw in him. Now, get back in this room. I'm almost finished. I think I saw a couple of blouses that these skirts would go great with. I want you to try the outfits on. You are gonna turn heads in these."

Sheila went into her bathroom and tried on one of the outfits. She came out and Max held out a pair of pumps for her to put on, too. The skirt was shorter than she was used to wearing. She tugged at the bottom of it.

Max swatted her had. "Stop that. That isn't going to make it any longer. You have great legs; you should show them off. He paired the skirt with a revealing top her godmother convinced her to buy one day when they were Christmas shopping. She never had the courage to wear it. Standing there with her legs and her breasts exposed, Sheila felt almost naked and uneasy, or perhaps it was the attractive man examining every inch of her. He told her to turn around and then stepped back to admire his handiwork. "You look hot, Ms. Sheila, H-O-T!" He touched her arm and made a sizzling sound. Sheila laughed.

A voice behind her said, "Dang, girl, where are you going?" Sheila spun around to find DaQuan standing in her doorway. He had a smile on his face and his eyes gleamed with approval.

"Doesn't she look gorgeous?"

"Yeah. Real nice." For an instant, Sheila was sure she saw desire in his eyes, but then it was gone. "Sheila, if your meeting is with a man I guarantee he's going to buy whatever you're selling. What kind of meeting did you say this was?"

"I agree. She's going to blow her dates' minds."

Sheila cringed. She did not want DaQuan to know she hired a matchmaker.

DaQuan raised an eyebrow. "Dates?"

Max was all too happy to give him the details. "Yes. I've arranged for Sheila to meet several highly successful business men in the city in hopes of finding love."

"What. Sheila? What's going on?"

Sheila let out a deep breath. She'd rather tell him than lie about it. "DaQuan, I'm tired of being alone. I haven't dated a man since you, and Max is here to help me get back out there."

"Wow. It's like that. Well, I can't tell you how to live your life. If you want to hire some dude to help you get a date, fine by me. Max, so you hook people up, huh? You look familiar. Do I know you from somewhere?"

Max smirked. "I doubt it. I'm quite sure that you and I don't move in the same circles. I haven't been to any Qwik Stops to buy malt liquor in quite some time. Nice suit, by the way. What is that? A JC Penny going-out-of-business special?"

Sheila saw DaQuan's jaw tighten, but he held his composure. "So you got jokes? I know I've seen you somewhere before, man. I'll let you know when I figure it out. Sheila, I'm out. Good luck on your dates."

"You do that," said Max.

"Good night, DaQuan. Thanks for tucking Xavier in. Let me walk you out."

DaQuan shook his head. "No need. I know the way. You stay here with Max. Maybe he can tell you what panties he likes to wear that might look good on you."

"Oh, good one," said Max and began clapping his hands.

DaQuan disappeared from her doorway and headed down the stairs. Sheila didn't appreciate Max trying to belittle him. Yes, he was rough around the edges, but he was a good man. She wanted to defend him, but she didn't want Max to think she wasn't over him.

"Max. I think that's enough for tonight," she said.

"Okay, sexy lady. Take that off and put it up for one of the more compatible men I'm going to hook you up with." He took a step closer. "You look absolutely beautiful, Sheila. If you weren't my client I'd try to date you myself." He chuckled, bit his bottom lip, and looked her up and down before walking over to the avalanche of clothes he made to put away the outfits he created as well as the ones he didn't use. He even had a pile of clothes he thought she never needed to wear again. He suggested she burn them or give them to the homeless.

She smiled from ear to ear. Max was flirting with her. She suddenly wished she wasn't his client and that unsettled her as well.

Chapter Twenty-Three

Leslie

Leslie's options were diminishing fast. With Simon and Cult no longer on the list that just left T-Money and Percy. As far as she was concerned, Pimply Percy was her very last option. She called T-Money to see when would be a good time to see him, but he didn't answer. She opened her laptop and logged onto the dating site she signed up for a few days earlier. She needed to polish up her profile. She initially posted a few pictures and wrote a short description. She didn't think it was very good, but someone must have liked it because she had five messages in her inbox. It might have been the provocative photos she posted of herself wearing a bikini as well. She received a text.

Out makin money. Hit u back. u tryin 2 do sum tonight?

By "sum," T-Money meant him. Beau had taken care of her needs the night before, but she was always up for another romp. Beau had a pretty boy vibe about him, but the streets educated T-Money. His take control demeanor kept her coming back for more. He was a boss when it came to his business and in the bedroom. She texted back: Yeah.

I'll swing thru n scoop u later. No panties.

Leslie laughed. That was T-Money's thing. Whenever she was around, he wanted her without underwear. At least he asked her to do something easy. Most days she didn't wear panties anyway. She didn't care for panty lines and she found thongs to be uncomfortable if worn for too long. Leslie closed her laptop. She'd look at those messages later. She needed to get ready for Mr. T-Money. She liked to look her best for him because he took great care in his appearance. His beard always looked like he just left the barbershop. He dressed in jeans and T-shirts that looked brand new and his sneakers, usually a pair of Jordans, never had a speck of dirt on them. She opened her massive closet and went to work selecting an outfit that would not only impress, but also make it appear they belonged together.

T-Money picked her up two hours later and took her to his place. He lived in a five-bedroom house in a quiet community in a suburb called Collierville. He said it was a little too quiet for his taste, but it allowed him to have easy access to the majority of his clientele. It also separated him from what he called low-level dealers. It was important for him to keep a low profile and stay out of trouble. He even ran a legitimate lawn care business. For some families, he was cutting the grass for the parents and selling weed to their offspring. He also sold more hardcore stuff like cocaine, but he would only sell that to clients who were twenty-one and older. He was a drug dealer with a conscience. Go figure. Everything in T-Money's living room was white. Leslie relaxed on a white leather couch drinking Jack Daniels and Coke, while T-Money took a shower or, as he called it, "washed away the work."

When he was done, he joined her, wearing basketball shorts and a doo rag. He was a sexy specimen of manhood. He didn't say a word before he handed her a bottle of Jergens lotion and sat next to her. Leslie smiled.

This was one body she had no problems putting her hands all over. His skin reminded her of decadent dark chocolate. T-Money had a cute lopsided smile, with a dimple in his left cheek. He also had a head full of long dreads that came to his shoulders. Whatever hair products he used smelled good. She put her face in his hair and deeply inhaled before she opened the bottle, squirted some of the lotion in her hands, and began massaging it into his strong, muscular arms. T-Money was handsome, intelligent, sexy, and rich. He could have just about any woman he wanted, but he'd always had a thing for Leslie. Last year, he took her to the Dominican Republic to help celebrate his birthday and let her know that whenever she was ready to make that move he would make her happy she did. He never pressured her about it though. He was patient and willing to let her come to him in her own time. He had plenty of other women to keep him company in the meantime. Lucky for him, the time had come. He placed a hand on her thigh and caressed it.

Leslie smiled. She loved the way he touched her. "Baby, why do you live this life? It's obvious that you're hella-intelligent. You could go legit and make plenty of money."

"Yeah, but it would take me much longer to get it. I don't plan on doing this forever. Drug dealing ain't no lifelong career. It's just a means to get where you're trying to go. I promised myself I'd be out in ten years tops. Then, maybe I'll settle down with a pretty thang like you and start a family or something.'"

Leslie straddled him. She kissed him deeply before rubbing some lotion on his shoulder and chest. She loved the way his muscles tightened in response to her touch. T-Money started flexing his left pectoral. That was like foreplay to her; a small show of strength and control that drove her crazy. She laughed and gently played with his nipple before continuing to moisturize his skin while telling him how she felt.

"Yeah, I know, but I worry about you in these streets. Did you know that guy that got killed last week? The news said he was a big time dope boy."

T-Money sat back, closed his eyes, and enjoyed the beautiful woman sitting on his lap. He thought it was sweet she was concerned about him. He cared for Leslie more than she would ever know. "Baby, let me hip you on game. Big time dope boys don't work the block. They have people who do that for them. The only time I'm on the block is if there's a problem that I have to handle personally. The guy who got killed was a middleman at best, but to answer your question, I knew him. We came up together, but he preferred the hood when I prefer a more refined clientele."

"Like little rich boys and girls with BMWs and trust funds."

"Exactly." T-Money opened his eyes, sat up and looked into Leslie's brown eyes. He then grabbed her gently by her afro and kissed her. Leslie didn't mind him being a little rough with her. She knew he would never hurt her. "Don't you worry none, baby girl. I know what I'm doing. You look good enough to eat. I brought you a little something to help you relax."

T-Money reached into his pocket and pulled out one of his popular little white bags. They were known in Leslie's circle as white diamonds. She moved so that he could put the powder-like substance on the glass coffee table in front of them in two lines. He put his head down and made one line disappear and then Leslie did the same. She lay back on the couch and waited for the drug to work its magic. It wasn't long before she forgot where she was and why she came.

Leslie awoke the next morning in her bed with all her clothes on, and she didn't remember how she got there. Her head was pounding and she felt a little queasy. She rarely used cocaine because she always seemed to space out afterward. Last night had been no different. There was a note by her bed.

Stop using that crap. I found you on the porch. You were too high to come in the house. I have to go to work, but we're all going to dinner tomorrow with Aunt Teresa. Get yourself together.

She was so tired of Ms. Do Good thinking she could tell her how to live her life. If Regina's life were so great, she wouldn't have ended up with such a lowlife boyfriend. Leslie smacked herself in the forehead. The conversation about her becoming T- Money's number one girl never took place. She pulled out her phone and called him.

"Hey. Yo, Les. You all right? You were pretty messed up. I took you home this morning, but you didn't have your keys. I'm sorry I had to leave you on the porch. I had some business I needed to attend to and had to go. Good thing it wasn't cold outside. I hated leaving you like that."

"Don't worry about it, baby. My sister brought me in. I meant to ask you something last night, but I got sidetracked. You know what you said about us being together like a couple when we were in the Dominican Republic?"

"Yeah. I remember."

"Did you mean it?"

"Yup. Me and you could have something special, Les. You're one of a kind."

"Well, I'm ready." She could barely believe she was offering to be committed to one man.

T-Money chuckled. "You sho? I'm not for the games, Les."

"Yeah and I'm all in. I want us to be official. Me and you together and see how far we can take it."

"I hear you, but you know you got to leave all those other fools alone to be with me."

"There's no one else. I already cancelled them all. You're the only one I want." T-Money didn't have to know that they canceled themselves.

"Well, that's what's up. My little rich girl finally came to her senses. I must have really put it on you last night."

Leslie laughed. She couldn't even remember last night. She just wanted her millions.

"Of course you did, Daddy. Let's do this," she said.

"I've been waiting for this a long time. I'm gonna make you happy, Les. Real happy. Those others fools you been wit' are gonna seem like a figment of your imagination."

"I believe you mean that, too," she cooed.

"I do. You just wait and see. Now, I gotta get to work. I'm gonna come back tonight and pick you up. You gon' spend the night with me as my woman and I'll show you what you've been missing. What you been getting is jump off treatment. I treat my woman like a queen. By the way, check your pockets. When I was going through your purse looking for your keys, I noticed you were a little light. That should help. I never found your keys though and you couldn't tell me where they were. At least you remembered the code to the gate."

"Sorry about that. I should probably lay off the coke. Thanks for taking care of me. I can't wait to see you."

Leslie hung up the phone, put her hands in her left pocket and pulled out a wad of money—one hundred dollar bills. There had to be at least one thousand dollars. This wasn't the first time T-Money had given her money, but he never gave her that much. He must have really felt bad about having to leave her on the porch. *I'm going to be Mrs—* then it hit her. She didn't know T-Money's real name either.

Chapter Twenty-Four

Regina

"Thank you for calling Precision Repairs and Auto Body. How may I help you?"

It was Regina's second day on the job and she still didn't quite know what to think. She had never done office work before, but she was very familiar with customer service. She gave a friendly greeting and a smile to all customers as they entered the shop. She offered them a beverage or a complimentary snack while they waited on their oil changes, repairs or arranged to have auto body work completed. She learned how to look up service fees in the computer. She knew how to take payments of cash or credit cards, but had a few problems with the shop's equipment. The cash register had to be at least twenty year old. She planned to talk to Chance about an upgrade.

The staff all seemed to like her. Maybe a little too much. She was the only woman and men were always trying to find a reason to come into the office to talk to her. She was pretty sure they were supposed to be in the shop repairing cars and not in the office asking what she was doing after work. Chance had come back to the office on more than one occasion and told whomever was with her to get back to work. She wondered how the shop was doing financially. There wasn't a steady stream of customers. She also wondered what kind of marketing strategy Chance was using to attract customers.

Regina looked online and noticed all they had was an outdated website and no social media accounts. She made a note to talk to Chance about that as well. With social media he could then offer some online discounts and coupons to try to increase business. Regina knew that with her help he could get more people through the door. When she wasn't dealing with customers, she worked on organizing the office. It was very cluttered and there didn't seem to be a logical filing system. None of the drawers were labeled and the folders weren't alphabetized. That kept her busy most of the day. The last customer left at 5:30 p.m., but she continued to work. At 7:00 p.m., Chance came into the office and sat at one of the desks. He looked angry. At first, he didn't say anything. He merely stared at Regina. She tried to act as if she hadn't noticed and kept straightening the office. The one thing she did notice was that Chance was an attractive man. Even when he was covered in grease stains.

When Chance finally spoke he said, "Ms. Regina, I think we have a problem."

That was the last thing Regina wanted to hear. "What? Did I do something wrong?"

"Yeah, a few things. First, you're giving away all my drinks and chips and those are for customers to purchase out of the vending machines. Secondly, I think you are too pretty to be working here. You're distracting all my mechanics and even a few patrons."

Regina began to panic. She needed this job at least until she could find a husband and get her money. She didn't know what to say, but she had to think of something fast. "I'm sorry. I didn't realize you were selling those snacks. At the boutique, where I worked, we always offered our customers a beverage. We didn't do snacks because we didn't want them getting food on the clothes. I'll replace the snacks I gave away with my first check. I can wear ugly clothes and no make up to make myself less attractive. Please don't fire me."

Chance started laughing. "I have no intention of firing you. However, I do need you to stop giving away my extra income and I need to figure out a way to keep my men out of the office. None of them are disrespecting you, are they?"

"No, they've all been quite kind, but they do pose a bit of a distraction with them coming in the office all the time. They want to talk, while I'm trying to work."

"I figured. Tomorrow I'm going to have a staff meeting and talk to the fellas and let them know that will not be tolerated, but I know my guys and they're still gonna try to come in here when I'm not looking. So, I will need you to lock the office door from now on. No one has any reason to come in here, but me and you. You will still have access to the customers through the service window. Is that okay with you?"

Regina nodded. "Yeah. I can do that."

"Good."

Regina decided that this would be a good time to offer her marketing assistance.

"Now, may I ask you something?" She didn't wait for Chance to answer. "Are you happy with the number of clients you're getting? I noticed that it can get really slow at times."

"No. Can't say that I am, but when that In A Jiffy opened up around the corner I lost quite a bit of business. I can't compete with those $19.99 oil changes they're offering. I'm not about to put cheap oil in my customers' cars. It's only going to cause them more problems later."

"I can understand that. I'd like to help. I took some marketing classes in college and I have a few ideas I think could help you attract some more business."

"I'm all ears. When would you like to chat?"

"Tonight is good, if you're not busy. You hungry?" Regina hoped he wouldn't think she was asking him out, but she skipped lunch and her stomach was growling. She needed to eat soon.

Chance looked at her and shifted nervously for a minute and then jumped up and said, "Yep. Let me go wash up a little bit and change my shirt and we can go get some chow. We can talk while we eat."

Chance walked out of the office as fast as he could. He wanted to get out of there before his new office manager realized the affect she had on him. He knew she was pretty, but now that he knew she was not only pretty, but smart, had ideas and wanted to help his business he was even more attracted to her. What a woman! It was going to be hard to be around her every day and he knew it.

Chapter Twenty-Five

Sheila

Dolled up and ready for her first matchmaker arranged date, Sheila squirmed nervously in her seat and tried not to drink too much water. She usually had to pee when she was nervous and she didn't want to keep excusing herself from the table in front of her date. A couple days earlier, she and Max went through several files of potential suitors and she picked out two she thought might be a good match. Her date tonight was Darwin who worked as a sports agent. He was divorced with one child, but what attracted her were his piercing blue eyes. A Black man with blue eyes was a rarity, especially, a dark-skinned Black man. She wondered if he was bi-racial. He didn't provide his nationality in his profile. Unfortunately, Darwin was late. What did men have against being on time? Her dates were always late, and DaQuan was usually late bringing Xavier home. It worked her nerves to no end. Her son was on a schedule and when he came home late, it threw everything off. Why was she thinking about DaQuan?

She took another sip of her water and looked up to see Max rushing toward her table. He was impeccably dressed as usual. Today he wore khakis, a brown shirt with a denim blazer, and a brown bow tie with blue polka dots.

Once he reached her table, he shook her hand and said, "Hello, Sheila. You look lovely. I'm sorry to have to break the news, but one of Darwin's major contracts with a pro NFL player is in jeopardy, so he has to work tonight. It seems his client's contract is almost expired and another agent is trying to woo him away. He sends his regrets and hopes you can understand."

Shelia didn't try to mask her disappointment. She was having the worst luck. No wonder she stopped dating. "I understand, but I was looking forward to meeting Darwin. Thanks for coming to tell me in person, but you didn't have to do that. You could have called."

Max patted her hand. "I know I could have called, but I didn't want you to look like you were alone. I remember you telling me how much that bothered you when your previous date didn't show. I haven't had dinner and I've been hearing how great the food is at this restaurant, so if it's all right with you, I'd like to join you for the evening."

Sheila smiled. "Of course, it's okay. I'd hate to waste a good babysitter, and I always enjoy your company. It was very sweet of you to come."

Max smiled and sat down. "I enjoy your company as well. By the way, your legs look great in that skirt."

She blushed. Max seemed to know the right thing to say to lift her spirits. Maybe he could make her feel important, desirable, and unforgettable. He got the waiter's attention and placed his drink order.

Three hours later, Shelia and Max laughed their way into her kitchen.

"Shhhhhh," Sheila whispered. "You're going to wake Xavier. He should be in bed by now."

"Okay. I'll be quiet. Let's get you upstairs. Where's your babysitter?"

"I don't babysit my own kid and that won't be necessary," said a male voice behind them. Max was startled when DaQuan appeared in the kitchen wearing jeans and a tight-fitting Superman T-shirt. "And you're right, Xavier, is asleep and usually you would be, too. I was beginning to get worried."

Sheila laughed, and said, "I'm cool," and gave him the peace sign with two fingers.

"No worries, she was in good hands," said Max. "Although, I fear our Nubian Queen had a little too much to drink tonight. I didn't want her driving and brought her home."

"Shelia doesn't drink," said DaQuan.

"And now we know why," Sheila said, before busting into a fit of giggles. She tried to hold herself steady on intoxicated feet and said, "Maximillian, meet my babysitter, baby daddy, ex-boyfriend and defender of all that's good. Faster than a speeding bullet! More powerful than a locomotive! Able to leap tall buildings at a single bound! Look! Up in the sky..."

"...it's a bird, it's a plane, its Superman!" she and Max said in unison.

Sheila laughed again, lost her balance, and began to fall.

"Sheila!" shouted DaQuan and moved swiftly to catch her. Max did, too and the three of them collided. Sheila was still laughing. DaQuan was not amused, and he didn't like Max putting his hands on Sheila, as if they belonged there. "I thought you were supposed to fix her up with other dudes, not yourself," he said.

"Not that it's any of your business, but her date was a no show and we ended up hanging out instead." Max turned his attention back to Sheila. "Let's get you to bed." He began walking toward the stairs.

"Thanks, dawg, but I got her," said DaQuan. "This is as far as you go…tonight. She's too drunk to play dress up."

Maximillian understood the insinuation that DaQuan didn't like seeing him in her room earlier in the week. He cocked his head to the side and raised an eyebrow. Did this homeboy from around the way think he was supposed to care about his likes and dislikes?

"Now boys, no need to fight over little ole me. I'm enough woman for both of you!" Sheila shouted before laughing again. "Oh, I'm sorry. Am I too loud? I'm going to wake up my son. DaQuan take me to see Xavier. I need to kiss him goodnight."

Maximillian was not a small man, but he was smaller than DaQuan. It was obvious he worked out regularly and he saw no need to get into a tussle over who was going to tuck a drunk woman in for the night.

"I guess I will leave you two to your parental duties." He took his hands from around Shelia's waist and straightened his jacket. "Shelia, thank you for a wonderful evening. We must do it again sometime."

"I had fun tonight Max-eee-millian. This was the best undate I've been on in a long time. Call me tomorrow?"

"Of course, my Nubian Queen." He watched DaQuan as he picked Sheila up and headed toward the stairs. "Good night, baby daddy and defender of all that's good."

"It's DQ. Lock the door behind you. I know I know you from somewhere and I'm going to figure it out sooner or later."

"Don't hurt your brain trying to think," said Max before he opened the door, turned the bottom lock, and saw himself to his car.

Chapter Twenty-Six

Leslie

Although Leslie had her eyes open, everything was pitch-black. "Can I take this blindfold off, baby? Why do I have to wear it anyway? I've been to your place before."

"Will you be patient and let me surprise my woman?" said T-Money.

"I'm trying, but the suspense is killing me!"

"You better be glad that I like you. You can take it off—"

Before he could finish his sentence, Leslie snatched off the dark blue bandanna he tied around her face. This was supposed to be their first official night as a couple and T-Money wanted it to be special. It started with dinner downtown at Felecia Suzanne's, followed by a short walk by the river, and them returning to T-Money's home.

Regina gasped as she looked around the room. They were standing in his bedroom. Like the living room, everything—the carpet, the furniture, even the comforter on the bed—was white. There were red and pink rose petals scattered over the bed and the floor. Candles illuminated the room, giving off the sweet aroma of vanilla. It smelled as if she were in her grandmother's kitchen, while the cook baked sugar cookies.

"Baby, this is so nice," she squealed and did a little dance. "No one has ever done anything like this for me before."

"That's because you've never had a real man who adored you, but you do now." He pulled her close to him and kissed her as if he were in the desert and she were a tall drink of water, engulfing her entire mouth with his and savoring her flavor. The kiss was forceful, but surprisingly sexy. When he seemed to have tasted enough of her, he pulled back.

"Wow! What do we do now?" Leslie asked seductively.

T-Money went to the bed and pulled back the covers. "Now I'm going to use these blessed hands of mine to give you a full body massage."

"That sounds lovely, but can I ask you something first?"

"Anything, baby."

"What's your real name? The one on your birth certificate."

"If I tell you, I'll have to kill you," he joked.

She crawled on the bed and looked up at him while crouched on all fours. "Then, pull out your gun because I want to know just that *baaaaaad*."

T-Money stood over her, enjoying the view the angle was providing of her ample cleavage. "You are such a bad girl. I could never hurt a single strand of this Indian woman's hair you got in your head."

Leslie fell on the bed laughing. Earlier in the day, she took the money he gave her and got a five-hundred-dollar sew-in done. She took the rest and bought an Apple watch to sync with her iPhone. She was excited to have a new gadget to add to her collection. "It's Malaysian. Now tell me," she said, before springing up and pulling him on the bed with her. They rolled around until Leslie was on top. She straddled him and shouted, "I said tell me!"

T-Money laughed. He could have easily thrown her off him, but he didn't want to. He loved Leslie's playfulness. "My names is Thaddeus Leon Lewis."

"Yes! That's a nice name. Can I call you Thaddeus?"

"Only when we're alone. Now lay down, girl, and let me make you feel good!"

He flipped her off him and began slowly taking off Leslie's clothes. When she was naked, he turned her on her stomach before reaching over to the nightstand where he had massage oil warming. He gave Leslie the most sensual massage she ever had, kissing each area of her body before he caressed it. Sometimes the feel of his touch was light and other times he added a little pressure. Leslie enjoyed the way his hands felt as they rounded her hips and behind. It was driving her insane and she begged him to make love to her right then, but he refused.

"We have a long night ahead of us. So, you're just going to have to be patient. I told you that my woman gets five-star treatment. We haven't even reached the three-star level yet."

Leslie knew she was in for a treat of epic proportions, as her body began to explode under the masterful caress of her man's hands. After his masterful massage, he carried her to his shower where he washed off the oil and made love to her under twin, pulsating jets. It was intense and passionate. Under normal circumstances, Leslie would have objected, but she didn't care that he was ruining her expensive weave and the cascading curls her stylist created. He was showing her a sensual side she never knew existed and she liked it. They had spent the night together multiple times, but never did he make her feel like she belonged to him, but more importantly he belonged to her. She could easily get used to this kind of treatment. She was glad he ended up being the one she chose.

T-Money wasn't a bad guy, but he was a dope dealer and Leslie wasn't about that life. She always thought she'd end up with a man who was part of the social elite like she was, but with the money she was going to inherit after marrying him, he wouldn't have to sell drugs. Leslie decided she wanted to be honest about her intentions. He dried her off and carried her to the bed where he made love to her again. They fell asleep intertwined in one another's arms. The next morning, she awoke, thanking God that last night wasn't a dream. Her prince charming was right in front of her the entire time and she was too blind to see him. He kissed her on her nose.

"You look beautiful in the morning," he said, pulling her closer.

"I bet you tell all the girls that."

"Nope. They don't get to spend the night in this house, but you're special."

They began talking and during the conversation, she revealed what prompted her to give them a try.

"So you mean to tell me that Old Lady Purdue put it in her will that all three of you had to get married in order for you to get your inheritance?"

"Messed up, isn't it?"

"Yeah. So is that the reason you wanted to get with me?"

"Yes and no. I always liked you, Thaddeus. I just wasn't cool with this lifestyle you're leading. When I sat down and thought about the men in my life who I could possibly share my life with and enjoy doing so, you were the one who rose to the top. The good thing is when I get my money you won't have to sell drugs anymore and that will no longer be a concern of mine."

T-Money kissed her. She didn't even care that it was morning and neither of them had brushed their teeth. "I'm glad you chose me., but Les, no real man is going to live off his woman's money and no real man is going to hinder his woman from getting her money either. I'll marry you and help you get your dough, but under one condition."

Leslie just knew he was going to ask to have an open marriage so he could keep seeing other women, a ménage à trois or something freaky like that. She'd been with a guy and a girl at the same time before, but she never expected to do it with her husband. Yet, she was willing to do whatever she needed to get her inheritance. She closed her eyes as if she were bracing herself for the worst and said, "Okay. I'm listening."

"No, open your eyes and look at me. I want to make sure you understand how serious I am." Leslie opened her eyes, but turned her head in another direction. She didn't want him to see the hurt in her eyes when he asked her for permission to share him.

T-Money gently guided her face back toward him. He looked into her brown eyes. He saw pain there. He didn't know what caused the pain, but he did know that he wanted to take it away. No one would ever hurt her again under his watch. "We are getting a prenup. It's going to state that your money is yours. I want you,

Leslie, and only you. I never cared about the fact that you came from money. I never wanted your money. All I want is a good woman to build a family with. So we can do this, but only if we do it that way."

Leslie blinked. Was he serious? She was about to inherit millions, probably more than he'd ever see in his lifetime, and he didn't want a dime? She was bewildered. In the world she grew up in it was all about the money. People planned their relationships and marriages around making the merger financially profitable. "That's it? That's all you want?"

He laughed. "Yep. What did you think I was going to say?"

Leslie was now embarrassed by what she was thinking. "I thought you were going to ask for an open marriage?"

"I'm not that kind of man, Leslie. I know I got money and for some reason people believe that all men with money have a basketball team of women and maybe I did at one point in my life. When I'm in a relationship, I'm loyal to my woman. My pops told me when I was a boy, 'If you gon' love a woman, love her right or leave her alone.' That's why I haven't been in any hurry to settle down because none of these women out her seemed worthy of my loyalty or my love, until I met you. It's obvious that you don't have any idea how special you are. I see more in you than just a hot body and beautiful face. You're smart, you're funny, and you're sweet. I see the real Leslie. Not this party girl exterior everybody else sees. Besides, with a freak like you, what do I need another woman for?"

Leslie laughed as her eyes welled with tears. "Baby, that's so thoughtful of you. I'll sign whatever you want.

These two days with you have been amazing. Just promise me it will always be like this. Promise me you won't marry me and then change."

"I promise and to prove it to you..." T-Money got off the bed, went to his white dresser, and reached into the top drawer. He came back with a small black box and got on one knee. "Leslie Priscilla Watson-Purdue, will you marry me?"

Leslie was in the bed with the sheet wrapped around her. At the sound of that question and her full name, she sat straight up and let the sheet fall from around her. She sat there topless, staring at the engagement ring T-Money was holding out in front of her. This was too much. Tears fell from her eyes. It was beautiful. This moment was beautiful.

"You remembered my whole name? I only told it to you once."

"I can't forget the name of the woman I want to have my children. Give me your hand, girl."

Leslie extended her left hand and he slid the ring on her ring finger.

"Thaddeus, when did you buy this?"

"I bought it a while ago. I almost asked you when we were in the Dominican, but I knew the time wasn't right. You gon' answer my question?"

"Yes, baby, Yes! I'll become Mrs. Thaddeus Lewis!" She pulled him to her, buried his head in her breasts, and kissed the top of his head. She brought his face to hers and lovingly kissed him on the lips.

When their mouths parted, T-Money said, "I know you want me to stop slanging and I will, but you gotta let me make a couple more deals to make sure that we're set up straight. Can you do that, Leslie? I promise you after that I'll go legit and just cut lawns for a living, bake cakes, mop floors, whatever you want."

Leslie pushed him away from her. "Boy, quit playing! You know you're too smart to be a janitor. Thaddeus, I really want you to stop right away."

T-Money took both her hands in his and kissed each one once. "Baby, the only way you get out the dope game cold turkey is to die or go to jail. I ain't planning on dying no time soon and my booty has a 'Do Not Enter' sign on it so jail ain't for me. I'll get out, but I have people who depend on me to take care of themselves and their family. I got to prepare my people for the change and then I'm out." He gently kissed her collarbone. Leslie moaned in response to the sensation that small kiss sent through her. She knew she was about to have the best morning of her life.

"You got to trust me. I'm doing this for us," he whispered.

"I know, baby. It's just I'm so scared I'm gonna lose you. The drug game is dangerous."

T-Money's lips traveled from her collarbone to her exposed areolas. Between licks, he said, "Baby, my number one goal each day is to make it back to you because I can't get enough of you. Now, let's get you pregnant."

Leslie laughed as her new fiancé gently pushed her back against his plush pillows and made love to her again. She felt better than she had in quite a while. Something in her life was finally starting to go her way.

Chapter Twenty-Seven

Regina

Regina was really enjoying her new job. She wasn't styling the elite of the South in the latest fashions, but in her mind, she was doing something better. She was helping a Black man with a good heart create a thriving business. A business that helped single mothers keep their cars running so they could get back and forth to work to support their family, see their kids play sports and transport them to church so they could worship as a family. Earlier that day, a college kid came in with a car some unscrupulous car salesman sold him that had so many problems it needed to be in a junk yard. On his lunch break, Chance went to the dealership and talked so badly to the man he refunded the young man his money and vowed to take the car off the lot.

Regina had to admit that she enjoyed their dinner the other night. She didn't have the opportunity to talk to very many men who openly professed their love for Christ. She believed in God. She was baptized as a child. She, Sheila and Leslie went to church regularly because their grandmother made them, but when she went away to college, she stopped going. Sheila was the only one still dedicated. She acted as if she were going to hell if she skipped a Sunday. Regina told all of this to Chance and he didn't judge her. He just said he hoped that while she was working in his shop he would say or do something that would make her want to give Jesus a chance again. He was a mighty good friend to have.

Today, Regina spent most of her time working on her marketing ideas. She opened several social media accounts and posted information about the shop and a coupon that allowed patrons to save 10% on services over $100. She also joined several online mechanic chat groups so she could gain greater insight on the industry from the experts. She then reached out to a couple of people she knew to see if they could help drive business their way. There was one person in particular she thought could help, but needed to get the number from her sister. She hoped she was in a pleasant mood. Leslie didn't come home last night so a phone call would give her a chance to make sure she was all right as well.

"Leslie, I need the number for Bart," said Regina.

"Bart?" Leslie sounded as if she were still asleep. It was one o'clock in the afternoon.

"Wake up, sleepy head. Yeah. You know, Grandma Grace's old driver?

Leslie yawned. "I haven't talked to him in years."

Regina refused to be brushed off that easily. "Leslie, did you forget who you're talking to? I know you guys slept together a few times. I need his number?"

Leslie let out a deep breath. "Sometimes I really hate you. I'll text it to you in a minute."

Regina hated that her sister thought it was okay to sleep with several men. She also didn't care if they were single or married. Regina believed her body was sacred and there was no way she would allow others, who haven't proven themselves worthy, to enter her sacred space. It also just seemed nasty to let random dudes inside you. "I love you, too. I noticed you didn't come home last night. Where have you been hanging out?"

"At my man's house," said Leslie matter-of-factly.

Regina didn't believe her. "Girl, please. Hoes don't have a man. Customers, but not a man."

"Shut up, Regina! I'm serious. I have a boyfriend and he's good to me and we're gonna get married and live happily ever after."

"Sis, you know I'm kidding. If you have found someone who makes you happy then I'm happy for you. When do I get to meet him?"

Leslie yawned again. "I dunno. I'm not ready to share him yet. You and Shelia are so judgmental."

"I'm sorry you feel that way. I won't push. We can meet whenever you're ready. I promise to keep an open mind about him. On another note, you haven't heard from Antonio, have you?

Leslie let out another deep breath. Why couldn't Regina see that leaving him was the wisest decision she ever made? "What are you worried about that fool for?"

"I'm not, but he's been kind of quiet lately, which is never a good thing. When I don't hear from him that usually means he's up to something."

"Maybe he's gotten it through his head that you are no longer interested."

"I hope so," Regina lied. The truth was Regina was missing him like crazy, but she couldn't bring herself to call him. She needed to send him a message that he couldn't keep mistreating her without consequences. "Well, I got to get back to work. Send me that number," were her closing words.

"I will," said Leslie. "Let that cheater go, Gina. You can do so much better."

Five minutes later, Leslie sent the number and Regina called Bart. She wanted to know which auto shop the local chauffeurs took their cars to and if they'd be willing to try a new place. Bart was a bit of a talker, but she hoped he would let her make it brief.

"Most of us go to Williams and Son, but since old man Williams has been ill and Junior is running the place, the customer service is crap and the quality of the work doesn't seem to be as good. Last time I went for an oil change, the dummy didn't tighten my screws good and I was leaking oil everywhere," said Bart.

Regina was glad he was dissatisfied. "Well, I'd like for you to try this new place I've been helping with their marketing. It's called Precision Repairs and Auto Body," she said.

"Oh yeah, I know the place. His grandmother used to work for the Levitts as their housekeeper. She and my grandmother were friends. She died a few years ago. A shame, too. She was a good woman. I'd be glad to come support him. If he does a good job, I'll spread the word among all us domestic workers."

"Thanks so much, Bart! He's a great guy and they do great work here."

"No, problem." Bart grew silent as if he were contemplating saying something. After a few seconds, he said, "How's your sister? You know I really loved that girl, but she couldn't get over that I was the help. As shallow as she was, I still wanted to make her mine." Bart's voice went from friendly to somber in two seconds. He was part of a long list of good men her sister bedded and then forgot existed.

"I know, Bart, but trust me, Leslie wasn't right for you. She would have only broken your heart. You lucked out by marrying Marina."

Marina was the daughter of Ms. Pearl. She and Bart had a beautiful wedding on the Purdue estate about three years ago. It was kind of sad though. While Marina was walking down the aisle to meet her groom, Leslie was telling Regina about the wild time she and Bart had the night before. It made her cringe to know he was kissing his bride with the same mouth he had just used to pleasure another woman. Her sister could be such a slut sometimes. She didn't even like him. Bart was at least fifteen years older than her and he used to take them and pick them up from school. It was a game to Leslie. She never liked Marina and she wanted to see if he was so in love with Marina that he would turn her down. He wasn't. She really hoped that this new guy, whoever he was, could tame Leslie. She really needed to slow down.

"Marina is a great girl, but you know how it is. Sometimes you wonder what if," said Bart.

"Yeah, but I've learned that everyone who comes into your life isn't meant to stay."

Bart chuckled. "How'd you get so smart, young lady? I need a new oil change. I should be by the shop today or sometime tomorrow."

"Great. I look forward to seeing you."

"Tell Leslie I said hello when you see her. Dang that girl is pretty." Regina shook her head, as she hung up the phone. Sexual hurricane Leslie had left another dejected penis in her path. Poor guy.

Chapter Twenty-Eight

Sheila

The next morning, Shelia woke up to a splitting headache and the room was spinning. She sat up and instantly regretted it. Nausea overtook her and she ran as fast as she could to the bathroom and threw up in the toilet. She couldn't remember the last time she felt like this. Maybe never. How many drinks did she have? She would have to lay across the altar and repent for being a drunkard when she went to church on Sunday, but in the meantime she needed God to grant her relief. She was afraid to stand for fear she would get nauseous again. She crawled over to the bathtub and pulled down a towel hanging from the shower curtain rod. She laid it on the floor and lay on top of it. The coolness of the tiles seemed to make her feel better. She started to doze off when she felt a pair of strong arms lift her up and carry her to her bed. She opened her eyes and realized it was DaQuan. Why was he in her room? Why was she only wearing her bra and panties and where was her son? She screamed.

"Sheila, calm down. It's me, baby."
"I know! What are you doing here?"
"You were drunk when you came in last night. I stayed to make sure you were all right and to make sure Xavier got to school."
"School? What time it is?"
"It's a little after one."

"One o'clock? Put me down! I got to get to work."

He held her firmly as she tried to kick herself out of his grasp. She was in no condition to go anywhere. "It's okay. I took care of everything. I sent your boss a text first thing this morning from your phone. I pretended to be you and told her you were sick. She wrote back and said it was fine. I gave X breakfast and took him to school. Baby, just relax."

DaQuan was right. She felt like crap and was in no condition to go anywhere. "You did all that?"

He lay her down on the bed and caressed the side of her face. "Of course, I did. I was worried about you."

Sheila welcomed the opportunity to lie down. The room was no longer spinning, but she didn't feel well. Her head was banging, as if someone were playing heavy medal inside it. She didn't want DaQuan to give up his day because of her. She rested her head on a pillow. "Don't you need to go to work?"

"I called in, too. I can't leave my baby mama when she needs me," he said, still caressing her face.

She had forgotten how sweet he could be. Sheila and DaQuan hadn't really spent any time together in years. Once Xavier was old enough to walk and talk, she lessened their communication and made it a point only to discuss matters that had to do with their son. She didn't see a need to have him in her personal life or her personal space if they weren't a couple.

"Thank you. I don't even remember drinking that much. I was supposed to have a date, but he had some work emergency and cancelled and Max ended up having dinner with me instead. I know I had a glass or two of wine, but after that everything is a blur."

"You never could hold your liquor." DaQuan crawled in the bed next to her and let Sheila rest her head on his chest. "About this matchmaker business… Why's it so important for you to find a man now? You never seemed interested in a relationship before."

Sheila may have been sick, but she wasn't so ill that she would tell DaQuan that she was trying to get married to get her inheritance. He didn't need to know and she surely wasn't going to marry him.

"I'm getting older. I'm ready to settle down and you know I never was much for socializing. Now with a demanding job and Xavier I really don't have time to go out. So a matchmaker seemed like the perfect choice to help me find love."

"Okay. How did you hear about this Max?"

"Vivian." Sheila nestled closer to DaQuan. She hadn't been this close to him since they broke up and that was before Xavier was born. Yet, at that moment, she was glad he was there. The strength she felt from the muscles underneath her head and the sound of his heartbeat seemed to help ease her agony. It was almost comforting and much better than lying on her cold bathroom floor.

"Your boss. You know I never liked her or trusted her. You've always been the brains behind her outfit, but she takes all the credit and takes the bulk of the money."

"DaQuan, she's not that bad. I make a good salary and it is her company. Can we talk about this another time? I just want to sleep. I have to get it together before tonight. We're all having dinner with Aunt Teresa to discuss some family business. Can you watch Xavier again?"

"Sure. You also need a breath mint, old vomit mouth girl."

Sheila smiled. He was probably right, but she didn't care. "Shut up, Superman. Thanks for being my hero," she said before she fell fast asleep while listening to the heartbeat of her baby's daddy.

DaQuan looked down at Sheila and kissed her on her forehead. He'd never really gotten over her, but it was obvious she was over him. He had secretly hoped that maybe one day they could try again. He knew he made some mistakes the first time. He was too stubborn and he kept listening to everyone else. They told him she was all wrong for him and she was changing him. His boys started joking that she was going to have him eating cucumber sandwiches and wearing men's hosiery. DaQuan was a product of the hood and he couldn't have his street credibility taken from him because of a woman. So, when she broke up with him he considered it a solution to his problem and acted as if he didn't care. Although, he did. The first few weeks he was miserable without her. When he found out he had a son on the way, he tried to use that as a way to get her back, but Sheila wouldn't hear of it. DaQuan didn't like the idea of Sheila using a matchmaker, but he couldn't do anything about it. Technically, it wasn't any of his business. He decided to stay there and enjoy this moment because as soon as she felt better she would be back to acting like she never loved him and telling him he wasn't setting a good example for his son. He didn't want another man coming into their lives, but if she wanted to move on he had to let her. Something just didn't seem right. He was absolutely sure he had seen Maximillian somewhere before and if Vivian was involved, he didn't trust it. He was going to get to the bottom of this because if they were trying to hurt Sheila, that hurt could ultimately impact his son and nobody was going to cause his family any harm as long as he had breath in his body.

Chapter Twenty-Nine

Antonio

Antonio found out Regina was living at the mansion, but he hadn't had any luck finding out if she was working and if so, where. He drove by the house all times of the night and day, but never caught a glimpse of her and since the property was protected by a security fence and monitored, he couldn't just go up and knock on the door. None of her friends knew. At least that's what they told him. He was running out of resources and needed to get his meal ticket back fast. The property manager he was sleeping with saw another woman leaving his apartment one morning, got jealous and gave him until the end of the month to get out. Did she really think she was going to be the only woman he was sleeping with? He smoothed things over with Olivia in hopes that she would be of some use, but so far, she hadn't been. She was clingy and getting on his nerves. She called constantly, wanting to know if she could come over. She didn't even have a job now because when her mother found out what she'd done, she fired her. She was looking for Regina as well so she could bring her back to the shop. She chose Regina over her own daughter! But, it wasn't surprising; Regina had plenty of style and a great attitude. Antonio had to admit that a small part of him missed her.

On top of that, he hadn't seen his number one lover in a while. He really didn't believe her when she said the last time was the last time, but every time he called, she didn't answer. When he texted her, she claimed she had a new job that was keeping her busy, but he knew better. The only skill that girl had involved taking off her clothes. Nobody would hire her except a pimp. His life wasn't looking so good and Antonio wasn't used to that. He had to devise a plan to get himself back on top and fast. The first step was to locate Regina and get her back.

Chapter Thirty

Family Gathering

The Purdue women gathered around the table for dinner and waited for Aunt Teresa to bless the food. It felt weird sitting at the big table in the dining hall without Grandma Grace. She and Teresa were nothing alike. Teresa was pretty, but she was tough. She had a "say it like it is" attitude she developed after serving over twenty years as a cop. She used to be an alcoholic, but she was able to get into a treatment program and get sober. As their grandmother's only surviving sibling, she was the only link they had to her. They didn't know why Grandma Grace made her the one who had to determine whether they got their inheritance. She was cool, but they didn't know her very well. Maybe Grandma Grace selected her because she was a cop and she would be able to spot a fake relationship a mile away.

Teresa bowed her head and they did, too. "Heavenly Father, thank you for this opportunity to gather together one more time. Bless the land that produced this food, the hands that prepared it, and the people who receive it. And help these girls find good men who will love them like Christ loves the church. This we ask in your son, Jesus's, name, Amen."

"Amen," said the girls in unison.

The food looked delicious. Ms. Pearl prepared them each a Cornish hen with cranberry stuffing, asparagus, and au gratin potatoes.

"Dive in, ladies. We can talk about how you're doing finding a husband while we eat. I'm not happy about what my sister did. I don't like being put in the middle of this nonsense, but I agreed to do it because I'm probably one of the few people who actually have your best interests in mind. I don't want your money. Our daddy left me plenty. I want you to have what's yours. I'm going to do everything I can to make sure you get it, but it's got to be within the guidelines that I've been given. I won't approve a fake marriage. I have to deem that you are each dating a man who loves you and wants you for you before I can sign off on anything. Understood?"

Sheila, Leslie, and Regina had food in their mouths and nodded to signify they understood. Nobody really wanted to be there, but they all had a common goal and that was to get their inheritance.

"We're about one month in, which means you've got about eight months left to find a suitable husband and get him approved by me. I'll do everything I can to help you short of choosing a man for you. That is completely up to you. I deal in legal matters, not matters of the heart. Now, I'd like to know what you ladies are doing to snag your Boaz. We'll start with the oldest. Sheila, how's it going?"

Sheila hesitated at first. She was always private when it came to her love life, but she didn't have a choice but to tell all her business. She needed Teresa to get her money. Besides, she was missing Bible study to be there so she might has well make it productive. "It's going slow, but I do have a plan in place. I've hired a professional matchmaker. He and I have selected a couple of candidates I like, but I haven't been on a date yet. I'm hoping one of them will be the one."

"I'm glad you weren't too proud to solicit outside help," said Teresa. "You were the one I was most worried about. I know that you really haven't dated since breaking up with Xavier's father. If this matchmaker is worth his salt, he should be able to turn up a suitable prospect or two. Good job. Keep me posted."

"Thanks, Auntie. I will, but why were you the most worried about me?"

"Of the three of you, you are the most reclusive. Let's face it, if it doesn't involve Xavier, work, or church you probably aren't participating. And, as much as you attend church, if you were going to find a man there you would have done so by now."

"Ouch," said Sheila. "Next, I'm done." Her family didn't know she hadn't been attending church as much as she usually did and she saw no need to tell them. Most of her evenings were consumed with her son and trying to find a husband.

Teresa turned to Regina. She was half-paying attention and playing with the asparagus on her plate. She hated asparagus and she hated being in the same boat as everyone else. She just knew she and Antonio would get married and she wouldn't have to play this horrible game her grandmother concocted. Why did her boyfriend have to be such a jerk?"

"Okay, Regina, what about you?" asked Teresa.

She looked around the room. "I don't know if you heard, but Antonio and I broke up. I always thought he would be my husband, but I guess it just wasn't meant to be. Aunt Teresa, I don't want to date. I spent seven years of my life with this man and now it's over. I can't just run out and try to find a new man. My heart is broken. The last thing I want is a new man in my life. Isn't there some clause in there for being emotionally unstable? The worst thing I could do to a man is bring him into this nonsense I call a life. I'm damaged, and I know it. I need time to heal."

Teresa reached over and patted her niece's hand. "Baby, I understand, but there's no such provision for that. The good thing is that you still have time. Maybe you two will get back together. If you don't mind me asking, what happened? I never really spent any time with Antonio, but I do know that Grace hated him. She actually came close to putting in her will that you couldn't marry him, but I told her that was unfair. Seven years is a long time. That's more than some marriages."

Regina picked up her fork and stabbed at her Cornish hen before answering. "I really don't want to talk about it. This food is delicious." Regina shoved a chunk of meat in her mouth.

"I'll tell you what happened," said Sheila. "He was beating her behind and if that weren't good enough he was sleeping with anything with a vagina. Grandma Grace wasn't the only one who hated him. I can't stand his no good, lying, conniving, flea-infested tail. You better be glad you called Leslie the day you moved out because if I had come over and saw what he did to your face, I'd be in jail and he'd be dead."

Teresa was taking a sip of her iced tea. After hearing that, she quickly put it down. "Is that true, Gina? Did that man put his hands on you?"

Regina didn't need or want her cousin's approval when it came to her love life. "Sheila, shut up! Nobody asked you anything. I don't expect you to understand. You've never been in love. You never loved DeQuan. I know because it was so easy for you to walk away. What

Antonio and I had was the real deal. You just don't give up on love. You fight for it! Don't you dare look down on me because I wasn't too scared to fight!"

"You were fighting for love, while Antonio was fighting you. You don't know a thing about what DeQuan and I had. And, if what you and that dog had was the real deal I don't want it. I'd rather be alone and miserable."

"Then you got your wish because that's exactly what you are," screamed Regina.

"Enough," said Teresa. "Your grandmother recently died. Don't you realize that you're all one another have now and you're here bickering like children? Stop it! You're family and family is always supposed to have each other's back. Even when you don't like or understand what one another is doing. Gina, that wasn't the first time he hit you, was it?"

"No, Auntie." Regina looked at her aunt with wide red eyes and a trembling bottom lip.

Teresa knew that look. She had seen that look of hopelessness and fear several times in the faces of other victims of domestic violence. "Baby, why would you deal with that? You know I'm a cop; I could put a bullet in his tail and claim self-defense."

"That's exactly why I didn't tell you. I didn't want you to hurt him," Regina said softly.

Leslie sat there quietly, hoping they would get to her soon. She couldn't wait to share the news about T-Money. She was so over Regina and her man problems. She didn't believe her sister deserved to be abused, but she chose to stay in that relationship. She had ample opportunities to leave. The one time she did leave, she went back to Antonio. So, evidently she enjoyed getting slapped around. Leslie couldn't understand how any woman could live with someone like that. She, on the other hand, had a good man that it didn't take her long to find. She was giddy with anticipation. She even put her ring in her pocket so she could surprise them with it when it was her time to speak. She was going to be the first one to get married and to get her money! She couldn't wait for Regina to stop whining so she could throw it in their faces.

"No matter how bad he treats me, I still love him," said Regina. "You think I didn't know about those other women. Of course, I did, but he never flaunted them in my face before. After he lost his job, he just became so resentful that I had an income and he didn't. He was mad that I quit my lucrative job to work in a not-so-lucrative boutique. He would take my car and go see whoever she was. It was as if all of a sudden, he didn't love me anymore and he didn't care if he hurt me. I tried to be a good girlfriend. I tried to let him know that we would be fine until he found another job, but nothing I did seem to be enough." Regina began to cry.

Teresa hated to see her niece cry. "Sweetheart, a man who truly loves you wants you to shine not hide your light under a bushel. He also doesn't take his problems out on you. That's not love." Teresa got up to hug her niece, while she cried. The girl was in pain, but she seemed to be in the worse kind of pain. The kind caused by blind loyalty to a useless cause.

"Ladies, I think that's all for now," said Teresa. "Leslie, I know we didn't get to you and I hope you understand. I need to attend to your sister right now. Domestic violence is a serious matter. We'll get together real soon and finish our talk. I know I'm not Grace, but I am family and you can talk to me about anything. No matter the problem, big or small, I'm right here."

"But I think I found someone, Auntie," said Leslie.

"That's good, baby, real good. If he's the one, he's not going anywhere and you can wait and tell me all about him next time. Okay? We'll start off with you."

Leslie didn't respond. They weren't really paying any attention to her anyway. She cut her eyes at the three of them. Sheila and Aunt Teresa were so busy trying to console the little princess they couldn't even find the time to listen to her good news. The first thing she was going to do when she got her money was leave this city. She and T-Money where going to run off somewhere and start over. She would make a new name for herself. A respectable one and prove to everyone she was just as good as her sister and her cousin.

As Leslie walked to her wing of the house, she got a text from Beau. As much as Leslie enjoyed their time together, she knew it was time for it to end. It was just sex and there was no future with him. She tried to tell him she had other things to do, but he kept texting. She finally stopped replying. Her grandmother didn't raise no fool. She was not about to let sex mess up the good thing she had going with T-Money. She turned off her phone, but then thought better of it and turned it back on. She needed to be accessible if her fiancé tried to reach her. She pulled her ring out of her pocket and put it back on her finger. So much for her big announcement! At least she still had an attentive man. He said he had some business to take care of tonight, but she would definitely see him tomorrow. She couldn't wait to feel his hands on her body again.

Chapter Thirty-One

Regina

Regina hated that she still loved Antonio so much. Her love life was horrible, but the one good thing in her life was her job. Bart got an oil change, as promised. He was pleased with the service, the work, and the price. He spread the word about the shop to all the domestic workers and business was picking up quickly. The chauffeurs, gardeners, housekeepers, and cooks of the city were bringing their vehicles to Precision Repair & Auto Body. It also didn't hurt that she was advertising their new oil change and tire rotation special on social media and people were responding to that as well. It was only 8:00 a.m. and the shop was full of customers waiting to be serviced. She was happy it was busy. That way she had less time to think about Antonio. Last night, Aunt Teresa tried to get her to press charges, but she wasn't interested. Regina just wanted to move on with her life.

The shop stayed busy all day. Regina was exhausted when it was time to close, but also satisfied because of a job well done. As they closed up the shop, Chance came into the office. It could get hot in the garage and he was sweating. The first two buttons of his shirt were open, revealing a few sparse hairs on top of a hard defined chest. His work Dockers fit him snugly and it wasn't hard to tell that his legs were as defined as his chest.

Today, Regina was wearing a fitted blue jean skit and a silk blouse. Chance was happy she relaxed her attire a bit, but did everything have to hug her sexy round behind? She was literally making it hard to be around her. He looked down at the front of his pants and hoped he wouldn't have to run out of the office like he did before.

He smiled at her. "Good job! We haven't had that many customers in one day in months. I also wanted to tell you that I enjoyed dinner with you the other night. I haven't laughed so much in a long time. It was nice to get out and be in the company of an attractive woman."

"Thanks! I enjoyed myself, too. I'm really glad you listened to my ideas and decided to give them a chance."

"No problem. They were good and, more importantly, cost-effective. There's no reason not to when they cost the company virtually nothing."

Regina opened her mouth to respond, but stopped when she looked up and saw a familiar face standing at the payment window. "What is he doing here?" she muttered under her breath.

Chance followed her gaze. "Who is that?"

"Someone I wish hadn't found out where I work."

"Do you want me to get rid of him? It's after hours. He shouldn't be here anyway." Chance started walking toward the door.

"No. No. I got it. I'll see what he wants." Regina got up from her chair and walked out of the business office.

"How did you find me?"

"Hello to you, too. It's such a pleasure to see you. I have my ways. You don't look happy to see me." Antonio found her by bribing their gardener with a one-hundred-dollar bill. He was all too happy to do a little investigating and divulge the information.

Regina scoffed. "I guess you forgot that the last time I saw you, you were taking my co-worker and friend to lunch, or did you make her lunch instead?"

"You know I did that just to make you jealous. I never wanted nor cared about that girl."

"Oh, I guess that's why you slept with her."

"I did no such thing. Come here, give me a hug. I've missed you." Antonio took a step toward her.

Regina raised her hand. "No, thanks. I'm good. I don't know where your hands have been. Why are you here?"

"What kind of question is that? Would Romeo let Juliet get a way? I'm sure Marc Antony would never have let—What was her name?"

"Cleopatra. Attend history class next time instead of getting one of the women you were banging to do your work. You are no Romeo or Marc Antony. What do you want, Antonio? I'm at work. You know that place most people go to, to earn a living." Regina wanted him to say whatever he had to say and leave.

Antonio turned around and scanned the room. "Yeah, I see. Are things that bad Gina that you're working in a garage? You have a degree. You love fashion. I'm sure you're not going to outfit that grease monkey I saw you talking to in the latest coveralls."

Regina snarled at him. "Antonio, I would thank you not to insult my boss. So far that grease monkey has proven himself to be a better man than you."

He looked at Chance, who was standing in the service window eavesdropping. "Oh really. Are you two swinging in trees together or something?"

"Our relationship is strictly professional, but he's a good guy. I'm going to ask you again, what do you want? You are not welcome anywhere around me."

"You're not gonna make this easy for me, are you? Gina, I know about your inheritance. There's no need for you to worry yourself about finding a man. You already have one. I know I messed up, but I can make it up to you. Think about it. All our problems started when I lost my job. If you marry me and we both become rich, I won't have that problem. I can go back to treating you the way I did before. I know I had no right to take my frustrations out on you. Gina, baby, I promise it won't happen again."

Regina wasn't buying it. Who told him about her inheritance, anyway? "What about her?"

"Her who?"

"Don't play dumb. You know who. That woman you would leave our home for in the middle of the night in my car. You still messing with her? How about the woman in the leasing office? I bet you didn't know I knew about her. Well I did. She was telling half the apartment complex about how good you were in bed."

Antonio knew that engaging that conversation would only start a fight. He didn't come to fight. "Gina, you're bringing up old stuff. Come home. Those women meant nothing to me. We'll get a new apartment and it will just be me and you. I promise. You're the one I want. You're the one I need. I miss you. You can't tell me that you don't miss me." He moved closer and kissed her softly on the lips.

Regina wanted to believe him. She wanted to take him at his word, but he'd broken it so many times before she'd lost count. She stepped away from him. She wasn't willing to go down that road again unless he could prove he had changed. "I do miss you, Antonio, but you have caused me a lot of pain. I didn't do anything to deserve any of it. I love you, but I don't think you know what love is."

Antonio took her hands in his and kissed her again. "I know that I don't have it without you in my life. Gina, I'm sorry. Tell me what I need to do to get you back. You want me to get on my knees and beg?"

He then dropped down to one knee. "Come home, woman!" He beat his chest like Tarzan.

Regina laughed. "Stop playing and get up!"

"Not until I do this." He reached into his pocket, pulled out a ring, and said, "Regina, will you marry me?"

Regina gasped and then stared at him in disbelief. It was beautiful and Antonio couldn't have looked more dashing at that moment. He was in black slacks with white a shirt, a black vest and cufflinks with the letters "R" for Regina. It finally happened. The man she loved had finally proposed. She felt like she was in a fairytale, but she was terrified there wouldn't be a happily ever after. He wasn't willing to do it before; she wondered if her money was the reason he was so motived to propose now. She wanted to believe he was there for her because he missed her, couldn't imagine life without her, and wanted to make everything right, but she knew better.

For the second time in two days, Regina was balling like a baby. The tears ran down her face. She was supposed to be happy. The problem was she had finally taken steps to put him out of her life permanently and she was enjoying the peace. She didn't have a reason to walk on eggshells and choose her words carefully so as not to evoke his anger and end up with a new bruise she had to hide. She stood there and let him slip it on her finger. It was beautiful. She knew he didn't have a job and wondered where he got the money. "I don't know what to say," she said.

"Just say you'll be my wife. I love you, Regina, and I want to spend the rest of your life showing you. Let me take you away from here and prove how good life can really be. You can't possibly want this." He held out his arm and swung it around him for emphasis. "Marry me. Get your inheritance and make all your dreams come true. You can have it all, baby. The good man, the dream job running your own boutique and the family. We can start having kids as soon as you want."

"That all sounds great, Antonio. I love you, too, but I need some time to think about it. This is a lot to process. I just stopped having to put makeup on my face to hide the bruises."

Antonio stood up and hugged her. "Okay. I'll give you your space for now, but we belong together. I'm going to prove it to you, if it's the last thing I do."

Antonio left and Regina found herself smiling and staring at her hand and the small but gorgeous ring on it.

Chance tried not to listen, while they were talking, but he couldn't help it. He appreciated the way Regina took up for him, but he didn't like what he saw. Antonio looked like a player, if he ever saw one. He couldn't have been more than one hundred eighty pounds, but had to nerve to put his hands on a woman. Especially one as delicate as Regina. Chance began to grow mad, but wasn't quite sure why. Regina was his employee and nothing more. He wondered what Antonio meant by "I know about your inheritance," but he didn't ask. It wasn't his business.

Regina didn't return to the office. Instead, she had a seat in one of the chairs in the waiting area. Chance went out into the waiting area to lock the door, but he really just wanted to check on her.

"That's some ring you got there," said Chance.

"Yeah," Regina said softly, looking at her hand.

"Are you okay?"

"I'll be fine."

"I didn't mean to eavesdrop, but you two were right in front of the window. I noticed that you didn't say yes."

"That's the guy I told you about the day you hired me. We've had some problems. We used to live together and I moved out. I'm not sure he's sincere about wanting to marry me. He's had years to do it and always had some excuse."

"I see. Well, pray about it and ask the Lord to help you make the right decision. You might even want to talk to someone about it. Can I give you some advice from a divorced man?"

She looked up and said, "Sure."

Chance sat down in the chair next to her. "When a man is the one, you don't need to think about it. You know before he even asks the question that the answer is 'Yes'. Also, getting married doesn't fix your problems. If anything, it amplifies them because you're not just being mistreated as the girlfriend, but the spouse. Whatever you decide, I wish you the best, but he was right about one thing."

"What's that?"

"I could use some new clothes. Do you think you could help me with that?"

A big smile spread across Regina's face. "I'd love to. Fashion's kind of my thing."

Chance looked her up and down. Her skirt rose up when she was sitting, exposing her brown creamy delectable thighs. "I noticed," was all he said before he got up and walked away. He wondered what it was about that woman that always had him on the run.

Regina didn't know why she cared, but she liked that she and her outfit had Chance's approval.

Chapter Thirty-Two

Sheila

Sheila agreed to go on another date with a different eligible bachelor. She was excited about this one. His name was Royal and he was an oral surgeon. In his pictures, he looked very handsome and his smile contained some of the whitest and straightest teeth she had ever seen. However, the heartfelt statement he wrote in his profile captured her attention. He talked about his parents. They had been married forty years and he was hoping to find that forever kind of love like they had. Sheila wanted the same thing. Having someone by her side, day-in and day-out, to share the highs and lows of life with, while raising their children, sounded good to Sheila. Although, DaQuan was an engaged father, she always felt like Xavier was missing out on something by not having a father in the home. A man hadn't been a priority for Sheila. The last few years of her life consisted of working hard to excel in her profession and taking care of her son. Now, her grandmother's ultimatum had caused her to reexamine things. She was thirty-five now. Maybe it was time to find someone special and she wondered if Royal could be that one.

Although Sheila was looking forward to the date, she was also a little conflicted. She had to admit that lying in bed with DaQuan was nice. Not only was it nice, it felt right, like he was supposed to be there. He carefully and lovingly took care of her and Xavier. He let her lay undisturbed for hours to recover and when she finally got up, he fixed her breakfast and a strong cup of coffee. While she was asleep, he cleaned the house and did the laundry. When Xavier got out of school, DaQuan picked him up and helped him with his homework. Sheila always knew DaQuan cared for her, but it was obvious his feelings still ran deep. She wasn't quite sure how she felt about him, though. He was her child's father. He was once the number one man in her life, but that was almost five years ago. Could there still be something there? DaQuan used to hint from time to time about them trying again, but when his hints continuously went unacknowledged, he stopped. It was kind of odd that neither one of them had been in a serious relationship since they broke up, but she was sure DaQuan at least had a lady friend he was seeing occasionally to get his physical needs met. After all, he was a man and a very nice looking one at that.

Sheila dropped Xavier off at Vivian's house and headed to the bar and grill where Max had arranged for them to meet. She arrived at least ten minutes early as Max instructed and wore another one of the outfits he styled: a beige pantsuit, with a pink top and multi-colored shoes. She really liked how he loved bright colors. Most days she wore black, grey and nude hues, but Max insisted she lighten up and stop dressing like she was going to a funeral. She followed his suggestions not only for her date, but also at work and was receiving compliments every day from men and women. To complement her new look, Shelia made an appointment at the salon and allowed them to straighten her natural tresses. The stylist curled them into a sexy bob that she loved. She even took the time to stop by the mall and let one of the women at the makeup counter put her on a new face. The pink eye shadow she chose brought out the pink in her blouse perfectly. For the first time in her life, Sheila found herself looking in the mirror constantly and taking selfies to post to her social media accounts. She felt beautiful and she owed it all to Max. Perhaps he was her fairy godfather.

Once Sheila entered the restaurant, she checked in with the hostess to see if Royal had arrived and was informed he hadn't, but their table was ready. Rather than being seated or going to the bar, she decided to wait for him on one of the benches near the door that were reserved for people who needed to be seated. She was hoping to catch a glimpse of him as soon as he walked in. She made small talk with an elderly woman sitting next to her to help pass the time. After fifteen minutes, a man came in that had to be Royal. He looked very much like his picture: mahogany skin, brown eyes adorned with long eyelashes and a gorgeous smile he flashed at the hostess as he approached her stand. He appeared to be about to ask her a question when he stopped abruptly. He turned around and used his right hand to remove the gold band on the ring finger of his left hand. Sheila gasped.

Royal heard her, turned his head, looked directly at her, and said, "Sheila?"

"No," she answered. "Wrong person." She hoped her new hair and fierce makeup would prevent him from recognizing her.

"Oh, I'm sorry. I'm here meeting someone for the first time and I thought you might be her."

"Is that why you just took off your wedding band?" She smirked and raised her eyebrow tauntingly at him.

The woman next to her snickered and whispered, "Get 'em, dearie."

He paused before answering as if he were trying to decide whether to tell the truth or concoct a good lie. "The wife and I are separated and...and sometimes I still wear it, but I realized that tonight it wouldn't be appropriate so I took it off," Royal stammered.

"Oh okay. Enjoy your dinner." She assumed he was lying, but even if he weren't, it wouldn't matter. What was it with all these married man who wanted to date before the divorce was final? Why couldn't they wait until all ties had been severed before moving on?

Royal was in such a hurry to get away from her that he didn't even respond. As soon as he turned his back, Sheila slipped out the door and hurried to her car. She was glad she that she hadn't given Max any money or she would be asking for a refund. She probably needed to leave him alone because if this was what he did for a living, he wasn't very good at it. Instead of going to Vivian's house to pick up Xavier, Sheila decided to go home for a little "me time." She rarely had time to herself these days and her present predicament provided the perfect opportunity to do so. She had a beautiful garden-style tub at home she hadn't soaked in, in over a month and that was exactly how she was going to spend the next hour. After she arrived home, Sheila ran her bath water and added Epsom salt and bubbles to the mix. She rolled her hair to preserve her style and shed her clothes. The steamy water and white mounds of bubbles looked so inviting. She was about to step in and enjoy when she heard someone beating frantically at her door. She didn't want to answer because whoever was at the door couldn't possibly compare to the Calgon "take me away" experience that awaited her, but curiosity got the best of her and she wrapped herself in a towel and went downstairs to investigate.

Chapter Thirty-Three

Leslie

T-Money was supposed to pick Leslie up for dinner, but he was three hours late. That was unlike him. He was very good about doing what he said he was going to do and if he were going to be late, he would let her know. He planned to take her to his favorite hibachi restaurant to celebrate their engagement and he said there was something important he needed to tell her. He loved to take Regina out and show her off. He called her his sexy little rich girl. Even though most of his clients came from rich families, she was the only one he dated. As far as she knew. He said he had run into too many rich chicks who were just trying to make their parents mad by dating a "hood nigga." Leslie assumed that since she had no parents, he didn't worry about that being her plan. He also said she didn't act all uppity and spoiled like the rest of them. She actually knew the meaning of the words "please" and "thank you." She attributed that to being raised by good old Southern people who didn't take their good fortune for granted.

Leslie and T-Money had only been together a short time, but things were going really well. He was a good boyfriend. He checked on her every day and made sure she had money in her pocket. He showered her with compliments and let her know she was important to him. She was surprised at how much she liked him and how he was so intelligent. She didn't expect them to have so much in common. All those years of servicing the elite of the city had helped him develop some culture and diverse interests. He was also a techie just like her and had a house full of gadgets. He recently purchased a contraption that cleaned the floors several times a day and something that looked like a speaker that talked and could answer any question you might have, play music and a bunch of other things. It even had a name.

Leslie paced the floor. Where was her man? She was now concerned and the cryptic text she received a few hours earlier from him didn't help matters. It contained the word "save" and six numbers. What were the numbers for? It was too short to be a phone number. She called him several times, but he didn't answer and now his phone was rolling straight to voicemail as if it were off or the battery was dead. She was looking forward to seeing him tonight. She got her nails and feet done for the occasion and even bought a new outfit. She was anxious to know what he had to tell her. Afterward, they were supposed to swing by his lawyer's house to talk about the prenup. She couldn't wait to get married. She wasn't sure what kind of wedding she wanted, but it really didn't matter. She just wanted to marry him, get her money, and live happily ever after. Who knew he was such a great guy?

Leslie was about to try and call him again when the screen on her phone lit up. She had an incoming call from Chareese, one of the girls she partied with from time to time. They went to high school together and both enjoyed a carefree lifestyle. If he didn't show up maybe she and Chareese could go out instead.

Before she could say hello, Chareese began screaming in the phone. "They killed him! He's dead, Les! He's dead!"

Leslie had no idea who she was talking about. "Calm down, chick. Who's dead?"

"T-Money. The cops killed him. Evidently, he was selling to an undercover cop and when he tried to run they killed him."

Leslie didn't believe her. T-Money didn't sell to people he didn't know. He had a solid, trusted clientele. "Are you sure it was T-Money?"

"I'm sure. His second in command, Silk, called me. He's dead, Les. My baby's daddy is dead."

T-Money wouldn't make a skank like Chareese his woman. She had been with everybody. "What? Girl stop lying."

"What reason do I have to lie? T-Money and I have been seeing each other for about four months. I'm pregnant."

Leslie didn't believe her. "Did he know?"

"Yeah. I told him after I missed my period last month. We were supposed to be getting a place together, but he said something came up and we needed to wait."

That didn't make sense to Leslie. "Really? Wow. Wait a minute. A place together? Why didn't you just move in his house? You being his baby mama and all."

"His house? What house? He lived with Silk. They were roommates. He even took me over there a few times." She sniffed.

"Oh yeah. I forgot." T-Money cared so little about this broad that he didn't even confide in her where he lived. Silk's place was his decoy spot.

"I'm sorry you had to find out like this. I know you two used to mess around. I was gonna tell you we were together. I just didn't know how. I love him. We were gonna be a family." Chareese sniffed and then blew her nose loudly in the phone.

Gross. "That's messed up, Chareese. I'm sorry to hear that, but better he leave you alone and pregnant than me. Let me clue you in; we didn't used to talk we were talking. That man never stopped wanting me and pursuing me. You're not that far along. It's not too late to have an abortion."

Chareese wasn't so sad that she couldn't yell. "You are such a whore! You would say something like that! Some of us actually open our legs to men we want to be with! I planned on marrying that man!"

"But he didn't plan on marrying you. I could tell you how I know that, but I'd hate to send you into a spontaneous abortion."

Chareese hung up in her face.

Leslie laughed. "Dumb chick didn't even know he was still sleeping with me. Dang, Thaddeus! How you gonna propose to me with a baby on the way by someone else? How you gonna tell me keep it one-hundred and you weren't? What were you gonna do, keep us both? That's what you get!" she yelled at the framed picture of the two of them she placed beside her bed earlier in the week.

Leslie punched her pillow. She tried not to shed a tear. Her entire future had changed in a matter of minutes. T-Money was dead and she was back to square one without even a prospect for a husband. She wanted to act hard, but she couldn't. She was actually falling in love with him, but he couldn't have loved her the way he said if he was harboring the fact he had a baby on the way with someone she knew. Maybe that was what he had to tell her. This sucked! Her plan for getting her money was gone. Her dreams for having someone who cared about her and loved her unconditionally were gone, too. For a brief moment in time, Leslie got to feel what it was like to be a priority. She hadn't felt like one since before her grandfather passed. While her grandmother was consumed with her business, her high society lifestyle, and philanthropic endeavors, Big Daddy made sure the girls were cared for and nurtured. He read her bedtime stories, held her when she cried for her parents and told her that she was his favorite wild child. He enjoyed her independence, quick wit, and desire to do things on her own terms. It was after his death that she became promiscuous, searching for a man to fill the void he left. T-Money had volunteered for the job and now he was gone!

"What am I going to do now? God must really hate me." She picked up the picture and threw it across the room. The glass shattered and the shards scattered across the floor making a mess that could injure someone if they weren't careful. That's exactly the way she felt about her life. It was dangerous mess.

Chapter Thirty-Four

Sheila

Sheila opened the door to Max standing on her front porch. He looked frantic. Without so much as a hello, he quickly pushed past her and into her foyer.

"Oh, thank God, you're okay. When Royal called to tell me that you didn't come to the restaurant, I thought something had happened to you. What are you doing?"

His eyes traveled from her exposed legs, to the top of her breasts protruding from the very large purple towel she had wrapped around her to her deliciously full red lips and doe-like eyes adorned with colorful mascara. Sheila looked good enough to eat. He'd always thought she was beautiful. He knew with the right clothes, hair, and makeup she could stop traffic. Now, there she was in front of him with the right makeup and no clothes. He didn't care that her hair was in rollers. He wanted to act on impulse and rip that towel from her body and attempt to make love to her right there in the foyer, but he knew doing so would be inappropriate.

Max stepped forward, closing the space between them. "You are gorgeous. Hello, bombshell."

Sheila became very self-conscious. She was standing in front of a man she barely knew wrapped in nothing but a towel. An extremely attractive man with impeccable taste at that. She pulled her towel tighter around her and blushed. "Thank you. I was about to take a relaxing bath. What are you doing here?"

"I told you, when Royal called to tell me that you didn't come to the restaurant, I got worried about you. I called you several times, but I kept getting your voicemail.

"I'm sorry. I probably should have called you after I left the restaurant."

Max raised an eyebrow. "So you did go?"

"Yes, I was there and I saw Royal, but I didn't let him know I was there after I saw him take his wedding band off."

"Wedding band? He told me he had been divorced for five years!"

"Well it didn't appear that way to me and I don't do married men. I was about to take a bath. Will you excuse me for a moment while I put on some clothes and we can talk? This isn't going the way I planned at all. Make yourself at home and I'll be back in a moment."

As she turned to leave, Max grabbed her right hand. Startled by the gesture, she released her towel slightly, exposing her right breast. Max pulled it back up.

"Careful, beautiful lady. I may be your matchmaker, but I'm still a man. Don't tempt me in such as fashion. You are sheer poetry in motion. A physical stanza of natural beauty if I've ever seen one."

Sheila pulled her towel tighter around her and blushed. "I'm sorry. It was an accident." She felt beautiful when she left the mall after getting her makeup done, but that feeling was nothing compared to the one she was experiencing at that moment. She didn't know what to do next.

Max continued talking. "Go put some clothes on and then come back down. I have something I need to tell you."

"Okay," was all Sheila said, as she scurried up the stairs.

Max had earned a thousand bonus points with her for being such a gentleman. She put on some jeans and a T-shirt and combed her hair before returning downstairs. She found him in her kitchen with food and ingredients laid out on her marble counter-tops.

"I hope you don't mind, but you did say make yourself at home. I took the liberty of raiding your refrigerator. I assumed you left the restaurant without eating, so how about I cook us something to eat? You have what I need to make steak with baby potatoes and artichoke hearts or baked chicken with baby potatoes and spinach. Which do you prefer?

She looked at the food he had spread out on her kitchen counter. This man seemed too good to be true. He was fine, intelligent, self-employed, and cooked. She wondered if he knew the Lord.

"How about steak with baby potatoes and spinach?"

"As you wish, my dear. Have a seat because it's your job to peel the potatoes, while I work on seasoning this steak just right."

Sheila sat on the barstool next to her island. A man like Max needed to be on her list of eligible bachelors. Spending time with Max was a light and playful experience. The two of them cooked and laughed like old friends. He made a special marinade for the steak, poured it on the meat, and let it sit for a few minutes.

"Sheila, I have a confession to make."

"Uh oh. That doesn't sound good," she joked.

"No. I think it's very good. I've enjoyed having you as my client. I enjoy talking to you, styling you, spending time with you. While I was picking out potential candidates for you, I found myself thinking that none of them was good enough for you. I mean, you're pure perfection. You're smart, you're funny, you've got a great body, and the most attractive thing is that you're so humble. I mean, you walk around like you don't know that you're all that and a bag a chips."

Sheila found herself blushing again and wondered from what book he gleaned these compliments. She shifted nervously. "I mean. I'm okay. I guess."

"No. You're better than okay. You are everything you said you wanted to be and you don't even know it. You are important. You are desirable and you are most definitely unforgettable."

"Thank you. Well if you don't think any of the men in your files are good enough for me, then who is?" she asked softly.

He grabbed her hand and stroked it softly with his finger. "Me."

"You?" Sheila found it hard to believe that a man like Max would be interested in a woman like her. He looked like the type of man who would have a supermodel on his arm. Not some plain Jane like her.

"Yes. You are the first client that has made me want to break my number one rule. *Never* date my clients. With your permission, I'd like to?"

Sheila smiled and decided she wanted to stop playing it safe and go for something that she thought was outside her reach. If a man this amazing wanted to make her happy, why shouldn't she let him? "I guess that would be okay. I mean, I enjoy your company when we're together and you are attractive. Actually, I think you're gorgeous."

"Then, Ms. Sheila Watson-Purdue, get prepared to partake in the Maximillian Beauregard experience."

Sheila laughed, but her jovial demeanor didn't last long. "I look forward to it, but there is something I should tell you. I hope it doesn't make you change your mind. You should know that I'm celibate. I'm a Godly woman, and I don't plan on having sex again until I'm married."

Max looked deeply into her eyes and said, "Some things are worth waiting for." He then gave Sheila a sweet kiss on the cheek and turned his attention back to preparing their dinner.

Chapter Thirty-Five

Leslie

Leslie didn't know why she was standing in front of Sheila's house. She and her cousin hadn't been close in years. Ever since she found Jesus, she was so condescendingly religious. She called her a whoremonger on more than one occasion and told she needed to change her heathen ways before Jesus came back for his chosen ones, but Leslie had no one to turn to. Her parents were dead. Her grandparents were dead. She didn't really know her Aunt Teresa so she didn't want to call her. Regina was busy mourning a no good man.

After spending an hour at the mansion crying while looking at pictures of herself and T-Money she had in her phone, she decided she needed to talk to someone. As she approached the door, she heard laughter. One of the voices was clearly Sheila's, but the other voice belonged to a man. Leslie wondered if Sheila was on one of the dates her matchmaker arranged. She hated to interrupt, but she needed her family. She took a deep breath and rang the doorbell.

Sheila came to the door and as soon as she opened it, Leslie fell into her arms.

Sheila fought to steady them both to prevent them from toppling to the floor. "Leslie, oh my God, Baby Girl, what's wrong?"

"He's dead?" she wailed.

Sheila was bewildered. "Honey, who's dead?"

"My fiancé."

"Fiancé?" Now Sheila was even more bewildered. She just found out from Regina that she had a boyfriend and now Leslie had a fiancé.

Leslie held up the massive rock on her hand.

Sheila's eyes widened and then she said, "Oh my. Come sit on the couch. I'll be right back. Give me a minute."

She helped her cousin to the living room and then returned to the dining room where she and Max had been eating dinner. "I'm sorry Max, but we'll have to finish our evening another time. I have a family matter I need to attend to."

He peeked at the forlorn-looking young woman slumped on Sheila's couch. "I completely understand. Do you want me to clean the kitchen before I leave?"

Where did this man come from? He does dishes without being asked. "Thanks, but no thanks. I think we need to be alone. I'll call you tomorrow."

Max stood and gave her a warm hug. "Okay, beautiful. Don't hesitate to call me if you need anything. I'll see myself out."

"Thank you. I appreciate that." Sheila then got on the phone and called Regina. "Cuz, you need to get over her. Something is wrong with Leslie. She needs us."

Sheila got her a box of tissue then made them both a glass of wine and waited for Regina to arrive. She didn't want Leslie to have to tell her story twice, but the suspense was killing her. She wondered why no one knew she was engaged. Who was this man and how did he meet his demise? Leslie was there in thirty minutes. They both sat in the living room and listened as Leslie told them how T-Money had swept her off her feet, proposed and gotten killed all in the span of one week.

Regina tried hard to keep her eyes off the massive rock on Leslie's hand as she spoke. She glanced enviously at it. Her ring looked like a chip of a diamond compared to Leslie's. Of course, it would though; she was engaged to her dope dealer. She, on the other hand, was proposed to by the unemployed.

Sheila struggled with not being judgmental. It was hard to find the silver lining in her promiscuous cousin agreeing to marry one of her lovers who also happened to be a drug dealer. She was no stranger to T-Money. He and DaQuan were raised in the same North Memphis neighborhood. She had met him once at one of DaQuan's mother's cookouts. He seemed nice, but he was contributing to the physical, mental, and spiritual demise of others in order to earn a living. His death was probably God's way of punishing him for his actions.

"Did you love him?" asked Sheila.

"Yes. I think I loved him. I wasn't in love with him. He had all the qualities I wanted. He was handsome, funny, intelligent, and he treated me well. Honestly, his only major flaw was that he sold drugs. He knew about my inheritance and he didn't care. Actually, when he proposed he made me promise to sign a prenup that stated if we ever split my money was mine and he couldn't touch it. All he wanted was me. No one I've ever been with said that. They all wanted something. My status, the money they thought I had, or sex, but not Thaddeus." She sniffed. "And now he's gone."

Regina felt herself growing more envious by the minute. She was with a man for seven years and he didn't propose until he found out she had money coming and her baby sister gets a man to propose in less than a week and he didn't want a dime. It was hard for her to feel sorry for her.

"Just be thankful that none of this went down when the two of you were together. He could have easily been killed when you two were out. You don't want to be a part of the drug life," said Regina.

"He was going to give it up. He promised he would give that life up, but he just needed time."

"I guess his time ran out," said Regina.

Sheila looked at her younger cousin and thought, *These two are so spoiled and catty.* "You're not helping, and what is that on your hand?"

Regina looked down at her hand. "Oh, this? It's my engagement ring from Antonio." Both Sheila and Leslie rolled their eyes.

"When did this happen?" asked Sheila.

"Earlier today. He found out where I worked and came to the shop. I didn't give him an answer, but he left the ring on my finger and told me to think about it."

"You're going to tell him no, right?" said Sheila.

"I haven't decided. I do love him. I want my inheritance. It seems like a feasible solution."

Sheila rolled her eyes again. "That's just it. He's a solution to a problem, but the problem is he's another problem, which makes him as the solution impossible. Tell me why you want to marry a man who doesn't have a job, beats you, and cheats on you with other women while using your car as the transportation to get him there? Let me and God hear you say that foolishness out loud."

"I swear I hate you heifers!" screamed Leslie. "I can't have my moment ever. You know why you're just finding out I'm engaged because at dinner nobody wanted to hear my news after "Miss I Always Got Drama" over there started crying. MY FIANCÉ IS DEAD! And you are more concerned about why she wants that lowlife. She has chosen this life. This abusive cycle and I, for one, say if she wants it let her have it. I, on the other hand, didn't choose to fall for a great guy, get engaged and then lose him in a matter of days. Can I, for one moment, have someone give a damn about me? Ever since Big Daddy died it's like no one cares about me and what I want. Grandma Grace used her money to control me and she's still doing it from the grave. Sheila, you're wrapped up in work, Xavier and Jesus, and Gina you were too busy with your job and catering to a man who will never treat you right. But, at least both of you had someone to come home to. Now that Grandma Grace is gone I have no one and when I finally get someone he gets taken from me!" Leslie fell into a fit of tears on the couch.

Regina and Sheila were dumbfounded. Neither of them had ever really stopped to consider how their life without their grandparents was affecting Leslie. Sheila went over to Leslie and cradled her in her arms. "Sweetheart, I'm so sorry. I'm so, so sorry. I didn't know."

"I miss you, Shelia. It's like you forgot about me. You're like my big sister. I need you. "

Sheila grabbed a tissue and wiped her tears. "I love my son and Jesus, but I'll always love you. We were raised together. I'm here for you. You were so busy partying and having a good time I didn't realize that you were in pain. I promise to make more time for you in the future."

Regina walked over and wrapped her arms around her sister as well. "I'm sorry, too. I didn't mean to neglect my little sister. I promise to make more time for us."

More tears escaped Leslie's eyes and she wiped them with the back of her hand. "Gina, he's a scumbag. Wake up and smell the manure you've been sleeping next to for years. Go on with your life; you don't need him! You deserve so much better."

"I hear you, but let's not talk about me, okay? Tonight, we're gonna make it all about you. How about we both spend the night here and have fun like we used to do? We'll watch a movie or something. Sheila, what do you have to eat around here?"

"Maximillian made steak and veggies. There's still some left in the kitchen."

"Maximillian?" said Regina. "You let a man in your house besides DaQuan and the Holy Spirit? What else have you let him into," she said with a sneaky smile.

Leslie laughed. "You should have seen him. He was *fine*. He looked like a light-skinned Idris Elba. Who knows what else he might have been cooking tonight if I hadn't come over."

Sheila nudged her gently on the shoulder. "Shut up, you two. Max is my matchmaker and a really nice guy. I had another bad date tonight and he just came over to check on his client."

"Mmmmm hmmmmm. I'm sure he did," said Regina.

Sheila decided to steer the subject back to Leslie. "Now, cuz, are you sure T-Money is dead? Have you seen a body? A story on the news?"

"No, but I got the news from a couple of pretty reliable sources."

"Who?" said Sheila

"His baby's mama and then his second in command, a guy name Slick, confirmed it."

"What? He has a baby mama, too? And you say I have drama?" said Regina

Shelia stood up to go retrieve her cell phone. "I'm calling my reliable source."

Chapter Thirty-Six

Antonio

Antonio sat alone in an empty apartment, pondering his present situation. He didn't expect Regina not to accept his proposal. He just knew by the end of the night they'd be somewhere making love and solidifying their reconciliation. He thought he'd handled it pretty well by giving her some time to think about it, but he had to put together a plan to make sure she took him back. He'd called her twice since he left her, but she hadn't picked up. He wondered if she was somewhere with that grease money he saw at the shop. He didn't like the way Chance looked at him while he was there. If he was interested, he was barking up the wrong tree. A woman as refined as Regina would never look at the likes of him. He was too far down the societal food chain. Although right now, that grease monkey had more money than he had. If it wasn't for that quick job he pulled last night, he'd be completely broke. He recently started working for an escort service to make some extra money. A man named Stacey approached him in a restaurant years ago after observing how he addressed a group a women who were obviously trying to get his attention. He explained how rich women were willing to pay an insane amount of money to have an attractive young stud on their arm for a few hours. He agreed to become a male escort but he didn't really enjoyed it because some of those ladies were hideous and wanted him to do things to them even money wouldn't entice him to do. However, when Antonio really needed some money, like now, he'd agree to take a high paying gig. To make sure Regina didn't find out, he did it in other cities. It was written in his contract that he must be flown to a different time zone.

His date last night was Eleanor Dandridge, a wealthy woman who was trying to make her soon-to-be ex-husband jealous. She saw his profile and specifically requested him. They went to a dinner party in Seattle and there was Mr. Dandridge with his new twenty-something girlfriend. Antonio played his role well, catering to the fifty-five-year-old woman's every need. He couldn't help but notice the ring she wore. It was small, but it was exquisite. She shared with him her husband bought it for her before he became rich and therefore, it had sentimental value. It must have been fate that made him notice it was missing when she came out of the bathroom. When she wasn't looking, he slipped in the bathroom and there it was sitting in the soap dish. She had forgotten to put it back on after she washed her hands. He made sure to keep her occupied *all night* so she never even noticed it was gone. The next morning, when he left her condo, she gave him a huge tip and an invitation to come back anytime. Once Antonio arrived back in Memphis, he took the ring to be cleaned. Once clean, it sparkled like it was brand new and no one was the wiser. He was such a bad boy and he loved every minute of it. If things didn't work out with Regina, maybe he could become Mrs. Dandridge's permanent boy toy to make a little extra money. She was quite attractive for her age and took pride in maintaining her body. He wondered why her husband was divorcing her.

Antonio decided to try to fill the time with his favorite treat, but she wasn't answering her phone either. He knew he was wrong for messing with her, but he couldn't help it. He texted her a picture of his penis with the words: *He misses you.* That usually got her. All he had to do was sit back and wait for her reply. As it turned out, he was wrong. Her reply never came.

Chapter Thirty-Seven

Sheila

DaQuan wasted no time getting to Shelia's house after she called. The streets were buzzing with news about T-Money's murder, but he didn't understand why his childhood friend would interest his ex-girlfriend. He arrived wearing a tight-fitting Captain America shirt. Once he learned the details, he realized the world was much too small.

"Wow. T-Money put a ring on it. He must have been really into you and you say he had a baby on the way? Baby mama was wrong though. He wasn't killed by the cops. Word on the street is T-Money was killed by one or some of his men who were trying to take over his territory and he was found by the cops. It's a shame, too, because if he was really getting out of the game, he probably would have given it to them anyway. Leslie, did T-Money tell you anything about his finances?"

Leslie and Regina were sitting on the couch drinking wine and listening to him speak, while Sheila sipped on hot cocoa. She wasn't ready to consume alcohol again after her last experience.

"No. Just that he had plenty of money. Why?"

"It's no secret that he was stacking paper, but no one knew where. He didn't trust banks so we know it wasn't there. He once told me he had a safe somewhere. Look Leslie, now that T-Money is gone, there will be a lot of people trying to come to his place and see if he left something behind. I advise you not to stay there anymore. If you have anything at the house you want, leave it there for a few days until the heat dies down and then if you want, me and my boys will escort you over there to get whatever it is. Can you do that?"

"Yeah, all I have over there are some clothes and my journal. I'd like to get those back," said Leslie.

"Okay. It's Friday. I'll take you over there to get your stuff Monday. Now don't go over there without me. When a dope boy dies people become like vultures. Where's his car?"

"I'm driving the Beamer. He took the Benz truck when he left," said Leslie.

"Ditch the car. It's very recognizable. Better yet, Sheila put it in your garage. We can go through it and then take it to the chop shop."

That didn't sit right with Sheila. She didn't want anything to do with a dope boy's car. "Is that really necessary? It's not ours. Items are supposed to go to the next of kin. We should give it to his family."

DaQuan hated that Sheila was such a do-gooder sometimes. "That's a thought, but I guarantee if she pulls up in his car she's in for a whole lot of questions she doesn't have the answers to. There's a reason T-Money didn't tell anyone he was engaged. He was trying to protect your cousin. If people were out to get him, they were out to get the people he loved."

Sheila had to admit that what he said made sense, but she wanted to do the right thing. "I'll put it in my garage until we find out a way to get it to his family without them knowing who it's from."

"Hello," said Leslie. "Did you forget I'm the fiancée? I should have the car."

"You can't keep that car. Now, if you want to make some money off of it so you can get something else, we can take it to the chop shop. I know one that will give you a fair deal."

"Then that's what I want to do. T-Money would want me to have it or at least something since I can't have him."

"As you wish," said DaQuan. "I'm going to get out of here and let you three have your little Hallmark moment. Remember, keep your mouths shut and stay away from his house. We don't know who killed my boy and whoever did may be waiting to see who surfaces at his place in hopes of finding T- Money's safe."

Leslie smiled and said, "Okay. Thanks for all your help," but she was thinking entirely different. *So that's what he texted me. It was the code to his safe. I've got to get in that house and find it before anyone else does.*

"No problem. I'm here for y'all. You like family to me. Sheila, walk me to the car."

Sheila did as she was told. Once they were outside, she said, "What's up?"

"I know it's none of my business, but I got a bad feeling about your boy, Max. Something doesn't sit right about him. He's got my Spidey senses on red alert."

She looked at his shirt. "I thought you were Captain America. What's up with all the superhero shirts, anyway? I asked you to come over here to talk about Leslie not me, but what makes you say that?"

"I can't put my finger on it."

"Then you're right, it is none of your business. Look, DaQuan, our son is four now. Eventually, one of us was going to move on. I'm actually surprised that you don't have a girlfriend. Women throw themselves at you all the time."

"That's the problem. None of those women compare to my baby's mama. Yeah, they try to get at me, but I'm looking for the total package...brains, beauty, and body. I had that with you, Sheila. I was just too blind to see it. I really enjoyed holding you the other night. You enjoyed having me near you, too. I know you did. I felt it." He pulled Sheila near him and wrapped his arms around her.

Sheila didn't push him away. "Thank you for taking care of me, DaQuan, but we are over."

"We don't have to be. You still do it for me, baby."

Sheila tried not to look him in his eyes. DaQuan had an uncanny way of looking into her eyes and decoding her feelings. "DaQuan, I care for you. I always will but—"

He cut her off by covering her mouth with his. To DaQuan, that kiss was like a lap dance to a man who was just released from jail after serving five years. His body shook as if she were shooting lightning bolts from her lips. He wasn't the only one affected. Shelia's body grew warm and a yearning she hadn't felt in some time awakened. She allowed her tongue to seductively dance with his. If a person were able to moan with desire internally, she was doing it now. DaQuan was the only man she'd made love to, and there was no denying he still did it for her, too.

Sheila broke their kiss. "DaQuan, stop! What are you doing? Just because I let you hold me doesn't mean I want you back in my life. Thanks for taking care of me. Thanks for coming over here to help with my sister, but if I have to deal with this every time you do a good deed, the next time I have a problem I won't call you!"

"What? Woman, you tripping. You just kissed me like you want me to take you in this driveway and now you're telling me you don't want me. Somebody's lying and I think it's that tongue of yours. I'm leaving. You can lie to yourself, but not to me. We're not over and you know it. You always did have to erect walls where none were needed. There's been nothing stopping us from trying again, but you and now I see that you don't even want to stop it. You're confused. Go back in the house."

DaQuan got in his truck and drove away, leaving Sheila standing in her driveway wondering how she went from one man interested in her to having two. She needed to pray extra hard tonight before she fell into the snares of Satan's temptation.

Chapter Thirty-Eight

Leslie

Sheila stayed with Leslie most of the morning, but left at eleven o'clock to go to work. Leslie assured her she would be fine. She had her own plans for the day and she knew Shelia wouldn't approve. She was also tired of Sheila praying for her and over her. Sheila rubbed Holy oil on Leslie's forehead and prayed last night and then again that morning. Leslie found it to be comical. Everybody knew that was just olive oil that somebody prayed over. It probably would have been better used if she sautéed some veggies in it.

Leslie didn't care much for religion. Especially since she wasn't living right and all the "Good Christian Folks" seemed to do was look down on her. As soon as she heard Shelia leave, she showered and got dressed. Even though DaQuan told her to stay away from the house, she just had to go and look for that safe. If it contained plenty of money she wouldn't need to get married and she could tell everyone to kiss her perfectly round behind. Once she entered the neighborhood where T-Money lived, she parked the car two blocks away and walked to the house. Everything looked okay. She started her search in the living room. She felt along the walls and the bookcases, hoping to find some secret lever to open a hidden door like she often saw in movies, but there was nothing. She went to the kitchen. She rambled though all the drawers, cabinets and canisters.

She actually found about five thousand dollars hidden in some flour in a canister on the counter and another five thousand dollars in one hundred dollar bills in a sandwich bag in the freezer, but no safe. She put the money in her bra and kept looking. When she didn't find anything else in the kitchen, Leslie headed for the bedroom. She went through all the drawers, but they only held clothes, a couple guns and some old pictures of a young Thaddeus with two women she assumed were his mother and grandmother. She bent down to look under the bed and was caught completely off guard when someone grabbed her from behind. Before she could scream, he placed his hand over her mouth and pressed a gun to her temple.

"Don't make a move or you're dead. If you make a sound, you're dead. Make me think you're about to do something stupid and you're dead. Nod if you understand." The voice sounded like gravel and sent Leslie's heart racing. She nodded frantically. He hoisted her up and threw her on the bed. "Well, what do we have here?"

The man was wearing a black ski mask and it only exposed his eyes and his mouth. He looked her up and down and licked his lips. "*Nice*. Money always did have fine-looking females. Who are you and what are you doing here?"

Leslie struggled to find her voice. It seemed to have escaped her throat when he pressed the gun to her head. "A…a…a friend of T-Money's," she stuttered. "I heard he was dead and decided to come see what I could find. I knew he left a little cash around the house."

"Some friend," said the man.

Another guy walked in. He was wearing a red ski mask. "I told you, bruh. These females ain't loyal. I recognize this one." This guy had a high-pitched voice almost like a woman.

"She had Money's nose wide open. He took her on trips out the country and everything."

"Is that so? I wonder what she had that made him act like that?" Black ski mask licked his lips again. He started to unzip his pants.

Leslie was afraid. She was in a house she wasn't supposed to be in with two men she didn't know. They could rape her and kill her and no one would ever know what happed. She wished she had listed to DaQuan. Why was she so stupid? She grew up around money and if anyone should know that money wasn't everything, it's her. Money couldn't bring her parents back. Money couldn't bring her fiancé back and it couldn't get her out of this situation either.

"We ain't got time for that. Plus, you don't know what this skank has. We need to find out where Money was keeping his dough. There was nothing at the warehouse so it must be here," said red ski mask. He looked at Leslie. "Did you find something? I saw where you wuz ramblin' downstairs."

Leslie shook her head.

"I don't believe you. The man came over and started putting his hands all over her body, patting her down like she'd seen security guards do guys at the club, only a lot rougher. The other one held the gun aimed steadily at her so she didn't dare try to move. Red ski mask started patting her breasts.

"Then what's this?" He put his hands up her shirt and tugged on her bra. The money tumbled out the bottom along with her cell phone.

"Stop lying," he said and punched her in the face. The force of the blow knocked the back of her head into the bed's headboard. She screamed. Black ski mask cocked the gun and said, "Make another sound and you're dead."

Red ski mask picked up the money on the floor and examined the amount before sticking it in his pocket. "If this is all she got then she doesn't know where his real cash is either. I know he's got millions somewhere. We just gotta find it. Put her in the closet. We'll deal with her later."

Black ski mask grabbed Leslie by the arm, pulled her across the room, and threw her in the closet. She landed on the floor with a loud thud. Before he closed the door, he said, "I'll be back for mine." He smiled to show yellow, crooked teeth in dire need of a visit to a dentist. He locked the door. Leslie was trapped. The closet was massive so she had plenty of room to move around. She felt along the walls until she found the light switch. She didn't know what to do, but she was most concerned about what they were going to do. Her face and her head hurt. She felt the back of her head to find a small knot forming there. She had to devise a plan because she wasn't going down without a fight. Maybe there was something in the closet she could use to defend herself if she needed to. She searched several boxes on the top shelf and found two thousand dollars and a small gun. She checked the clip and it had two bullets. If she had to shoot them, she had one bullet for each of them and she couldn't miss.

Leslie pressed her ear against the door in an effort to listen to what was happening on the other side. She heard a scuffle then a loud thud as if something had hit the floor and then a second one. Suddenly the door flew open, but there was no one standing in front of it. She waited to see if anyone would appear, but no one did. She held the gun in front of her and slowly made her way out of the closet. On the floor of the bedroom were the two men who put her in the closet. They had both been shot in the head and appeared to be dead. Blood was oozing from their masks and onto the snow-white carpet. She went over to the one who had taken the money she found and dug in his pocket. It was still there. She put it back in her bra and then began looking for her phone. She was aided by the fact that it began to ring. She followed the sound until she heard it under the bed. It was an unfamiliar number, but for some reason she answered it. A voice she didn't recognize said, "If you want to live get out of the house now. Leave the truck and don't ever come back. T-Money is dead and no one can protect you. Stop being stupid."

That sounded like great advice to Leslie. She ran back to the closet and grabbed a leather backpack she found while she was rambling. She put her journal and the few clothing items she had in the house in the bag. She grabbed a small cedar chest where T-Money stored his diamond stud earrings and watches and put that in the bag along with some other jewelry that was lying on the dresser. She decided to leave the car. Although, she really didn't want to, but the last thing she needed was for someone to recognize it and think it was T-Money. Leslie was glad she wore her workout clothes as she sprinted out of the back door. It seemed like the best way to go to keep the neighbors from seeing her because T-Money had a privacy fence surrounding his property. She climbed over the fence and ran into the woods behind the row of homes on that block. She knew that on the other side of the woods were a parking lot and a strip mall. She would call one of her friends to pick her up once she got there. Someone had saved her. She didn't know who or why, but she was grateful. Maybe that Holy oil Sheila used on her was good for more than sautéing vegetables.

Chapter Thirty-Nine

Sheila

Sheila went to work with a smile on her face. Having two men interested in her was a big boost to her ego. She was glad last night provided some time to bond with her family and realized how much she missed their company. They would have to get together more often. Although her cousins shared what was going on in their lives, she needed to seek counsel for her life elsewhere. Telling her business around Leslie wasn't wise. She never was good at keeping her mouth closed. Sheila no longer shared details about her life with her godmother after the last date she arranged. She obviously didn't know what she was doing.

Vivian, however, was her best friend and a great person to confide in. When she arrived, she went straight to her office and found Vivian at her desk typing away on her computer. She was only a few years older than Sheila, but she seemed to have found the secret to living a happy, fulfilling life. Vivian had a very upbeat disposition and always looked so happy whenever Sheila saw her. She looked happiest when she was with her husband and kids. Sheila hoped she would have that same glow one day.

"I know we're at work, but I need a sister chat," said Sheila.

"Well, you know I don't like to discuss our personal lives on company time because the boss doesn't like it, but I suppose I can allow it this once," said Vivian.

Sheila laughed. "But you are the boss, Madame CEO."

"That's right. Well, I guess that makes it okay. What's up, Madame CFO?"

Sheila gave her a quick rundown of how her search for Mr. Righteous was coming. She even told her about how Max had asked her to stop being his client and be his current love interest. She was quite conflicted.

"DaQuan has been coming around to help me with some family problems and I think there is still something there."

"DaQuan! The hustling homeboy! No! You have the opportunity to be with a man who doesn't live in the hood or drink out of forties. Why would you damage your family's legacy like that? Does he even have a legitimate job, yet? What is that loser doing to earn a living these days?"

Sheila didn't care for the way Vivian reacted or her tone of voice. "When I met him he was working at a warehouse, but he went to barber school and now he cuts hair for a living. He's quite good at it, too. I'd thank you not to refer to my child's father as a loser. He's not a loser. He's a good guy and a great father. He was just raised in a different type of environment."

"Calm down. I'm sorry. You're my best friend. In my opinion, you deserve so much better and I guess I got a little bit too passionate. DaQuan had his chance. An ex is an ex for a reason and I think you should really consider giving Max a chance. I don't know him very well, but you could." Vivian gave her a naughty smirk.

"Girl, stop!"

"Gon' dust those cobwebs off that thang. When's the last time you got laid anyway?"

She looked at her friend and shook her head. Sometimes it amazed her what came out of her mouth. "Too long, but you know I'm trying to live right. Would Jesus tell me to dust off my vajayjay?

"You're talking about the thirty-three-year-old virgin, right? Probably not. Okay. You don't have to sleep with him, but I think you'll regret it if you don't give him the opportunity to make you happy. You keep saying you want what I have. Well, maybe this is your chance. You said yourself that Max was attractive, smart, and funny and a successful businessman. Sounds like he deserves a green light to me."

Sheila bit her bottom lip. "You're probably right. I'm just so confused by these feelings I'm having for DaQuan."

"What you're feeling for DaQuan is nostalgia. Days of old gone by. He'll always be a part of your life, but he doesn't have to be the number one man in your life. He's not a good fit and he never was."

Sheila didn't respond. She just nodded. "Thanks for letting Xavier stay with you last night. My cousins and I really needed some family time."

"No problem. He had a blast and the hubby dropped everyone off at school this morning."

Vivian's assistant, Sylvia, stepped into her office. "Sorry to disturb you two, but Ms. Watson-Purdue has a guest by the name of Maximillian Beauregard here to see her."

"What?" said Sheila. "I wasn't expecting him."

"Yes, ma'am. I seated him in your office. If you don't mind me saying so, he is quite handsome and he is causing a stir with the other ladies in the office. I figured it was best if I got him out of the common areas. You would think they had never seen a man before."

Both women smiled. "Thank you, Sylvia," said Vivian.

Sylvia walked out of the office, closing the door behind her.

"Seems like someone wants a continuation of whatever was interrupted last night," said Vivian.

Sheila smiled. "He probably wants to take me to lunch or something, but don't worry. I know I just got here."

"It's okay. Go. I may be your boss, but I'm also your friend and I know how important a date is during this time in your life. As a matter a fact, take today off. Spend time with Max then go check on your cousin."

"You sure?"

"I insist. I officially declare it Sheila's Fun Day. Enjoy!"

Sheila did a little dance. "Hallelujah! Thanks, Viv!"

"Now get out of here and stop making that gorgeous man wait."

Sheila returned to her office. Her door was closed, but several women were peering in the window that separated her space from the hall, staring at Max. They reminded her of people staring at animals in the zoo through thick glass.

"Ladies, there's nothing to see here and you're certainly not getting paid to stare. Please return to your desks and do some work," she said.

Five women turned around and were greeted by Sheila's "I mean business" look. They scurried away like roaches when the lights come on. "Lucky, Sheila," said one woman as she retreated.

Sheila took a deep and then turned to knob. What she saw nearly took her breath away. Max in all his splendor wasn't a new sight, but the two dozen red roses sitting on her desk was.

"Max, you shouldn't have! They're beautiful. Thank you."

"I wanted to. I didn't have to be in the room to know that last night something real serious occurred. Come here." Max stood up and collected her in an embrace. His arms were warm and welcoming. His cologne smelled heavenly and as the divine scent wafted into her nostrils, it, along with the heat radiating from Max's body, ignited in her the same desire she felt with DaQuan the night before. She knew she needed to step away, but didn't. Instead, she laid her head on his shoulder and took a deep breath to calm herself. Her heart was beating a mile a minute.

"I needed that."

"Anytime. How are you? Is your cousin okay?"

"As well as can be expected when your new fiancé that no one ever had the chance to meet gets killed."

"Sorry to hear that. Sounds like you could use some friend time. Let's get out of here, go get some lunch and talk. Then maybe we can catch a matinee at the movies."

Sheila was glad Vivian gave her the day off. Spending time with Max would be nice. "Sounds like a plan to me. Lead the way, handsome."

She looped her arm in his and enjoyed the looks of envy from several women as they walked down the hallway to the elevator. She actually felt kind of lucky.

Chapter Forty

Regina

Regina was looking forward to work because she agreed to take Chance to do a little shopping after they closed up shop. She hadn't had an opportunity to style anyone other than herself since she left the boutique. She let Chance know she had a family emergency and that she would be late. He said he would run the front office until she arrived. Regina ate breakfast with her sisters and then went back to the mansion to change. Leslie stayed at Shelia's house. She said she had no desire to be at their massive dwelling alone and she had promised DaQuan she wouldn't go back to T-Money's alone. Knowing her sister, she wasn't going to listen, but Regina didn't feel the need to protect Leslie from herself. She was grown and whatever bed she made she was old enough to lie in it.

When she arrived, the waiting area was crowded and Chance was busy taking information, getting customer's cars to the service bays. When Regina walked in, he gave her a smile of relief. He was usually pleased to see her, but this time he was elated.

"I was beginning to think you weren't going to come in."

Regina thought he had the most welcoming smile.

"I'm a woman of my word. I just needed to make sure everyone was all right before I left."

"Is there any way I can help?" he said.

"That's very sweet. I think we've got it under control, but if that changes I'll let you know."

"That's fine. Now please take over this window. I hate doing customer service."

She gave him a reassuring pat on the shoulder. "I got it. Now go get under a hood or something."

"Yes, ma'am." Chance left the office and didn't come back until it was time to leave.

After work, Chance wanted to go home and change, and gave Regina his address. She would meet him after finishing a few tasks. When she pulled into the driveway, she checked her GPS to make sure she put in the address correctly. She had to have had the wrong house. It was exquisite. Why was he living in a gorgeous house like this and dressing as if he made minimum wage? It was located in an exclusive community. He had to have money to live here but that wasn't all. To purchase a house there he also had to be approved by a neighborhood committee. She rang the doorbell and Chance answered wearing jeans that looked like they were at least ten years old and a T-shirt that used to be black, but after being washed one hundred times or so was now a deep gray.

"Come in," he said.

Regina stepped inside onto marble floors and looked around. The white walls were completely bare. Not one picture or piece of art. To her left was an area she assumed was the sitting room, but the only thing to sit on was a wooden chair. To her right was probably the dining area, but it, too, contained no furniture.

"Chance, your house is very nice, but where's your furniture?"

Chance shrugged. "I've really never been into decorating. I always figured that when I get a girlfriend I'd let her decorate it for me, but I never got one. I got a nice bedroom suite upstairs though and a state of the art man cave complete with a theater and game room."

Regina laughed. "Only the essentials, I see. How long have you lived here?"

"Five years."

"Why do I get the feeling that the shop is doing better than I thought or you have another job you're not telling me about."

Chance smiled. "Let's just say that I know how to invest wisely with the money I do have. I own several rental properties and I'm a silent partner in my brother's commercial real estate company."

Your last name is Chambers, right? You mean to tell me that Chadwick Chambers of Chambers Properties is your brother? He's got over twenty million in properties. I was looking at one of them for the boutique I want to open."

Chance raised an eyebrow. "So you keep up with my brother's business?"

"No, not really, but his wife and your mother do. They are regulars at the boutique where I used to work and they were always bragging about how successful he is. Dropping names and figures wherever and whenever they could."

"First, his mother is not my mother. Second, he started that company with some of my money and I'm proud to say it was one of the best investments I ever made. He does all the work and I reap some pretty hefty benefits." Chance pretended as if he were popping his collar.

"Impressive, but I don't get it. You act like you're broke. You bring your lunch every day, you drive an old antique Ford truck, and you dress like this." Regina let her eyes travel from his dirty run-over tennis shoes to his head, which was in dire need of a haircut.

"I'm not materialistic, Regina. That truck belonged to my dad. He taught me everything I know about cars. I bring my lunch because I have a sensitive stomach and I enjoy my cooking better than anything they serve in a restaurant. I'm a simple man. I just want to go to work, do a good job, and come home to a nice house and my woman. I thought I had that, but it didn't work out so well. I got rid of the woman when I realized the only reason she married me was because of my money. Just because I can afford for her to go shopping all the time doesn't mean she should. The very least a woman can do, if a man is funding her extravagant lifestyle, is cook him a hot meal and give him some loving when he needs it. No man likes being taken for granted. Especially when he's doing his job as a husband, but the last straw was when I found out she was secretly taking birth control. She knew I wanted kids more than anything, but she didn't care. Talkin' 'bout she wasn't ready to have a baby. Well, she should have told me that before I married her!"

Regina didn't mean to open up old wounds with her questions. She realized her boss was a prime example of how you shouldn't judge a book by its cover. The man was loaded.

"Well, let's take your mind off the past and get back to the present. Why do you want to go shopping?".

"Two reasons. I've been asked to be in a magazine that wants to talk about my business and I have a fancy business dinner to go to with my brother next week. Last time I went to one with the clothes I have I looked like I belonged in their gardens pulling weeds compared to the other men in the room. I don't want that to happen again."

Regina smiled and grabbed him by the arm. "You've come to the right place. Where's the truck. Let's go!"

Chance escorted her to his garage. He opened the door and turned on the light. "We're not taking the truck today. That's just for work."

Regina's mouth dropped open. The garage held four cars. She was used to seeing the truck, but next to it was blue antique convertible Corvette and next to that was a newer model black Jaguar. There was even a Harley Davidson motorcycle. Each one shone like a new penny. She was no stranger to seeing nice things, but she never would have expected such an array of cars from a man like Chance.

"All these belong to you?"

"Yep. When you can fix anything, there's no reason for you not to have plenty of vehicles at your disposal. Which chariot would you like to take, m'lady?" He bowed and held out his hand to help her step into the garage.

"It's such a nice day, let's take the Corvette, and ride with the top down."

"Excellent choice," said Chance. "You can drive."

Chapter Forty-One

Leslie

"I missed you," Beau said, nuzzling his face in the back of Leslie's neck before wrapping his arms around her waist and pulling her closer to him. His finger played with her belly button. "We belong together, you and I. I'm sorry I haven't been able to make that happen, but maybe we can do something about that."

Leslie remained silent. She wanted him to stop touching her. This felt wrong. She didn't know how she ended up in Beau's bed. She ran as if she were being pursued, although there wasn't anyone behind her. Once she reached the strip mall, she tried several of her friends, but none of them answered. She didn't dare call Sheila or Regina. She had no desire to listen to a lecture about how she wasn't supposed to go alone. When she emerged from the woods, she was covered in small cuts from the trees that threatened to capture her as she ran. She had almost been killed and thanks to an unknown hero, she was still alive. She shuddered to think what those men were planning to do to her when they pulled her out of the closet.

Beau continued talking when she didn't say anything. "You've had a long day. Get some sleep. We'll talk about it later." He kissed the nape of her neck and laid his head on her pillow.

Leslie called Beau when she couldn't reach anyone else. He immediately came to get her. He looked like a million bucks and smelled as if he'd showered himself in cologne. Evidently, he came into some money, and had gotten himself a new car and new clothes. Leslie was too shaken to go home to the empty mansion and she didn't want him to drop her off there for fear that someone might see them. Instead, she let him take her to his apartment. She wanted to tell someone what happened, but she knew not to tell him. She told him she had gotten into a fight with one of her friends and when she pulled a gun on her, she ran. She prayed silently that no one saw her enter or leave the house and once the bodies were discovered, no one would come looking for her. A Purdue in jail would certainly be the scandal of the year and she was sure she wouldn't look good in a prison jumpsuit. The only good thing that came out of her adventure was the money that was now safely hidden in the backpack she took from T-Money's house.

Beau listened attentively and held her while she cried. Afterward, he gave her a bath followed by some additional TLC as he applied ointment and Band-Aids to her cuts. This was not the selfish, self-serving Beau Leslie was used to. She should have known it was too good to be true because less than an hour later, he was pawing at her looking for "payment" for his good deed. Leslie just wanted to be held. That was all the comfort she desired, but Beau thought she needed more. Just like every other man before T-Money, he thought he could use her body at will. Like sex was all she wanted or needed. No, Leslie didn't need extras like love, romance, and genuine affection. As he entered her, a tear rolled down her face. Beau thought it was her reaction to the pleasure he thought he was evoking, but she was mourning the life she could have had with the man who asked her to be his wife. He had been stolen from her and she had no idea who did it. She hoped whoever took his life would pay for their crime. She wondered if it was the two men who lay bleeding on his snow-white carpet. It was obvious they knew him and DaQuan said people believed it was his own men. If so, they got exactly what they deserved.

After he climaxed, Beau told Leslie to get some rest, but how could she on a queen-sized mattress on the floor that served as his bed. How desperate was she to have sex with a man who didn't even have furniture? Leslie lay there listening and waiting for Beau's breathing to become steady. Once she heard soft snores escaping his person, she slowly unwrapped herself from him. She watched him and prayed he didn't wake as she slipped into on her clothes and shoes. He looked so pathetic. What did she ever see in him? She left, vowing never to return.

Sheila and Regina had been calling and texting most of the day. She didn't have the energy to talk to them right now. As she walked to a nearby gas station to meet the cab she called, she sent them a quick text letting them know she was still alive and safe.

Chapter Forty-Two

Regina

Chance and Leslie had a great time shopping. She took him by her favorite men's boutique and helped him pick out four casual outfits and he was fitted for a suit that would make him look like he belonged at the millionaires table when he went to his meeting. Regina was in awe of how great his body looked. When he put on a pair of jeans from this decade, he looked younger than his forty years of age. She even got him to purchase a couple of stylish close-cut T-shirts that showed off his chiseled chest and arms. She convinced Chance to wear the jeans and shirt out of the store. Then she took him to get a haircut and a shave before they went to get a few pairs of shoes. One of them included a pair of tennis shoes that didn't look like they belonged in the trash. Now, Chance looked like the owner of a successful business.

After their outing, they went back to his house and Chance made turkey burgers to put on the grill, along with a few vegetable skewers. He fired up the grill and waited for the coals to reach the right temperature. While they waited, they took their shoes off and stuck their feet in his heated pool. When Regina saw his feet, she almost passed out. They looked like they belonged on Big Foot, the Abominable Snowman or possibly the Loch Ness Monster, but certainly not on a human being. Her purse was sitting nearby. She took out the personal grooming kit she carried and tried to clip his toenails.

"Do I have to? Please don't make me do it," Chance whined.

"Yes. You have to clip these talons. When's the last time you had a pedicure?" Regina looked down at his feet in disgust.

"Never. Men don't get pedicures."

"That is a lie from the pit of hell that they tell men who have feet that look like yours and, for some strange reason, aren't ashamed of them. I think you might have a fungus; I'm glad I spotted these before I left."

Chance protested, but she was not having it. He had to do something about those daggers he called toenails and he had to do it right then and there.

His mind was working overtime to figure out a way to get out of it. "Well, let's do it after I finish grilling so I don't burn the burgers. I'm sure this won't be an easy fix. Better yet, how about I let you schedule me to let some foreign woman that barely speaks English work on my feet instead?"

Regina clicked the toenail clippers in her hands repeatedly. She enjoyed taunting Chase. "Fine, but if I leave you alone today you have to promise me that you'll go with me to get a pedicure tomorrow."

"Deal!" He jumped up quickly before Regina had a chance to change her mind. "Regina, you really need to loosen up. I know what you need. You need to go for a dip." He picked her up and acted like he was going to throw her in the pool. Now it was Chance's turn to taunt her.

Regina screamed. "Don't you dare! Put me down!"

Chance continued to act as if he were going to throw her in. "You're in no position to make demands, madam! My house, my rules."

Regina softened her voice and batted her eyelashes. With an exaggerated southern accent she said, "Please, kind sir, won't you put this damsel down? I'd forever be in your debt, sir. I prefer not to ruin my clothes, hair, and makeup in such a ghastly fashion."

Chance looked down into her eyes. Even in the diminishing light of the setting sun, they glistened. He also took in her pouty, cherry-red lips and the form fitting dress she wore that accentuated the roundness of her ample breasts. He put her down and to his surprise, Regina kissed him squarely on the lips. Chance opened his mouth and took her in slowly like a fine wine he wanted to savor. He normally didn't mix business with pleasure, but something about Regina made him go against his better judgement. Besides, this was the first time he had employed a woman who looked like someone he would want to date.

When the kiss ended, she said, "Sorry. I don't know what came over me."

Chance smiled. "I don't know either, but I liked it. Do it again!"

Regina granted his request. This time more hungrily and she pressed her body as close to him as possible. She wanted him. She saw no reason why she couldn't have him. With her mouth still tasting his, she began pawing at him like a dog in heat, stripping the shirt he bought off his body and throwing it on the cement patio that surrounded the pool.

Chance pulled back. "Are you sure you're not just doing this because you're trying to prove to yourself you don't need Antonio?"

"I'm doing this because I want to forget Antonio ever existed. Can you help me?" Regina slid her dress over her head. Unfortunately, the sultry move didn't go as smooth as she hoped and it got stuck around her neck. She had forgotten that this particular dress had a small neckline and required her to use the zipper in the back. So much for trying to be a sexy seductress! She struggled with it for a moment before saying, "Can you help me?"

Chance laughed softly, but made no attempt to relieve her of her dress. Instead he stood there with his arms folded and admired the view. This was confirmation for him that he shouldn't make love to her. One, she was his employee. Two, she was fresh out of a relationship. Three, she was wearing another man's ring. And four, he could easily fall for a beautiful woman like her. His eyes scanned her partially nude body. Her red satin bra and panties seemed to be challenging him to remove them. He was like Adam in the Garden of Eden being enticed to eat that red juicy apple. Forbidden fruit. Regina didn't seem like the aggressive type, but maybe he had misjudged her. He continued to stand there and watch as she struggled to get the dress off. She was awkwardly breathtaking. He couldn't remember the last time a woman that beautiful was willing to get naked for him and it wasn't in hopes that he wouldn't charge for expensive repairs to her car. Chance was a mere man, but he knew it would complicate things for the both of them if he succumbed to his carnal lustful desires. Regina had to make a decision regarding Antonio before they crossed that line.

Regina continued to struggle with her dress for a few more seconds before pulling it back down. She laughed and then batted her long eyelashes at him seductively. There was now a red smudge on the front of her dress where the fabric rubbed against her lips. "Well, are you?" she asked.

"Yes ma'am. I do believe I'm the man for the job, but not like this. I've made a lot of mistakes in my time, but one of my biggest is rushing into a relationship and then a marriage. I like you, Regina, and today was the first of many outings together, I hope. I'd like to get to know you before I *get to know you*. If that makes any sense," he said. "I'm going to go in the house and grab our turkey burgers and skewers and cook us a great meal that we can sit by the pool and enjoy as we talk and get to know one another better." He retrieved his shirt from the ground and left Regina alone.

This was the first time Regina had tried to sleep with someone other than Antonio and she was rejected. There was no way she was going to sit there and eat turkey burgers and veggies like she wasn't completely embarrassed.

When Chance returned with the food to put on the grill, Regina was gone. He wasn't happy, but neither was she.

Chapter Forty-Three

Sheila

Shelia was late picking up Xavier. The school had already called twice. She was having so much fun with Max that she lost track of time. She was so late that she didn't have time to go back to her job and pick up her car. She and Max drove to the Little Scholars Learning Center as fast as they could. She exited the car and ran to the door and, as she was about to enter, Xavier and DaQuan emerged from the building.

"Oh crap!" she said. "What are you doing here?"

"The school called me because you were taking too long to pick up X from after care." He looked at Max sitting in the car. Max smiled and waved. DaQuan gave him the stank face. "So is he why you were too busy to pick up your son?"

"We were conducting business," said Sheila. She usually didn't lie, but this was not the time to be truthful. She turned her attention toward Xavier. "Hey, baby! You ready to go?"

He grabbed his mother around the legs and squeezed. "Hey, Mommy! Who's that?"

"That is Mommy's friend, Max. He's going to take me to my car and then we're going home."

"Naw. It ain't going down like that," said DaQuan. "I don't like my son around strange men. X can stay with me. I'll bring him home later."

Sheila picked up her son. "Oh no you don't. You can't dictate whom my son spends time around when he's with me. I told you, Max and I had business to conduct."

"Yeah. Tell that to someone slow, Sheila. First, you go drinking with this dude and come back too wasted to make it up the stairs, and now you show up with him at my son's school. That's not protocol for any business I've seen."

Unbeknownst to Sheila, Max had exited the car and was now standing behind her. "I know it's none of my business, but this really isn't a conversation you need to have in front of your son. How about a compromise? Sheila and I are finished conducting our business. Why don't you take her back to her car? That way, Xavier doesn't have to witness his parents fighting outside of his school and you won't have your son around *strangers*, as you say."

"I'm not going anywhere with him," said Sheila.

Max looked at her sternly and said, "Sheila, look at the bigger picture. This isn't worth the fight."

"Yeah, listen to Fonzworth Bentley over there. This ain't what you want, cuz, I'll take it to the mat for mine," said DaQuan.

Sheila grew furious. "FINE! You can be so hood sometime. Xavier has been around my business associates before. He knows Mommy has to work, but if you insist on acting childish then so be it. Max, thanks for everything. I'm sure our arrangement is going to work out just fine."

"I know this is going to work out in both our favor. Enjoy your evening and we'll talk soon. Xavier, it was nice to meet you, little man."

"Bye, Mr. Max," said Xavier. He was such a happy child and danced around the schoolyard as he waited for him and his parents to leave. He seemed oblivious that his parents were having a heated exchange.

"Catch you later, DQ," said Max.

"Fa Sho! I'll be right here. I ain't going nowhere."

Max understood what he meant, but he wasn't afraid of a little competition. Actually, he didn't view DaQuan as competition at all. He was more like a fly who invited himself to the picnic. No one wanted him there; he was annoying and he served no purpose. Max walked back to his Mercedes and drove off. Sheila watched him with desire in her eyes. What a man! She was actually turned on by the way Max took control of the situation. She wished he didn't have to go. Sheila began walking toward DaQuan's truck. "You coming?"

He watched the jiggle of her booty as she moved ahead of him and his son. To him, she was one of the most beautiful women God ever made. There was no way some preppy dude was going to take her from him.

"Sure," he said. "But I promised X we would go to Clown Burger so I hope you feel like fries with that attitude because we're all going to eat."

"Yay! I love Clown Burger!" shouted Xavier, as he jumped up and down.

Sheila did not want to sit in a restaurant with him acting as if she were happy to be there. "You two can go just take me to my car."

"No can do. Clown Burger is two streets over and your car is on the other side of town."

Even Shelia couldn't argue with the fact that taking her to her car would be out of the way. She could have demanded it, but she couldn't bear to see her little man disappointed. He was a good child and he deserved a treat like Clown Burger from time to time.

"Fine," she said and continued to sashay to the truck with DaQuan staring at her derriere.

****

"Mommy, I had fun today," Xavier said, while his mother helped him put on his pajamas.

"Really, what did you do at school that was so much fun?"

"Not school. With you and Daddy at Clown Burger. We did something together. We never do stuff together."

Her son's words made her pause. He was right. "How does that make you feel?"

"I dunno, but today was nice. It felt like when I hang with Auntie Viv and Uncle John, except this time it was my mommy and daddy."

Sheila hugged him and helped him get under the covers. "I see."

Xavier kissed her on the cheek and they did their nightly ritual of rubbing noses. "Did you have fun today, Mommy?"

"Yeah, baby, I did." She smiled at her only son and kissed him on the forehead.

Sheila had a great time at lunch with Max. He took her to Pesto, a new Italian restaurant in Midtown. The conversation was so good they sat there for two hours. Afterward, instead of going to a movie they went to an art gallery and viewed a new exhibit in the downtown arts and fashion district of South Main. She was impressed by his knowledge of painting techniques and artists. Although, she had to admit that she also had fun with DaQuan and her son…once she stopped being mad. DaQuan had a hilarious sense of humor and the three of them laughed all through dinner. On the way to her car, he put in his greatest hits of the 90s CD and played some of her favorite jams. Artists like Joe, Xscape, Babyface, Prince, Jagged Edge, SWV, Tupac and more had her bobbing her head and singing along. Max brought the mature adult experience, but it was DaQuan who allowed her to just relax and have youthful fun. Sheila was now even more confused about her feelings than she had been before. Was Vivian right? Was what she felt with DaQuan really nostalgia because the emotions he brought forth when they were together felt like real time?

"Mommy, Mommy, did you hear me?" asked Xavier.

"I'm sorry, baby. What did you say?"

"Can we do more things together? You, me, and Daddy?"

Sheila didn't know if that was something she could agree to. If she decided to pursue whatever was going on with her and Max, spending time with DaQuan would be a problem. But, the joy emanating from the most important person in her life was undeniable.

"We'll see, baby," was the only honest answer she could give. "Now, say your prayers."

She listened quietly, as he recited his nightly prayers. He wasn't the only one who needed to pray. She needed direction from her Heavenly Father concerning her love life and she needed it soon.

Chapter Forty-Four

Regina

Regina was in pure ecstasy. She'd never known pleasure like this. Antonio was the only man she'd ever been with as an adult. She had a couple of meaningless trysts in her teens, but that was just curiosity getting the best of her. Once she had sex with Antonio during her senior year of college, she knew she didn't need or want another lover….until now. She realized that what she'd been getting all these years was mediocre, at best. Chance took her to the pinnacle of ecstasy several times. Each time when she thought it couldn't get any better he did something she'd never experienced before the next time to show her that it could. She just hoped this was the beginning of a dream and not a nightmare.

"Good morning, princess," he said before kissing her lips. "What are you thinking about?"

"I'm wondering if this is too good to be true."

Chance smiled at her and kissed her again. "Of course it is, darling, because you're dreaming. Wake up."

Regina felt someone shaking her. She opened her eyes to Leslie standing over her eating a green apple. "Wake up, nasty. You're in here moaning a groaning like you have company. I had to come see for myself because I just knew Ms. Goody Two Shoes didn't have a man in here and I was right."

"What? No I was not!"

"Oh yes you were. Who's the lucky man of your dreams?"

Two times in less than twenty-four hours, Regina had been thoroughly embarrassed. "I don't know what you're talking about? Give me a bite of that." She reached for the apple.

Leslie moved it out of her grasp. "Eww, no. You just woke up. I bet you have a serious case of yuck mouth. Your mouth has probably been on whoever was just rocking your world in HD. You should have heard yourself 'Ooooh. Ooooh Oooooh. Don't stop, Daddy! Don't stop!'" she said, mimicking her. "I bet your panties are soaked."

"You can be such a brat. Please change the subject. How are you? Are you feeling better?" said Regina.

"A little bit. I came to ask you if I can get your car while you're at work today. I'd like to do a little shopping therapy."

"Work?" Regina dreaded seeing Chance again. If she didn't need the money, she would call in and quit. "Sure. Just don't wreck it. It's not mine."

"I promise to be careful with that old car. I bet Booker T. Washington took George Washington Carver to lunch in it when they were alive." Leslie pulled out a wad of money, peeled off three one hundred dollar bills, and laid them on the bed. "Thanks for giving me money to help you move, but you can have it back."

Regina just looked at it. "Where did you get that?"

"Chill. I found it in T-Money's car," Leslie lied.

Regina lay back down. "Keep it. I don't want his whack drug money."

"You are so critical. He didn't just sell drugs, he also had a legitimate lawn service." Leslie picked up the bills.

"Fine. I'll keep it. Speaking of whack, have you heard from Antonio?"

"Not since he proposed. I guess he's giving me some space to think," said Regina.

"Have you made a decision?

"No, not yet."

"I don't think you should marry him. You deserve better, Big Sis."

"I know, but Antonio is all I know. My entire adult life it's been me and him."

Leslie took a bite of her apple. It was so juicy some of the juice dribbled on her lip. She licked it off and started talking with her mouth full. "Exactly and he's always been a jerk. You're beautiful, smart, and talented and he doesn't appreciate you. You should go out and find someone who does. I want the money as much as you do, but dooming yourself to a lifetime with him is a fate worse than death."

"Close your mouth. You're getting juice and spit on me. He's not that bad, Les."

"Yes, he is."

Regina sat up in the bed and stared at her sister. "What do you know that you're not telling me?"

Leslie held her poker face. She had knowledge of several of Antonio's trysts. He'd been cheating on her sister for years. "NOTHING! But, I've dealt with enough creeps to know one when I see one. You hungry?"

Regina didn't believe her, but she didn't press the issue. "Yeah."

"I'm going down to the kitchen. Ms. Pearl was in there cooking yesterday. She said she left something in the fridge. I'm going to warm us up whatever it is. You can finish masturbating and come downstairs when you're done."

"Shut up! I was not doing that!"

"Whatever. You know I love you, right?"

"Of course, I do. We're sisters. I love you, too." She opened her arms and Leslie bent down to hug her.

"I've made a lot of mistakes and if I ever hurt you, I'm sorry."

Regina was not used to seeing Leslie emotional or apologetic. "Where is this coming from?"

"T-Money's death has made me put a lot of things in perspective. We're only on this Earth a small amount of time. I've been wasting mine, and I want to do better. I'm thinking about going back to school."

"That's a great idea. You're smarter than you give yourself credit for. Start using that brain for something other than manipulating men."

"Yeah, I know."

"Maybe you should give whoever you were dreaming about a chance," said Leslie.

"How do you know I wasn't dreaming about Antonio?"

"I just do."

"I'll think about it."

"You might as well. Sounds like you already boned him."

"I wish," said Regina. Last night was an experience she never wanted to have again, but the dream she had was definitely a reality she could handle.

Chapter Forty-Five

Leslie

It was really messed up that Grandma Grace willed her car to her driver and left Leslie with no wheels. Not even a scooter to drive. She'd bought Leslie three cars over the years, but after she wrecked the last one while driving drunk, Grandma Grace refused to get her another one. She used to tell Leslie, "I'm not going to always be here so you need to learn to take care of yourself. The money your grandfather and I earned was not so you can become a professional bum." Grandma Grace just didn't realize that Leslie's idea of earning a living was different from hers. Although, she hadn't quite figured out what she wanted to do to earn a living. Until she did, sexing men with money seemed to work well.

She had found enough money in T-Money's house to buy a used car, but Leslie wasn't quite sure if she wanted to spend thousands of dollars in one place. She had to reserve her funds until she knew when she was going to get more. She had to find a husband. Leslie planned to go shopping, but she really wasn't even in the right frame of mind to do so. Yesterday, she was running for dear life, and she believed she was safe now. Although, she wasn't one hundred percent sure but the fact that the police hadn't shown up to ask her about the dead bodies in the house was a good sign. The mall wouldn't be opened for a few hours. So, Leslie drove around aimlessly and eventually found herself parked in front of Percy's house. He was her favorite geek. She hadn't seen or talked to him since Grandma Grace's funeral.

Percy routinely left his doors open so Regina just let herself in. She found him in his room asleep. Although she wasn't physically attracted to him, he was a source of comfort for her. Percy was a great guy, but he would forever find himself in the friend zone. His room was a mess, as usual. She was going to give her friend a rude awakening. Leslie began to pull back the covers and almost screamed when she noticed that there was a body in the bed other than Percy's. A petite woman with an afro was pressed against him wearing nothing, but a pair of boy shorts. The light peering through partially closed blinds was the only illumination in the room, but even in sparse light, she could tell she was beautiful.

Leslie tried to place the covers back without disturbing them, but Percy opened his eyes. He didn't seem the least bit startled to see her standing next to his bed. He actually looked happy to see her and smiled.

"Hey," he said shyly and yawned.

"Hey. I'm sorry, I didn't know you had company. I was trying not to wake you or *her*," Leslie whispered and nodded toward the partially nude woman who was snoring softly against his chest.

"Yeah, that's my girl, Tabitha."

Leslie felt a pang in her heart. She didn't know why, but she didn't like the sound of Percy loving another woman other than her. He'd asked her plenty of times to give them a try and each time she declined.

"I'm happy for you. I'll just let myself out."

"No. Don't go. I haven't had a chance to talk to you and see how you're doing. Tabitha sleeps like the dead.

Go downstairs and fix us some coffee and I'll be down in a minute."

"You sure?"

"Yeah."

He smiled, again. Leslie missed his smile. They used to hang out a lot. He was the only man besides T-Money who tried to engage her in intelligent conversation. He treated her like she had a brain and not just a body. Leslie did as instructed.

Percy's kitchen was normally as messy as his room, but evidently Tabitha was good for more than sex. It was spotless. No dishes piled up in the sink. There wasn't even a fork in there and the stainless steel shone as if it had been freshly polished along with the floors. She went to the Keurig carousel of single serving cups and picked out a breakfast blend for her and a dark roast for Percy. He came down just as she finished brewing both their cups and was taking her first sip. When she looked up, she spat her coffee on the counter. Percy looked great! His skin was clear. He wasn't wearing his glasses and he had lost weight. She ran to him and gave him a huge hug.

"OMG, Percy, you're hot! What did you do?" She patted him on his chest and stomach and felt nothing but muscle.

"You like it?" he said bashfully. Over the past couple of months, he'd heard similar compliments from women, but he still wasn't used to it. "Tabitha did it. She showed me what products to use to clear up my acne and had me change my diet to curb my allergies. Turns out that certain foods were triggering my mass mucus production. I used to be on a slew of medicine and now I'm down to two pills. She's also a health nut so I'm eating better and working out regularly. She convinced me to start wearing contacts. I got a new haircut and now I can't keep the babes off me," he joked. "I feel good though. Better than I've ever felt."

For the first time, Leslie found herself attracted to Percy. "I bet. She's really good for you. What is she, some kind of doctor?" Leslie looked into his dark brown eyes and wondered why she never noticed how handsome he was before. She was probably distracted by the craters in his face.

"Better. Tabitha's a scientist. She works for St. Jude helping to develop treatments for cancer. She's amazing. If she wasn't asleep, I'd introduce you. Maybe we can all link up another time. I'm sure you'd like her." He took a sip of his coffee. "Hey, you remembered the way I like it. You got the cream and sugar just right. Thanks."

"You're welcome." Leslie continued to stare at Percy. He looked like a new man. She could have slapped herself. All this potential was in front of her for years and she never saw it. She was happy for him, but she had to admit that she was a tad bit jealous. She didn't deserve a man like Percy. She was a wreck and she knew it. He deserved so much better. He deserved a woman like Tabitha.

"How did you two meet?"

He took another sip of his coffee before answering. "We met on a dating site."

"Really? Those things actually work?"

"Heck yeah, but you have to be careful. There are a lot of liars out there."

Leslie reached on top of the refrigerator for some bagels, pulled two out of the plastic bag, and put them in the toaster. "I signed up for one, but I haven't been out with anyone yet."

"You? Why? You've never had a problem getting a man." He went to the refrigerator, opened the door, and got out the strawberry cream cheese.

"Oh, I dunno. I've been thinking that it's time for me to slow down. Stop all the partying and find someone decent to come home to. I've even been thinking about going back to college and finishing my degree."

"Thank God! I hope you mean that, Les. I've always been worried about you. I pray for you all the time. I was afraid that you'd overdose one day or go home with the wrong guy and end up dead or catch a venereal disease or something. That life you were living is dangerous." Percy gave her a hug and kissed her on the forehead. "You're important to me, Leslie."

"You're important to me, too, Percy. You were praying for me? When did you get so religious?"

"I've always believed in God. That's one of the other things Tabitha has been helping me with. I'm developing a relationship with Him because of her. We've been going to church and everything. I even got baptized." He stuck his chest out proudly. "I admit we're not perfect because we're fornicating, but I hope to end that soon. Tell me what you think of this."

Percy reached into his pajama pants, pulled out a blue velvet box, and opened it. Inside, sat one of the most gorgeous rings Leslie had ever seen. It was a large, blue sapphire surrounded by several small diamonds. The setting and the band were either silver or platinum, but she wasn't sure. It didn't matter because it was exquisite.

"I designed it myself. Blue is her favorite color. I know it's not traditional, but she's not the kind of woman that's hung up on tradition," he said.

Leslie pulled it out and put it on her own ring finger, which was now empty because she was no longer wearing the ring T-Money had given her. "It's gorgeous and I'm sure she'll love it. When are you going to propose?"

I don't know. We've only been dating three months. But, when you know they're the one why wait? I can't imagine my life without her, Les. I never thought I'd feel about another woman the way I felt about you, but the way I feel about her is twice as strong as what I felt for you. It's probably because she loves me back. I feel invincible when I'm with her. It's like I can accomplish anything with her by my side. I'm just so scared. I know she'll say yes, but I want it to be special— no magical."

Leslie began to tear up. "That's beautiful, Percy. The only time I've seen your face light up like this is when you're working on one of your gadgets. She must be amazing. Let me help you propose. Leave it to me; I'll plan everything."

Percy looked at her quizzically. "You'd help me propose to another woman?"

"Of course I would. You've been an amazing friend. When everyone else saw me as a dumb party girl, drug addict, you saw me as smart and funny. I never treated you the way you deserved to be treated and I'm sorry. I'm at a point in my life where I want to be a better person. Let me show you some of the kindness you've shown to me."

"Thank you, Les. I'll never forget you. I know if you put it together it's going to be fantastic!" He gave her another hug.

Leslie hugged him tight. She stood on her tiptoes and kissed him on his cheek. "You are welcome. All I want is an invitation to the wedding. Now sit down and tell me some of her favorite things and let's get this proposal done."

For the next hour, Percy and Leslie talked about how to make his proposal like something out of a romance novel. She left his house with a renewed sense of purpose. He was going to propose the next afternoon at the family mansion. She planned to pull Regina in to help with the decorations and she was going to pay for it with her own money as partial repayment for all the loans Percy gave her that she never bothered to repay. It felt good to do something for someone else. She decided right then she was going to do it more often. She was also going to get back on that dating site and find herself a husband.

Chapter Forty-Six

Regina

Regina dreaded going to work. She almost called in sick, but she knew Saturday was one of the shop's busiest days and they needed her. Regardless of how wounded her pride was she still had a job to do and it was a job she enjoyed. She usually came in early, but today she only came in five minutes prior to open time in order to leave no time for chatting if Chance wanted to talk.

When they saw one another, they greeted each other cordially. Regina didn't quite know how to feel. She knew she needed to talk to someone and after she put in the repair orders for the first few customers who had gotten up early to meet them at 7 a.m., she went to the bathroom and called her big cousin. She normally didn't like Shelia's advice, but that's because she was usually right. After she explained what happed, Sheila wasted no time in setting her straight.

"Let me get this right. You're upset because a Godly man chose not to treat you like the whore of Babylon and bed you before getting to know you."

"Sheila, can you drop the sarcasm. I offered myself to him and he turned me down cold. My feelings are hurt."

"And? You can't have everything you want Regina, including sex with a man. The man didn't tell you he didn't want you. He didn't even say he didn't like you.

He said he wanted to get to know you and treat you like the lady you were raised to be. You should fall on your knees right now and thank God that He sent a good man your way. You're so focused on the physical that you don't realize what Chance is offering you."

"No. Tell me," said Regina.

"The opportunity to have the type of man you deserve. For years you've been with a self-serving bastard who only wanted you because you are a Purdue, but you've been too stupid in love, or should I say sprung, to realize it. Wake up and smell the good man coffee brewing, girl. Your problem is that you have never really dated. Antonio was the first man you felt passion with and you latched on for dear life. Dating is spending time with someone with your clothes on to see if the two of you could have a future together. My advice to you is take sex out of the equation. Go slow. You said yourself that you had a wonderful time shopping with him. Go out and have more wonderful times with your clothes on."

Once again, her cousin was right. "I get what you're saying, but how do we get through this awkward phase?"

"That's easy. When you talk to him just say can we forget last night happened and start over. That way you don't have to talk about it and you both can go back to being pals. Act like pals instead of potential lovers."

"Thanks, Shelia. You really think it's that simple?"

"You're welcome, hot to trot. Men aren't like us. They don't obsess over things. I'm sure he'd love to move past what happed, too. Go take a cold shower before you ruin what could be the best thing to ever happen to you besides me being your cousin."

Regina laughed. "Okay, now your turn. How are you? I haven't heard you say anything about how your search for Mr. Righteous is going."

Sheila sighed. "It's going." She had no desire to talk to Regina about her love life. That girl may have been in her mid-twenties, but she sometimes had the maturity of a nineteen-year-old. Her solution to her problem would probably be sleep with Max and DaQuan and see whom she had the best chemistry with. There was so much more than that at stake. She had to pick who was also best for her son, too. She decided to change the subject. "Did you give Antonio back his ring, yet?"

Regina looked down at the sparkler on her finger. "No. I plan to when I tell him I'm not going to marry him."

"When do you plan to do that?"

"As soon as I find time."

"You're stalling, Gina. Give that fool back his dollar store trinket and tell him to kick rocks."

"Shelia, what if this is my only chance at getting a husband by the New Year? There are millions at stake."

If Sheila could have squeezed her body through the phone and got in Regina's face she would have. "No, what's at stake is the safety of your face and his because I swear if he puts his hands on you again I'm going to get DaQuan's cousin, Drake, on him. You remember him, don't you? He's the killer in the family."

Regina gasped. "You wouldn't."

"Try me. Grandma Grace is no longer here to look after you. So it's my job and if I have to put Antonio six feet underground because you don't know when to run for your life, I will."

"I see why Grandma Grace didn't like DaQuan. You picked up his bad habits. You're all hood and stuff now."

"When it comes to the people I love….fa sho!" Shelia said, using one of DaQuan's favorite phrases.

Regina giggled. "I gotta get back to work."

"Okay. Just let me know if you want me to go with you when you break it off. I dare him to give you a hard time with me standing there."

"I'm sure I can handle it," said Regina.

"I know you can, but I'm here if you need me. Bye."

Regina walked out the bathroom and almost hit Chance with the door.

"Hey, watch it. That's my face; I may need that," he said.

Regina marveled at how handsome he looked with his fresh shave and haircut.

"You okay? We had some more customers come in. I tried not to disturb you while you were taking care of your lady business, but you've been in there a while."

Regina knew that he was really asking if *we're* okay. "Yeah. Sorry I took so long. Sometimes lady business takes a minute. Hey, about last night—"

Chance cut her off. "This may not be the right time. We've got work to do."

"Yeah, but I'd rather not spend this entire day feeling awkward. What I have to say won't take long. I just wanted to know if we can forget what happened and pretend like the evening ended at shopping."

"Is that what you really want?"

"Yeah. I was completely out of order. I'm totally okay with taking things slow and getting to know each other before we go there."

Chance let out a deep breath. "Thanks for making this painless. I'm happy to see you can be mature about this. I was scared what happened would make it hard for us to work together."

"No. I don't want that, but I don't want you to go anywhere, either. We're adults. We can do this. Give me a hug." She opened her arms and Chance stepped into them. He took one hand, rubbed the back of her head, and then whispered in her ear. "I'll forget about everything that happened, but that kiss. I don't think I'll ever forget that."

"Me either," she whispered back.

He broke their embrace. "And the way you looked in your underwear. Now, get back to work. We have a lobby full of people who need their vehicles serviced."

Leslie blushed. "Yes, sir. Right away, sir," she said. Then saluted him and headed for the lobby.

Chapter Forty-Seven

Sheila

Sheila was happy when Sunday finally arrived. It felt good to be in the Lord's house one more time. She loved to worship. The choir sang one of her favorite hymns, "His Eye is on the Sparrow." It was a moving rendition. She could feel the Holy Spirit as it descended on the congregation. Sheila had been a member of Faith Cathedral of Praise and Worship since she was a child. She attended every Sunday with her parents and their grandparents. It was a massive church with over ten thousand members. Each Sunday there were three services to accommodate the many congregants. Xavier loved children's church. She enjoyed going to the 8 a.m. service. It was the one most of the elderly members attended, including Grandma Grace. The two of them used to worship together faithfully. Her cousins had fallen by the wayside, but Sheila felt it was important to keep her connection with Christ and she used to use it as her bonding time with her grandmother. Every Sunday they went out to dinner afterward. Her grandmother could be a stern woman, but there was no doubt that she loved the Lord and her family. Sheila knew she was forcing her granddaughters to find a husband because she thought they needed a man to protect them and provide emotional support and other things money couldn't buy. Especially since she was no longer around. Sheila wished she had found another way to express it.

She wanted a husband, but she wanted to receive the man God had for her on His time, not her overbearing grandmother's.

Bishop Noel Proctor preached a mighty word. He talked about how God will save you from the snares of the enemy in times of trouble. The scripture came from 1 Samuel 23. It was a familiar story of how God delivered David from the hands of Saul. Sheila knew God would give her the desires of her heart and help her make the right decision regarding her love life. She just wished that when He delivered His message, it would be so clear she couldn't possibly get it wrong. Deciphering God's will wasn't always easy. After the message, Bishop gave the invitation to Christ. It always warmed Sheila's heart to see another soul won for the kingdom. A family of four walked down to the altar and joined church, and she clapped loudly. What a blessing it was for a husband and wife to lead their son and daughter to the Lord. Then, a teenage boy joined. When Bishop asked him why he wanted to join, he talked about how his father died and he'd been in and out of a juvenile facility, but when he started to attend the church's after school youth program he saw there was a better way and there were people who cared for him. His testimony almost brought tears to her eyes. She loved that she belonged to a church that invested in the community. Then an adult male stood before the church. She thought he looked familiar, but she was sitting in the balcony and wasn't quite sure her eyes weren't deceiving her, but when he spoke there was no doubt who he was.

"What's your name, son?" asked Bishop Proctor.

"I'm Max Beauregard."

"And Max, why do you want to be saved?"

Max hesitated and then said, "I want to be a better man, Bishop. Recently, God has placed someone in my life who has a strong connection with the Lord. I see what He's doing with her and through her. She's kind, she's smart, she's got a good heart. She's loyal to her family and anytime one of them needs her she is there. The more I've come to know her the more I see that it's the God in her that causes her to be such a beautiful person. The joy of Jesus is all up and through her and He has a calling on her life. I want that kind of joy."

"Praise God, but I have to ask you is this a young lady you are interested in?"

"Yes, Bishop. A woman like her won't settle for anything else than a man of God. So I guess I don't just want to be a better man for myself, but for her, too. She deserves that. She and her son. I want to be a good example for him of how a Godly man should treat his woman."

Bishop Proctor smiled. "God bless you. Somebody say, 'Won't He Do It!' See ladies you can be a good influence on a man by just letting your light for Christ shine. You better get on your knees and pray for God to change that man. If he truly wants to be with a righteous woman, he will. This is an attractive young man. Look at him. He's articulate, well-dressed and probably has a good job. He don't want no hoochie that's trying to get him to finance her lifestyle. He wants a hard-working, good God-fearing woman and he's willing to get right with God to get her."

"Hallelujah!" shouted one of the mother's in the front row.

Bishop turned his attention back to Max. "Now, son, does this young lady know you're doing this?"

"No, sir. She has no idea. I've been attending here off and on for a few months. I usually go to 11 a.m. service, but this morning I just knew it was time to do what I've been putting off. God has been calling me. Today, I had to get here early and answer."

Bishop motioned for one of the elders of the church to bring him the Holy oil. "I'm going to ask the Lord to lead and guide you so you can be the man of God you want to be. I know you can." He rubbed oil on Max's forehead and placed his hand on the top of his head. Several of the men of the church surrounded Max, placed their hands on his shoulders, and bowed their heads in prayer.

Sheila bowed her head, too, and asked God to give Max the desires of his heart. Tears streamed down her face in gratitude. Max had to be talking about her and Xavier. To think that the few times they were together, he saw the light of Christ in her. That's all she ever wanted in addition to being a good mother to her son and help care for her family. "God, draw him closer to you," she prayed. It wasn't far from her thoughts that as God was giving Max the desires of his heart, He could be providing for the desires of her heart as well.

"Amen, Father. Do it. Do it for me," she said, as Bishop closed out the prayer.

Chapter Forty-Eight

Leslie

Leslie did as she promised and planned a perfect afternoon brunch for Percy to propose to Tabitha. Percy was now at the mansion, nervously waiting for Tabitha to arrive in the limo Leslie arranged to pick her up. The two of them were going to have a romantic meal in the rose garden. After they ate, Percy was going to propose, while a violinist serenaded them. It seemed simple enough, but he was a ball of nerves. The temperature was in the sixties, and the roses were just beginning to bloom.

Percy was extremely grateful to the Purdue family for helping him. Everyone chipped in. Regina did a wonderful job on the decorations. She created a lovely centerpiece for the table along with other accent pieces to create the right ambience for the big moment. Sheila arranged for the dinner along with the violinist. Leslie helped him pick out his clothes. He looked quite handsome in the purple shirt and pink tie with flecks of gold and purple. Everything was perfect! When Tabitha arrived, she looked breathtaking. She wore a strapless pink dress with a pearl necklace and teardrop earrings. Percy stood and greeted her with a hug and then pulled out her seat for her.

The Purdue women stood nearby to observe, but far enough away as not to intrude.

"Oh, P. Diddy, this is exquisite," Tabitha squealed. "I didn't know you had rich friends with houses like this."

"P. Diddy!" giggled Leslie.

"Hush," said Sheila. "I can't hear."

"You're not missing anything. He's not supposed to propose until the crème brule comes," said Leslie.

"I don't care. I don't want to miss a thing," said Sheila. "I've never witnessed a proposal before."

A server approached them with their appetizer. Percy told Regina that she liked shrimp so Shelia arranged for a shrimp cocktail appetizer. He set it on the table.

Instead of eating, Percy took a deep gulp of his water and said, "Look, I gotta do this before I lose my nerve." Percy looked in the Purdue girls' direction. "Can you guys send the violinist out now?"

Tabitha looked in the direction he was speaking, but she didn't see anyone. "P. Diddy, who are you talking to?"

"My angels," said Percy.

Regina ran and got the violinist who was in the house waiting. A few minutes later, Arturo walked out of the house and began playing a lovely rendition of Stevie Wonder's "A Ribbon in the Sky."

Percy stood up, walked next to Tabitha and cleared his throat. "Tabitha, the day you inboxed me on meetsomeonewonderful.com I thought you had the wrong guy. Why would someone as beautiful as you want to spend time with a geek like me? I really thought it was some kind of joke, but after talking to you, I realized that you weren't only beautiful, but smart, funny, sweet, and just genuine. You saw all my physical and emotional flaws and you met every one of them head on. All my insecurities with my acne, weight and allergies, you helped me conquer them. Then, you went to work on my self-esteem. I don't deserve you. You're like a dream come true, but if I'm dreaming I hope I never wake up. If I'm in a coma, I hope I never come back to the miserable existence I had before. Life without you would be just a shell of the one I have now. I love you, Tabitha." He then got down on one knee and pulled the blue box he'd shown Leslie the night before from his pant pocket.

Tabitha began bouncing in her chair. "Oh, my God! Oh, my God! Oh, my God!" she squealed.

"Will you do me the honor of being my wife? I want to spend the rest of my life making you as happy as you've made me!"

"Oh, yes, P. Diddy. Yes! Yes Yes!" she squealed, as he placed the ring on her tiny finger. She looked at it and exclaimed. "It's blue and absolutely beautiful! I love you, too, baby."

They kissed. Arturo switched to playing a more upbeat number no one recognized. Leslie, Regina, and Sheila emerged and engulfed the happy couple in an embrace. Tabitha hugged them all with tears in her eyes and then looked and her fiancée and said, "P. Diddy, who are all these beautiful women who were hiding in the bushes?"

They all started laughing.

"These, my darling, are the women who helped me make this moment possible. They grew up in this home. Allow me to introduce you to the Purdue girls: Shelia, Regina, and one of my best friends, Leslie. Thanks to all of you for making this the magical moment I wanted for Tabitha."

Tabitha looked at each of them with gratitude. "I don't know if Percy is allowed to have friends as pretty as you, but if you arranged all this I think I can deal with it. Thank you!"

"You are so welcome," said Leslie. "Thank you for making this amazing man happy because if anyone deserves happiness it's him. Now, we're going to go in the house and leave you two alone. Enjoy your meal and stay as long as you like."

"God bless you both," said Shelia.

"I wish you an abundance of joy and prosperity," added Regina.

Leslie, Regina, and Shelia beamed at the happy couple as they locked arms and retreated into the mansion.

"Do you think we'll find men who love us that much?" said Regina.

"Dear God, I hope so," said Leslie. "Did you see the way he looked at her?"

"Yeah, like if she ever left him he'd stop breathing right on the spot," said Leslie.

"Like life has no meaning if she's not in it," said Sheila.

"Yeah. She's one lucky woman," said Regina.

"Y'all wanna hang out for a while and watch a movie?" suggested Leslie.

"Sounds like a plan to me," said Sheila. She was no longer confused about which man she should focus her attention on. If Max Beauregard wanted a shot at capturing her heart, she was going to give it to him. She was still in disbelief that he was willing to get right with God to be with her and her son. She felt warm and fuzzy every time she thought about the testimony he gave in church.

"You guys go ahead," said Regina. "There's something I have to do." She went to her room to get her purse and then ran out the door.

Chapter Forty-Nine

Regina

Regina reached her destination and stood nervously in front of her old apartment. The place that was once home to her and the man she thought she wanted to marry. She knocked on the door and waited for Antonio to answer. He came to the door wearing clothes she had never seen before. He looked surprised to see her.

"Regina! Why didn't you call and tell me you were coming?" He stood squarely in front of the door to block her entrance.

"I'm sorry. I just took a chance that you would be here. I have something to get off my chest and it couldn't wait."

"Well, it's kind of a bad time. I've had a long weekend, and I'm really tired. Why don't you come back tomorrow?"

Regina laughed. "This is so you. You proposed to me, but you have another woman in the house we used to share that you are no doubt planning to sleep with today if you haven't already. You are such a dog. I must have been out of my mind to think you were worthy of me." She held out her left hand and used her right hand to take the ring off. "It doesn't matter who you have in there. I came to give you this back." She grabbed Antonio's hand and placed the engagement ring in it.

"What? No! There's no woman here. I'm just tired. I was doing like I said and giving you time to think about it. That's why you haven't heard from me. Baby, I got this for you and our future."

"I did think about it, and I decided that I don't want to be your wife. This is the end for us, Antonio. Enjoy your evening with whatever skank you have in there this time."

Regina turned to walk away. Antonio grabbed her arm and pulled her back with such force she almost fell. "What are you doing?!" she screamed.

"Stop playing, Regina. You know you belong to me. I just signed a lease on a new condo downtown for us. It's got a great view of the river. We even have an extra room for your studio. You can create all the clothes you want there. Don't botch your only chance at getting your inheritance. Marry me."

"My inheritance? Who told you about that and how do you know they told you the truth? I haven't said a thing. No amount of money is worth me coming home to a liar and a cheater every night. You'll never see one dime of my family's money. Let me go!"

Regina tried to squirm out of his grasp, but the grip Antonio had on her arm was almost like a steel trap. "I deserve every dime you're going to give me for putting up with your spoiled, winey, frigid behind all these years. You can't cook, you don't clean, and you don't even give decent head."

Regina grew angry and started beating him with her fist. "I gave you seven years of my life. I was good to you. I stood by you, but now I hate you. I will not marry you. I deserve better and there's a man who wants to give it to me. Let me go!"

Antonio tried his best to deflect her jabs while holding on to her tightly. "Who are you talking about? That grease monkey on your job? I saw the way he looked at you. That's supposed to be better? He doesn't know the first thing about dealing with a high-maintenance, whiny debutante."

"He's not a grease monkey. He's kind, honest, loving, sincere. Everything you aren't."

Antonio continued to hold her. "Are you sure this is what you want, Regina?"

"I'm sure. Get out of my life and leave me alone! Let go. You are hurting me. Help! Somebody, help," she screamed.

Antonio looked around and loosened his grip a little. The last thing he needed was for someone to call the police. "You can go, but that's only because I'm busy, but know that this isn't over. You're in for a rude awakening, Regina. Very soon. So enjoy your grease monkey, but remember this, the only reason we appreciate pleasure is because we know what it's like to be in pain."

He pulled Regina to him, forced a rough kiss on her lips, and then shoved her away so hard she fell squarely on her butt onto the grass below. Ouch! Although, her enlarged derriere provided some cushion between her and ground, it still hurt. Antonio went in the apartment and closed the door behind him. A couple walking their dog approached her.

"Are you all right, ma'am?" asked the woman, as the man reached out his hand to help her up.

"I've never felt better in my life," said Regina. "I just kicked the devil out of my life."

"Good for you!" said the woman.

"Yes, that is good news, but I hate to have to tell you that you landed in dog poop," said the man.

Regina twisted her body around to find he was telling the truth. On her behind of her purple dress pants was indeed a large clump of brown poop. She screamed. Antonio was such a jerk!

Chapter Fifty

Leslie

Leslie had never been so sad in her life. She arrived at T-Money's funeral early in hopes of having a few moments with the body to say goodbye, but was informed it was a closed casket funeral and that wasn't possible. She sat in one of the church pews and waited patiently for the family to arrive and said a little prayer to a God she wasn't quite sure she believed in to allow T-Money's soul to be at peace and for whoever killed him to be brought to justice. Once the family arrived, she approached his mother to give her condolences, but stopped dead in her tracks when she saw Chareese with them, as if she were his girlfriend. She was putting on a show, too. The tramp was dressed in black from head to toe with a long veil that hung down to her breasts. She was crying on anyone's shoulder that would let her and she was even trying to poke out her stomach as she walked so that everyone could see she was pregnant. When she saw Leslie, she smiled at her and rubbed her stomach in an effort to make her jealous. Regina began looking at the obituary to avoid seeing her sickening display. It contained pictures of him in his youth with his mother, sister, and grandmother who were now deceased. It talked about how he was a scholar and standout athlete in high school. She was surprised to see that he attended college for two years. She smiled while reading the sweet words his family members wrote, but her smile quickly changed when she read a sentence the mentioned Chareese as his special friend.

She should have taken someone with her for moral support. This was one time she wished she hadn't tried to go it alone. She refused to let Chareese get to her. Leslie gazed down lovingly at her ring. She knew she was the one who held T-Money's heart, even if no one else knew. The church was packed with family and what Leslie assumed were other drug dealers. She didn't really recognize anyone other than Chareese. Leslie decided she didn't need to be there and left before the funeral even began.

Chapter Fifty-One

Those Purdue Girls

The next two months were something out of a fairytale storybook for Regina and Sheila. Regina and Chance took their time getting to know one another and fell in love. At work, they tried to keep it professional, but once the last customer left the two were inseparable. The combination of work and play seemed to be a winning formula for them. Thanks to Regina's marketing, the shop had more customers than ever before and both of them couldn't have been happier. The age difference didn't seem to matter. Chance brought stability and security to Regina's life. He was even a blessing to her family. A few times, Xavier spent the day with them and it was obvious Chance was going to be an excellent father. Regina even took it upon herself to decorate his house.

Regina brought excitement and light to Chance's world, which had been a dull existence for quite some time. He loved her wide-eyed approach to life. Everything was an adventure and she planned to enjoy it to the fullest. Simple tasks like grocery shopping and selecting art and furniture became a fun-filled activity. She made him feel young and alive. He knew his life was better with her in it.

Sheila and Max were quite cozy as well. He became a usual sight at her job as he came to escort her to lunch several times a week. It wasn't uncommon for him to cook meals for her and Xavier at her home. He even started attending church with them. Sheila broke the news as gently as she could to DaQuan that she was dating Max. He didn't like it and he never wavered in his distrust of Max, but Sheila didn't care. As far as she was concerned, Max was her Mr. Righteous. The one thing that bothered her was that Xavier didn't seem to care much for him either. He had gone so far as to start sleeping in her bed instead of his own as if he were trying to prevent Max from spending the night with her. When Max came over to the house, Xavier would go to his room and stay in there the entire time to avoid him. If he cooked, he wouldn't eat. Anytime Sheila tried to plan an outing and include Max, Xavier would misbehave the entire time and ruin the experience. It got to the point where she only went out with him on the nights that Xavier was with his father or Vivian. Sheila didn't know what to do.

She didn't understand why her son didn't like Max. He seemed so perfect. Max had fresh flowers delivered to her job at least once a week. He wrote her poems and texted them to her phone. They did all her favorite things, which happened to be Max's favorite things, too. Their dates included plays, ballets, operas, and other cultural events like museums and festivals. He respected her celibacy and never tried to entice her to have sex, so Xavier's plan to keep him from spending the night was for nothing. Although, some nights when Xavier was away, Max did spend the night and hold her. She loved being wrapped in his arms. Sheila had never dated anyone quite like him before. She really liked Max, but how could she be with someone her child disapproved of so strongly? She prayed to God often about it. She needed Him to bring peace to her situation soon.

Chapter Fifty-Two

Leslie

Over the next few months, Leslie tried to move on with her life and her quest to find a husband. She tried desperately to connect with someone wonderful via online dating sites like Percy, but she wasn't having much luck. She went out on several dates and each one was worse than the last. The first one looked nothing like his picture. She agreed to go out with a thirty-year-old man with a six-pack and a head full of gorgeous hair. The man who showed up had to be at least fifty-five, balding and close to three hundred pounds. When Leslie arrived, and realized she had been deceived, she pretended to have a headache and cut their evening short.

Another man she met looked exactly like his picture. He was fine. His body reminded her of her favorite wrestler of all-time, The Rock. He seemed to have some potential until he told her he was a recently released felon with no job who lived with his mother and three pit bulls he called his girlfriends, even though one of them was male. She stayed until the end of the evening, but never called him again.

The last guy Leslie went out with made her delete her profile from all the sites. His name was Wallace. He was handsome, with a nice smile and flawless skin. He looked very nice and seemed like the perfect gentleman. He pulled her chair out, complimented her on how nice she looked and when his food came out before hers he refused to eat until hers arrived. During the course of the conversation, he told Leslie he was a follower of Satan and he could be her escort to the gates of hell. When she declined, he tried to sell her burial insurance. She was afraid he planned to kill her because she didn't want to worship Satan and began to talk to herself throughout the evening. Her plan was to make him think she was mentally ill so he would leave her alone. When Wallace asked her what was wrong, she told him she was schizophrenic and forgot to take her meds that morning. Wallace pushed back from the table as if he were about to leave. Leslie thought she had successfully scared him away until Wallace reached in his pocket, pulled out several pills and asked what she was taking. He told her that he was being treated for the same disorder and may have something to help her. Leslie excused herself to go to the restroom and never returned. She was done with online dating!

Even though Leslie vowed to never see Beau again, she resumed spending time with him. He was better than no one. It was kind of weird because he began treating her as more of a love interest than an occasional lay. He moved into a new place with a magnificent view of the Mississippi River. He invited her over a couple times for dinner. Afterward they sat on the couch and talked, played games on his X-box or watched a movie. She spent several nights with him and in the morning, he would fix them breakfast. In the past, after sex, they would each go their separate ways. She was enjoying the attention. It helped her get over the disappointment of losing T-Money. One morning, after a night of intense sex, Leslie told Beau about what happened between them. Beau held her while she cried over the only possibility of finding love and her only shot at gaining her inheritance.

A tear streamed down Leslie's cheek and Antonio, who she called Beau, licked it away. "You know you're the only woman I'm seeing now?" he said, kissing her lips.

"Quit lying. When have you ever dealt with one woman?"

"Now. I wasted so much time dating your sister when I should have been with you all along."

"I don't know what to say. I'll admit we've had a lot of fun together these last few weeks, but I don't know if I'm ready for the backlash we'd receive if we went public," said Leslie.

"Regina and Sheila are busy with their new boyfriends. They could care less about what's going on with you. Your fiancé was killed and instead of being around to comfort you they went and found someone for themselves and forgot all about you. You don't owe them anything. Besides, don't you deserve to be happy, too? They're going to get their inheritance. They don't seem the least bit concerned about helping you get yours. If it makes you feel better you can consider this a business arrangement with great fringe benefits."

Leslie had to agree. The Purdue girls' family time together had been scarce since Sheila and Regina both found their dream guys.

Antonio continued. "So, why do they get to live happily ever after, but you don't? Because I used to date your sister? That's not fair. If they really love you as much as they say they do then once you tell them about us then they should be happy for you."

Leslie laughed. "That's not going to happen. You didn't just date my sister. She was in love with you and you dogged her out. You asked her to marry you. You've been sleeping with me. Those really don't give cause for celebration."

He kissed her neck. "That's my past. I'm trying to build a future with you. I could be faithful to you. I was unfaithful to Regina because I was bored. You are more than capable of keeping my attention. I say let's do our thing and not worry about them. Stop torturing yourself by going out with those losers from the Internet. We belong together. We always did. I just met Regina first."

Leslie bit her bottom lip and looked at the tattoo of Regina's name on Antonio's chest. This was one of the few times she didn't demand he cover it up while they had sex. "If we do this, you've got to let me tell my sisters in my own time. We've still got a few months before we have to be married. Besides, I have to convince my Aunt Teresa that this is true love in order to get my money." A harrowing thought entered her mind and another tear escaped her eye. "Do you promise never to hit me?"

Antonio was caught off guard by her question, but he hid it by placing more kisses on her neck. "I never meant to hurt Regina. She was just so frustrating at times. I lost my job and I didn't feel like she was there the way she should have been. Those were not my proudest moments. I'm sorry I ever did it. I'm sorry I hurt her in that way. You have a legitimate fear, and I promise you that I won't lay a hand on you." He kissed her neck again. "I care for you, Leslie, and I know it wouldn't take much for me to fall in love with you. We can do this your way. We'll keep it on the low until you're ready to reveal that we're dating. This is a win-win situation. You get a man who will be there for you. I get a beautiful woman with a great body who also happens to be an insatiable sex fiend, and we both become filthy rich."

"Yeah a win-win. I need some time to think about this."

"Take all the time you need. As long as we can keep doing this while you think, I'm good." Antonio began placing soft kisses on her body in a trail that led to her love below. Leslie tried to clear her mind and enjoy the moment, but it didn't escape her that Antonio didn't say anything about her being smart, funny, creative or any other adjective that didn't have to do with her looks, sex or her inheritance. She also knew she was about to turn the two people she loved most against her. At least she would be rich. Maybe she could buy a new family.

Chapter Fifty-Three

Sheila

"Vivian, I've never been so happy and miserable at the same time," said Sheila.

"What do you mean?" She chomped down a delicious leftover lobster tail that Max fixed for him and Sheila the night before.

"I'm falling in love with Max and I know it, but it's hard to let myself fall completely when my child hates him so much. Xavier's not warming up to Max at all. His birthday is in a couple of months and when I asked him what he wanted, he said for me to stop spending time with Mr. Max. When I asked him why he doesn't like Max, he said he didn't know.

Vivian pulled some more of the juicy meat from its shell. "Do you think DaQuan is influencing him?"

"No, DaQuan is a lot of things, but petty isn't one of them. He doesn't say anything about me dating Max. He's been so cold lately. When he comes over, he doesn't even want to talk to me. He just picks up Xavier and leaves."

"When John and I first got together, Aiden didn't like him either."

"Really?" Sheila found that hard to believe. Her child treated John as if he were his biological father. He gave him Father's Day gifts and bragged about how good he was to him. It was obvious they had a great relationship. She assumed it had always been that way.

"Yes, really. That boy would always come down with a cold, a toothache, or some other pain on the nights John and I were supposed to go out. I just had to keep reassuring him that no matter who I brought into my life he would always be number one. Be patient. Xavier will come around eventually. Speaking of coming? Have you and Max done it?"

Sheila was so embarrassed by the question she almost choked on her glass of juice. "Nooooo," she coughed out.

Vivian patted her on the back. "Sorry," she giggled, "I forgot that you still think you're wearing a Chastity belt. Why not? You said yourself that he's Mr. Righteous. Well, if he's the one, why wait? I think that's why you're so stressed. You need to get some. I bet he's great in bed." She giggled some more.

Sheila shook her head. "See that's why I need to stop hanging with heathens like you."

"I love the Lord, too, but a woman has needs and you've been neglecting yours for far too long. You should really give some thought to giving yourself a treat. You do so much for others. You're on a winning streak right now. The company is doing well and you are partially responsible. Regina and Leslie are okay. You're a great mother. You should go on vacation and take Max with you. I'll even let you use our beach house in Florida."

"A vacation would be nice but—"

"But nothing. I'm your boss and your son's godmother so I can give you the time off and watch the little one, if needed. It's settled. Take next Friday off and spend a three-day weekend in sunny Florida with Mr. Righteous getting your engine *revved*." Vivian balled her hand into fists and acted like she was gripping the steering wheel of an imaginary car.

"Girl, you are crazy!"

"And a heathen. Don't forget that I'm a heathen," joked Vivian.

"You're not supposed to enjoy being a heathen."

"Then you're not doing it right!" Vivian snapped her fingers three times and rolled her neck.

Chapter Fifty-Four

Regina

Regina and Chance were now a legitimate couple. He was her man and she was his woman. Regina was glad she took Shelia's advice and took sex out of the equation. They spent a lot of time talking, going out, learning about each other's likes and dislikes. The more Regina found out about him the more she wanted to keep him in her life. Chance was a good man. He worked hard. He loved the Lord. He gave to charity regularly. He treated Regina with respect and kindness.

Chance confided in her that he was a little jealous of his brother and that he would love to be able to move in the circles Chadwick did and attract major investors. He wanted to create a franchise of garages that allowed him to help people keep a major investment—their cars—running well. By now, it was no secret that Regina was a Purdue and part of the city's elite group of rich African Americans. She decided she wanted to help Chance make his dreams come true. She began using her connections and the Purdue name to assist her man in making major moves. She taught Chance the right verbiage to use, the right mannerisms and revamped his entire wardrobe. When she was done, Chance was able to communicate comfortably with arrogant millionaires, as well as the mother on public assistance who showed up at his garage needing his help.

The couple went to several high-society fundraisers and social events together. Regina introduced him to the movers and shakers of Memphis and Chance would turn on the charm. Everyone said they made a handsome couple and they were quickly dubbed as one of the "it" couples in Memphis. A lot of people were surprised to learn that he was the brother of the famous real estate mogul Chadwick Chandler, but that's what happens when you make yourself a silent partner in a company. Chance was every bit as suave and debonair as his younger brother and the media was having a field day with him. It was nice to be with someone others thought was good for her, for a change. For Regina, this best part was that Chance loved her just because she was herself. He was also faithful, but the newfound attention had its drawbacks as well. Once the female elite got wind of him, the vultures—single and married—started circulating. Chance turned every one of their advances down cold. Some even had the audacity to show up at the shop pretending they needed to talk to him about their cars. He told them that all business was handled by the office manager who also happened to be his girlfriend and they had to speak directly to her. Of course, those conniving women didn't want to do that and often left the premises without getting their car so much as diagnosed. Regina chuckled every time it happened. She had an amazing boyfriend! Chance never gave her a reason to get jealous or upset. Although, sometimes she did. Each time she let her ugly side show, he reassured her she was the only woman for him and those other women didn't have a chance with her Chance.

The two took things slow in the beginning, but eventually felt enough time had passed for them to become intimate. Regina was pleasantly surprised when reality far exceeded her dreams. Chance was an amazing lover. His entire purpose seemed to be to please her. She found herself relaxing in ways she never could with Antonio. She realized that the problem wasn't that she was frigid, it was that she was with a man who made her feel uncomfortable and inadequate.

Regina hadn't heard from Antonio in weeks and she was grateful. Having a good man in her life made her see everything she had missed out on while she was painstakingly trying to please the wrong man. She realized there was another person she hadn't seen much of either. Leslie was spending several nights a week away from the house. She was very secretive about where she was going and with whom. Regina knew it had to do with a man because she was always smiling, but if he made her sister happy and Leslie was staying out of trouble, whoever it was couldn't be all bad.

Chapter Fifty-Five

Sheila

The week seemed to move slowly as Sheila counted down the days until her vacation. Work was nothing out of the ordinary, but every day was special because of the new man in her life. Tuesday she received a bouquet of roses and Wednesday a gift certificate to get a manicure and pedicure to make sure she looked her best on the beach. Sheila was still undecided about sleeping with Max, but she did agree with Vivian's observation that she needed some alone adult time with him. After she told Xavier she was going out of town with Max for the weekend, he became a terror. He talked back. He was defiant and he threw his toys. She had never seen him behave so badly. She needed a break from him, if nothing else.

Thursday finally arrived. It was DaQuan's weekend with him and he agreed to pick their son up a day early. He arrived at her house that morning wearing a Spider-man T-shirt. When he asked where she was going, Shelia didn't lie. She told him that she was going on vacation with Max.

"Look, Sheila, I don't like this, but if he makes you happy, I'll respect your decision. I personally think it's a little soon to be taking a trip together. How long have you been dating, three months? Just make sure you don't do anything you're going to regret. Please give me the address of where you will be just in case anything happens and I need to reach you."

Sheila didn't like his request. "Why? You have my cell phone?"

"Just do as I say, woman. If you come up missing at least the police will have a starting point."

"Okay," Sheila said reluctantly. "But I better not look up and see your big head anywhere around."

"I got better things to do than check on you. If this is what you want, then who am I to stand in your way?"

Sheila grabbed DaQuan's hand and squeezed. "You know that really means a lot to me. You'll always be my baby daddy and my first love."

He squeezed back. "I know. Have fun, but not too much fun, if you know what I mean."

"I know exactly what you mean," were the words that came from her lips, but inside her head, Sheila's response was, *I can't make you any promises.*

Chapter Fifty-Six

Family Meeting

The girls and Aunt Teresa met at the mansion for lunch to give updates on their husband hunting progress. Ms. Pearl prepared various sandwiches, a fruit tray, and homemade cookies for them to eat while they talked. Teresa's schedule had been particularly busy as of late. Crime in the city was on the rise and she was investigating several homicides. The four of them sat out on the patio behind the home and took in the last of the nice weather. It was sunny with a cool breeze, but it was bearable with a jacket. It was early fall and before they all knew it, it would be the end of the year and time would run out for getting married and getting their money.

"I promised to start with Leslie the next time we got together. How's it going sweetheart?" said Teresa

Leslie shifted uncomfortably in her seat. "I don't really have anything to report. I've been seeing someone, but it's not serious. We have a lot of fun, but I'm not sure he's husband material. I tried online dating, but that was a dead end. There are a lot of weirdos out there. This is a lot harder than I thought it was going to be."

"That's because we were out of God's plan," said Sheila. "The Bible says, *he that findeth a wife, findeth a good thing*. I believe that's why things are going so well for me and Regina. The man found us instead of us finding him. Although, it was during the course of trying to find a man, but Max chose me and Chance chose Regina. Stop looking, Leslie, and let him find you."

"That's easy for you to say," said Leslie. "We're already six months in, which leaves only three months for me to find someone."

"I can see if Chance knows someone," said Regina.

"I can ask Max to take you on as a client," said Shelia.

Those two irritated Leslie. "First, I'm doing it wrong and now you want to help. No, thank you, Sheila. I'm not paying to find a man, and I don't want any of Leslie's grease monkey boyfriend's friends."

"Girl, have you seen my man lately? Evidently you don't read. He's been featured in the newspaper and two magazines in the past three weeks. He looks like an ad for a men's fashion store. The only time he's covered in grease is at the shop and he's slowly phasing out of working on cars and doing more work in the office to lay the foundation for his franchise. You need to shut up," said Regina. Regina was normally docile, but when it came to her boo, she was ready to draw blood. She was proud of her Chance.

"Calm down, Leslie. They were only trying to help," said Teresa.

"I don't want their help. What I want is my money without these stupid rules and stipulations. What I want is my fiancé back. What I want is a man who only wants me and not my money, but I can't have any of that, can I?"

"What in the world are you talking about?" said Sheila. "Is the guy you're seeing trying to get you to marry him so he can get your money? You told him about it?"

"I never said that," said Leslie.

"You haven't said much of anything other than he exists. Who is this guy?" said Sheila.

"Sounds like another Antonio to me," said Regina. "Beware, sis."

Leslie stood up and almost knocked a pitcher of water over. "Ugh! Will you get over Antonio! You're happy in love with another man and you're still bringing up his name. I'm sure he's found someone else by now and he *never* mentions you."

"What has gotten into you?" said Regina. "No one here is interested in Antonio."

"Why are you so combative?" said Teresa.

"Because neither of these heifers care about anyone other than themselves. Since they got boyfriends, we don't spend any time together and we barely talk. They get a man and forget about the other people who love them. I'm miserable and nobody cares!"

Sheila had heard enough. Her cousin was jealous and trying to bring rain to a "Happy I Found Love Parade."

"Look, I'm about tired of your spoiled behind. If you want to talk to us, all you have to do is call. If you want to see me, you know where I live. I admit I've been spending a lot of time with Max, but I can still make time for you. I'm not a mind reader. You need to tell us these things instead of throwing a fit when we do get together. You act like we're not there for you. Regina and I dropped everything to be there for you when T-Money was killed. Then the next day you and his car disappear without so much as a phone call. Big Daddy spoiled you rotten, but no one here at this table is going to continue to do it. Grow up, Leslie!"

Leslie became enraged. Shelia was always jealous because she was Big Daddy's favorite. He had nothing to do with this conversation. "Well, you know what's on my mind right now...leaving!" Leslie stood up and began walking toward the mansion.

"Don't go," said Regina. "Let's talk. I'm sorry. We can hang out tonight when I get off work."

"Let her go," said Teresa. "Whatever is eating at that girl is much bigger than the two of you and when she's ready to talk about it, she will. This food looks delicious. Let's eat and you ladies can tell me what's going on in your lives without throwing a damn tantrum."

Chapter Fifty-Seven

Sheila

After Sheila left their family lunch, she went home and finished packing. She wondered what was going on with Leslie. She needed to stop acting like a spoiled brat and learn to talk about her feelings. She put on her calendar to call her when she returned in case she forgot. Right now wasn't a good time because she didn't want anything to put her in a foul mood before her trip.

She and Max left Memphis at 3:00 a.m. They made a few stops along the way for shopping and sightseeing and they arrived in Florida during the early evening. Vivian's beach house was gorgeous; it had five bedrooms. The master bedroom was spacious, with its own patio that was perfect for watching the water, as waves crashed into the sandy white beach below. Afterward, they went to eat at a seaside restaurant. The seafood was delicious. Sheila had never tasted anything so fresh. It made her wonder if the lobster and shrimp were caught that morning. On the way back to the house, they stopped at the grocery store to pick up a few snacks. Later that night, they went to a neighboring couple's house. They were having a beach party and invited them over. She and her husband, who looked after Vivian's home while they were away, invited them over. Max and Shelia danced and laughed until 2:00 a.m. They returned to the house in good spirits and crashed on the couch.

"I can't remember the last time I had that much fun!" yelled Sheila.

"It was good to see you let your hair down. You have some moves, girl. I didn't know rich girls knew how to do the Cabbage Patch and the Roger Rabbit," Max teased.

"I'm not rich. My family is, but I'll have you know that old school dances are my specialty sir."

Max grabbed her and kissed her hungrily. "Sheila, I want you," he said. "Show me some other moves I've never seen you do before."

"I want you too, but not yet," she panted.

"I'm in no hurry. I'm a patient man; we can wait until you're ready. I just thought you should know that whenever you want to take that step, I promise to make you glad that you did."

"Thank you, baby. That means a lot to me. I'm sure it will be a memorable experience for both of us."

"I'm looking forward to it," said Max.

Sheila laid her head on his chest and fell asleep in his arms, thinking, *This man is just too good to be true*. Mr. Righteous indeed!

They got up early the next morning and participated in a yoga class on the beach. Then they went to a small bistro for breakfast before returning to the house to shower and change clothes. It was a great day to let the top down on the convertible mustang they rented and enjoy the sunshine. They had no plans and wherever they ended up was where they ended up. While trying to find their next great adventure, they drove through a lovely neighborhood and admired the houses. The architecture in South Florida was beautiful. Max stopped the car in front of a stately house with white columns surrounded by and a massive lawn with beautiful trees, flowers, and shrubbery.

"Could you imagine living someplace like this?"

Sheila realized he had never been to the mansion and had no idea she grew up in a house twice the size of the one before them. "I could if I was with you," she said.

"Me, too. I can see myself pulling up to the house and you coming outside to greet me in a flowing white dress, pregnant with our child. Xavier would be there, too, with the family dog."

Shelia smiled and laid her head on his shoulder. "That sounds nice."

Sheila knew she wanted this man to make love to her. The question was when. Max cared for her and it had nothing to do with her family or her family's money. He did a background check on her when she became his client so he was well aware of whom she was and how much her family was worth, but not once during the entire time they'd been dating had he mentioned it. If it became a topic, she brought it up. They spent many evenings together in conversation about the past, present, and future. He listened as she cried at the memory of losing her parents and her beloved grandparents. His words of comfort were, "You have me now, babe. And I'm not going anywhere." He always seemed to know the right thing to say. She listened as he talked about being raised by a single mother. He never really knew his father; he left when he was three. He said his mother was heartbroken when his father left and she never really had a healthy relationship after that one and eventually just gave up. She passed away two years ago after a lengthy battle with breast cancer. One of the reasons Max became a matchmaker was to help women like his mother, who desired to find love again. With his help, the odds of doing so were more in their favor.

They drove around some more, found a mall and did some shopping. Sheila bought souvenirs for Xavier and others. Max got a few items as well. When they returned to the car, he surprised her with a teddy bear that read: "Life would be a BEAR without you." She was moved by the sweet gesture. Her life was better with him in it as well. Then, they went to a favorite spot with the locals that had karaoke on Saturday nights, Sheila almost lost her mind when Max pulled her on stage and sang a beautiful rendition of Luther Vandross's "Never Too Much" to her. She had no idea he could sing! His voice was amazing.

As Max finished his song, he kissed her passionately in full view of everyone. The room erupted with howls and whistles. Sheila hugged him tightly and whispered in his ear, "You make me so happy. Take me back to the house, *NOW*."

Max looked into her eyes and saw such desire that he was fully aware of what she meant without her having to explain.

He whispered, "Are you sure?"

Sheila nodded.

He grabbed her by the hand. "Your wish is my command."

As they drove to the house, Sheila played in Max's hair. Periodically, he would grab her hand and kiss it. He was so handsome, but more importantly, he made her feel special and she wanted him to know it. When they entered the beach house, she told him to fix them both a drink and make himself comfortable. She had a surprise for him. Sheila took a quick shower and put on a black, lace teddy she purchased earlier in the week, and six-inch, strappy, red heels. She applied baby oil to her arms and legs. If Max thought she was unforgettable before, after tonight she would be seared in his brain like a brand. Her finishing touch was a light spray of one of her favorite fragrances from Dior. She looked at herself in the mirror. She looked good. She felt good, but most of all, she felt desired and loved.

Sheila was a ball of nerves as she stood at the top of the stairs and prepared herself to walk down and make her entrance. She'd never done anything like this before, not even for DaQuan. There was never any presentation involved with them. They just ripped each other's clothes off and did their thing when it was time to do it. As she descended the stairs, Sheila heard soft music playing by Maxwell, one of her favorite artists. She couldn't wait to see Max's reaction when he saw her. She walked down each step carefully because she didn't want to fall and embarrass herself. When she reached the bottom, she got the surprise. DaQuan was holding Max face down into the cushions of the living room loveseat. She could hear his muffled shouts as he struggled to get up.

"What the hell are you doing? Stop before I call the police!" she screamed.

Chapter Fifty-Eight

Regina

"What do you mean I'm fired!" screamed Regina. "Who fires their girlfriend?"

Chance put his hands in his pockets. Why did Regina have to be so dramatic? "I'm not firing my girlfriend. I'm firing my office manager who, quite frankly, is doing a crappy job. Baby, you have great customer service and marketing skills, but you're giving away the store. Last week I lost one thousand dollars in revenue because you want to give almost everybody who comes through the door a discount."

"Those people could really use a break. Do you have any idea how much car repairs cost?"

Chance gave her a bewildered look. "Of course I do. It's not like I'm gouging my customers. We use top of the line parts and products here and I have top-notch mechanics and auto body technicians. Those things come with a price tag and it's not a cheap one. My prices reflect the stellar service we provide. Baby, I'm running a business not a charity. Since you've been here, I've taken a loss every month, which is crazy because, thanks to your marketing, our customer base has almost doubled. I probably would have let you go sooner, but I like looking at you." His attempt to lighten the mood with a compliment backfired.

"So that's what I am to you, a pretty face and a nice booty? I can't believe this. What am I supposed to do for money? This is my only source of income."

"Your boyfriend has money. I'll float you until you get another job. Perhaps we can look into opening up that boutique you want?"

"Oh no! You can't buy your way out of this one and you can't fire me because I QUIT! I QUIT being your office manager and I QUIT being your girlfriend!

Regina thought her last statement would rattle Chance, but he remained calm and said in a monotone voice, "You're overreacting and being childish. If you want to be in business, you better learn to separate business from your personal life. I've never begged a woman to be with me and I'm not going to start now. Are you sure this is what you want?"

The conversation began to sound too similar to the one she had a few months earlier with Antonio. He had also insinuated she was being a brat and it would be her loss if she left him. Well this time she was going to be the one in control. She put her hands on her hips and readied herself for battle.

"No, are you sure this is what you want, Chance? Women like me don't come along every day, but you can't have it both ways. You can't run this business and our relationship. Something has to be a partnership. You didn't even talk to me about doing better. You just fired me. Am I that expendable? I'm the reason that your business is booming. I'm the reason you've been able to make connections that will allow you to open your franchise. I made you," she said.

Chance dug his hands deeper in his pockets and let out a deep breath. He didn't expect her to be happy about the decision, but he didn't expect Regina to behave like this. "You're acting like this was an easy decision. It wasn't, but it needs to be done. Gina, baby, it doesn't have to be this way. You're making this personal and it isn't. I still want and need you around. Furthermore, you may have opened some doors for me, but it's my quality service, reputation and ability to deliver that has gotten me those deals you claim you're responsible. My business didn't just spring up when you walked through the door crying, young lady. I was made before you ever met me. All you did was help me let other people know it."

Regina jutted out her chin as a sign of defiance. "So, am I still the office manager?" She narrowed her eyes as if she were daring him to say yes.

"Regina, be rational. It doesn't make good sense monetarily for me to keep you in that capacity, but I don't want to lose my girlfriend either."

She picked up her purse, headed toward the door and said, "You just did."

Chance had always been a proud man and he just couldn't will himself to run after her even though he desperately wanted to. The last few months with Regina had been like heaven on Earth. He didn't think it was possible to experience that type of joy and no physical interaction had taken place. Then when they did make love, it was explosive and he knew it was because he was in love. Regina was truly one of a kind. She was amazing in almost every way…except as his office manager. Why couldn't she see that one had absolutely nothing to do with the other? His chest tightened as he watched her walk out the door.

Regina couldn't believe he let her leave. She just knew Chance would come running out to the parking lot and tell her she could continue working at the shop. She shook terribly from the emotional tears that erupted before she even reached her car. Not the Acura he let her borrow, but her car, the one that brought them together. Her BMW looked brand new. Chance fixed it for her and didn't charge her a dime for the repairs.

Chapter Fifty-Nine

Leslie

Leslie scooped up the last bit of cherry vanilla ice cream from her cup and said, "I give up. If you want me, I'm yours. I can't do this anymore. Regina and Sheila both have someone and I have no one. I've found love and lost love. I've almost been raped or killed or both. I've had a mentally ill, Satanic worshipper try to sell me burial insurance. One person can only take so much. Let's do this."

She and Antonio were sitting at an ice cream parlor in Overton Square. This was their first official date. In the past, they never went out in public together for fear of people seeing them. Now, neither of them cared. Leslie wasn't sure how she was going to break the news to everyone, but she would somehow.

"I'm glad you finally came to your senses," he said. "Now let's hurry up and finish this ice cream because I have a taste for something else. We need to go to your spot tonight."

"Why?"

"It's closer and I can't wait. This ice cream is nothing compared to your dessert."

Leslie giggled. "You're so bad."

"No, I just need you bad."

Chapter Sixty

Sheila

DaQuan twisted Max's arm behind his back. He lifted him slighted from the couch so he could speak.

"Tell her," he said. His voice was venomous and his eyes held pure hatred.

It was obvious Max was in excruciating pain. "It was a set up!" he screamed. "It was all a set up. She paid me to be a matchmaker and then make you fall for me. I'm supposed to marry you. Get access to your money and then give her a cut."

Sheila stood there in horror. There had to be a logical explanation for all of this. She didn't like seeing Max in agony. She wanted DaQuan to let him up, but she needed more details. "No, that can't be true. Who is she? Who would do such a thing?"

Max looked like he wanted to cry. DaQuan twisted his arm some more "Tell her before I snap your arm in two!"

"Viviaaaan! It was Viviaaaaaaan! Don't break my arm. Please!" screamed Max.

Sheila walked over to them. "Let him up."

DaQuan released his grip and pushed him on the coach. Max closed his eyes and lay on his side as if he were trying to block the two of them out.

"Tell me everything now or I'll let DaQuan beat you until you're in a coma."

Max opened his eyes, sat up, and breathed a sigh of relief. He rubbed his arm in the place where DaQuan once had his hand. "Vivian is one of my clients. I'm a professional escort, if you will. We've been sleeping together on and off for years. She called me a few months ago and said that she had a plan that would give us both a big payday if I had some acting skills. She told me about your inheritance and how you had to find a husband in order to get it. This entire thing was her idea. I was supposed to send you on a couple of crappy dates with a couple of fellow escorts and then present myself as an option. I'm sorry, Sheila. I know what I did was wrong, but you gotta believe me when I say I fell for you, too. I didn't expect for you to be so beautiful and wonderful. Every compliment, every kiss, every touch, it was all sincere."

DaQuan hit him in the face.

Max grabbed his jaw. "Ooooooooow!"

"You still lying, punk. I went to see your baby's mama. I saw that rock on her finger. She went on and on about how you got some new job making lots of money and you were a changed man. Y'all still live together. That new baby y'all had together ain't even a year old yet. How you gon' have a whole family and be sleeping with other women for money?" said DaQuan.

Sheila was in disbelief. This was too much. Why would someone do something so deceitful? She had never done anything to either of them. "Vivian put you up to this? You're engaged? You have a baby? You're a prostitute?" Her eyes began to tear up, but she refused to cry.

"That was before I met you. I had every intention of breaking it off so we could be together. I haven't seen any clients since we became serious. You gotta believe me. Everything I said is true. I want you, me and Xavier to be a family," said Max.

"How much is she paying you?" asked Sheila.

Max looked down. "It's not about the money. I really care about you. I can see a future with you. I want a future with you. I've been trying to figure out how to tell Vivian our deal was off. The last thing I want to do is hurt you."

It was all beginning to make sense now. No wonder Max was so perfect. He had been coached on what to do and what to say.

"How much!" screamed Sheila.

"Ten thousand dollars, initially, to help me pay for all the things I needed to look the part of a man that you would want. I was supposed to funnel some money to her once we got married and you began to trust me with your finances. Once her company was in the clear, I would also get a lucrative stake in that as well."

Sheila continued to try to choke back the tears. She had a lump in her throat the size of a lemon. She was actually about to break her vow of celibacy for this man because she thought they had something special, when the entire time he was just trying to get his hands on her money and to think that her best friend Vivian orchestrated in all. She was a fool. Before she knew it, she had balled up her fist and hit him in the face with all her might. Max's body bounce back on the couch with such force he came forward and hit the floor face first. He was knocked out cold.

"Good shot, baby. I'm impressed," said DaQuan.

"Thanks," said Sheila, before crumpling into a ball of tears.

DaQuan caught her as she descended to the floor. "I got you, woman, in every way. You don't need him. If you need someone to love you, you don't have to look any further than the man in front of you. I'll be whatever you need."

A flood of tears cascaded down her face. How did she let this happen? "DaQuan, I feel like such a fool. I should have known he was too good to be true. How did you find out?"

"I knew that I knew him from somewhere, but I just couldn't remember where. Then, yesterday when I was washing my car, I remembered that I met him years ago. His baby mama used to date my cousin, Peanut. She's his baby mama, too. He was always complaining about how he didn't want a man like my brother, meaning hood, around his kid. This dude ain't no good. Peanut had to go over there a couple of times and have a talk with him when he tried to include his son into a couple of his schemes. He's always been a liar and a hustler. He's just better dressed and more refined now. He also used to have dreads and a beard. That's why I didn't recognize him. He definitely ain't no one that you or Xavier need in your lives. Max ain't even his real name."

She looked up and noticed that today DaQuan was wearing a Batman T-shirt. She planted a sweet kiss on his cheek. "When did you become such a super hero? It seems like you're always there to save the day."

"That's what a man in love does for his family. Look Sheila, I'll never be one of those rich dudes with good table manners you grew up with, but I have grown up. It was selfish of me not to try to expand my horizons and go to plays, operas, museums, and fancy dinners with you. I was so afraid you'd damage my street credibility. I was the fool. I let the best thing that ever happened to me get away. You don't have to make a decision today, but consider giving us another chance."

Max moaned, making both of them turn in his direction. He appeared to be coming to.

"I'll give it some thought, but in the meantime we need to get the police over her before this liar wakes up. I can't believe Vivian would do something like this. She actually thought she was going to get her hands on my money. She's supposed to be my friend. If she needed a loan all she had to do was ask."

"I told you I never liked her. You need me to handle her, too."

Sheila laughed. "Naw, she's all mine. Wait a minute. How did you get here?"

"I took a plane."

"What? I thought you were afraid to fly."

"I was, but I needed to get here before you did something crazy like marry Max." He looked Sheila up and down. If circumstances were different and she was wearing that form-fitting teddy, DaQuan wouldn't have been able to control herself.

"Did you two—"

Shelia suddenly felt self-conscious. She was so upset she forgot she was standing there in he-gon'-get-it-tonight attire. "No, but we were going to. You interrupted that. DaQuan, you are still the only man I've been with."

"If I have it my way, it will stay that way. You look hot! I want to marry you, woman."

Sheila didn't know how to respond. For the past few months, she had been falling in love with another man who turned out to be an imposter. "I better go change before the police get here," was all she could say for now but she would definitely give some thought to the rest.

"Yeah, probably, but before you do—" DaQuan kissed her. Sheila didn't pull away nor did she stop him when his hands began to roam across her ample behind. The sensual motion of his tongue coupled with the caresses of his hands ignited a small flame inside her. A soft moan escaped her lips indicating the passion he was provoking. When the kiss ended, Sheila nestled her head in his shoulder and let out a deep breath. He was right. She still loved this man. Everything she was looking for was always right in front of her: a husband, provider, protector and live-in father for her child. Most importantly, it felt right. She couldn't deny that her heart still belonged to her child's father. Max had been a pleasant distraction.

"I want my family, Sheila," whispered DaQuan.

She didn't have to think long. "Okay," said Sheila and then kissed DaQuan as if she never wanted him to leave her side again.

Chapter Sixty-One

Regina

Regina ran through the house looking for her sister. She needed someone to talk to and Regina was out of town. How in the world could Chance fire his girlfriend? Leslie's rental car was outside, but she was not in her room, the kitchen, the study, or the den where she normally watched television. She looked out the window and noticed that the light in the barn was on. Her sister was probably getting busy, but she didn't care. Regina was curious to know who she was with anyway. She had been spending a lot of time away lately and very secretive about where she'd been. Besides, she really needed her sister. She called Sheila twice, but she didn't answer and neither did Aunt Teresa.

Regina tried to be as quiet as she could going up the wooden stairs, but the creaking sound didn't compare to the noise her sister and her lover were making. Leslie was screaming at the top of her lungs like he was killing her and he was grunting like a madman. She began to reconsider her plan to interrupt. This obviously wasn't a good time. But, who was this mystery man sneaking around with her sister? Why didn't she bring him in the house? Grandma Grace was gone and they could have any room inside the mansion they wanted. Curiosity about who her sister was with got the best of her. Regina decided to creep up to the top of the stairs and get a quick peek before she went back to her room and tried to call Sheila or Aunt Teresa again. She had to talk to someone.

The glow from the lamp on the desk was bright so Regina would have no problem seeing. She giggled a little at the naughty thing she was about to do. They probably wouldn't even realize she was there. She heard her sister say, "Tell me I'm the best you've ever had!"

"Baby, you're the best I've ever had. I wasted all that time on the wrong woman. I'm gonna marry you, girl!"

Regina froze. That voice! She would know it anywhere, but it couldn't be. She no longer felt the need to peer over the steps and hide herself. Regina boldly mounted the top step and stood in full view of Leslie and Antonio as they were entangled on the bed as naked as the day they were born and engulfed in the throes of passion. They both looked like they were in sexual bliss. Regina screamed in emotional agony. Leslie turned toward her. If shame were a color, it would have been instantaneously painted all over her face.

"Oh my, God, Gina!" she said and tried to push Antonio away. He was in the middle of his climax and couldn't move, but when he opened his eyes and saw Regina standing there, he smiled. He was enjoying her pain. No one walked out on him. He told her she was in for a surprise. This shocking revelation was better than anything he could have planned.

Regina couldn't breathe. She had to leave. The sight was sucking the air from her lungs while burning a hole in her chest and upsetting her stomach. She turned around and ran down the steps. All that time Antonio had been cheating on her, she never would have suspected that one of his lovers was her own sister.

Chapter Sixty-Two

Sheila

DaQuan called the police while Shelia changed clothes. When they arrived, Max was conscious and sitting on the couch with DaQuan standing in front of him, daring him to try to escape. He was going to bash his head in if he did. The police arrested Max and he was charged with criminal impersonation.

Sheila found out Max's real name was Stacey Leaks and he had been arrested a couple of times for prostitution and theft. He even had an extortion case against him at one point. He tried to get money out of one of his clients in exchange for not telling her husband. The case was thrown out of court for lack of evidence. He confessed to his role in Vivian's plan and agreed to cooperate with police. He told them how Vivian gave him personal details about Sheila that were guaranteed to impress her. He even told them that the night Sheila thought she was drunk he put a drug in her drink. The plan was to take her home and have unprotected sex with her in hopes of getting her pregnant to help him convince her to marry him quickly. The Florida authorities contacted the Memphis Police Department and Vivian was arrested. Shelia called her Aunt Teresa and told her what happened. Teresa made sure she conducted the interrogation and investigation herself. Vivian wasn't going to get off easy for this one.

Vivian's motive was extreme debt. Her husband had a severe gambling habit and they were in danger of losing everything they owned, including their businesses. The picture perfect marriage Sheila thought they had wasn't so perfect after all.

After receiving a frantic call from Regina, Sheila and DaQuan packed up and drove back home the next morning. Regina was at Chance's house. Their silly fight no longer mattered. After fleeing the barn, she ran straight to the comfort of her man's arms.

During the drive, Sheila called Leslie to find out exactly what was going on. Leslie informed her that she and Antonio had been sleeping together for over a year. Not only that, but the two of them were now dating and she fully intended to marry him. It was a business arrangement to get her money. Leslie was sorry that she hurt her sister, but she had to look after herself because no one else was going to do it. She knew Regina was devastated, but the good thing was that Regina and Antonio were over and she had Chance to help her pick up the pieces. She also went on to say how Antonio was a changed man and he treated her pretty good, so nobody needed to worry about him hitting her. She hoped they could all get past what she'd done.

Sheila couldn't believe what she was hearing and hung up the phone in Leslie's face after giving her a piece of her mind. Deception and manipulation seemed to be the popular way to get what you wanted. She expected that from Antonio, but not Leslie. They were family. That girl was a lost cause and wasn't worth the breath she used trying to make her understand how what she was doing was causing irreparable damage to her family. She didn't care. First, Max and now Leslie and

Antonio. The entire world was full of selfish liars and cheaters who didn't care who they hurt. Sheila wished Grandma Grace were alive to put her in her place. She was the only person who could put a leash on that wild child.

DaQuan dropped her off at Chance's house and went to go check on Xaveier at his mother's house. Chance led Leslie to his den where Regina sat looking forlorn and dejected. DaQuan leftAs soon as she saw Sheila, she grabbed her in an embrace and cried like a child who had just been whipped with a switch. Those tears were in addition to the hundreds she had already shed.

When she was able to speak, she said, "How could they? I thought they loved me? I always knew Antonio was a dog, but Leslie?"

"Leslie is a misguided whore. She's been one for years. She doesn't care about anyone, but herself. I imagine all the deaths in our family did it to her. She was the youngest and the least able to cope. Grandma Grace probably should have put her in therapy after Big Daddy died." Sheila rubbed Regina's back in a circular motion. Her cousin's eyes were bloodshot red and had massive bags underneath. Sheila could tell she hadn't had any sleep.

"You didn't know, did you She-She?" Regina hadn't called her that since they were children.

"No, sweetheart. I had no idea. I would never try to hide something like that from you. I know this isn't easy, but you've got to stop all this crying over a no good man. Especially when you've got a good one who loves you. Marry him and get your millions and the two of you can live that amazing life you deserve."

"I don't care about the money anymore, Sheila. If this is what money does to people I don't want any of it."

"Now you're talking nonsense. This isn't just money. This is our inheritance. This is money our family worked hard for so they could leave a legacy. They wanted us to have it. You and Chance can have a wonderful life and if not for you, accept this money for your unborn children. You and generations to come can be set for life," said Sheila.

"You're right, but I keep thinking of what I need to do to get them back. I can't let them get away with treating me like this. I heard him say he was going to marry her. How am I supposed to love two people who have broken my heart into a million pieces? I've never felt so betrayed in all my life."

"Vengeance belongs to God. The reason he says give it to Him is because people who seek revenge end up making their lives about others. Hate takes residence in their heart and they're no longer about enjoying this wonderful gift of joy we've been given. You'll get through this by clinging to the people who love you and would never hurt you. Whenever you need me I'm a phone call away."

Regina squeezed Sheila tighter. She now understood when her Aunt Teresa said they were all each other had. She would have loved to be able to run to her parents, Big Daddy or Grandma Grace, but they were no longer around. She was extremely grateful for Sheila and the bond they shared.

"Thank you, Sheila. I love you."

"I love you, too."

Sheila and Regina sat in silence for a good part of the evening with Sheila rocking her like a child. Words weren't really needed at that moment. All Regina needed was the presence of people who loved her. Eventually, she fell asleep. Sheila closed her eyes and prayed for Regina and then she prayed for Leslie. She had never wished bad things on anyone in her life, but she asked the Lord to deliver swift justice and allow Leslie, Antonio, Vivian and Max to get everything they deserved and a whole lot more.

"Avenge us, oh Lord. Keep hatred out of our hearts because I don't want anyone or anything to obstruct our joy, but please avenge us. Such behavior does not deserve to go unpunished. Feel free to let them burn in hell. Amen."

Chapter Sixty-Three

Regina

Regina had no intentions of ever going back to the mansion or speaking to her sister again. She was heartbroken in the worst way, but Chance was there for her day and night. It was a good thing he fired her because she was in no shape to work. She didn't do much of anything. She couldn't eat. She couldn't sleep. All she did was cry. Leslie tried to contact her several times, but she refused to speak to her. She deleted her texts without reading them and never sent a response. As far as she was concerned, she was now an only child.

Chance didn't even seem to mind that some of her tears were over another man. He said he understood. He held her, he rocked her, he urged her to eat. He let her stay at his house as long as she needed. Regina considered going to Sheila's house but didn't after she found out that she and DaQuan were back together. She didn't want to intrude. She had always liked DaQuan and wanted to give them as much privacy as possible. Teresa said she could stay with her and her husband as well, but Regina knew she needed to be near Chance. Some days he was the only thing that made her feel better.

Chance prayed for her incessantly. He also asked God to give him the strength to be the rock that she needed. He hated seeing the love of his life so distraught. He started working half-days at the shop so he could be there for her. Some days he went in early. Others he went in late. This particular day he decided to go in early. Before he left, he went to check on Regina. She appeared to be sleeping soundly. She looked almost angelic to him. Her soft brown hair was spread over her pillow. She looked so peaceful. He was patiently waiting for the day when they could return to the way things used to be before their joy was interrupted by the pain of betrayal. She always seemed so sad. He kissed her on the forehead and left. He was halfway to the shop when he realized that he left his wallet and returned to the house.

He entered through the garage door and had an uneasy feeling that something wasn't right. The house was cold and it was warm when he left. He noticed that the glass patio door leading to the pool was wide open. He hadn't been out there and as far has he knew, Regina was still in bed. He went to go close the door and noticed a large mass floating in the pool. He moved closer to investigate and realized that it was Regina face down.

His heart was racing as he ran to the pool and dived in. He hoped he wasn't too late as he swam toward her, grabbed her body and flipped her over. Evidently, Regina hadn't been in the pool long because she was very much alive and began coughing up water.

"Let…me…go," she said and coughed some more. "I…have…nothing…to live…for." He pulled her out of the water and hit her several times on the back to aid her in coughing up more water. When she was better, he brought her in the house. He stripped off her wet clothes and wrapped her in a blanket. He suggested that she go to a mental health facility and talk to someone, but she refused to go. He knew that her care was now beyond what he and her family could do. She needed to be under the watch of a professional.

"Why would you do that?" he said.

Regina sniffed. "I'm trying to end my pain. It's like someone took a knife and stabbed me in my heart, twisted it and left it there so I could slowly bleed to death. I don't want to live like this."

"What do you mean? You have plenty of reasons to live. You have me. Regina, I love you. I want to marry you. I was just trying to give you time to deal with this."

She looked at him with her doe-like eyes. "You want to marry me? As messed up as I am. Look at my family. Why?"

"Yes, I do. More than I've wanted anyone in my entire life. All of you, messed up family and all. I can't think of nothing better than to give you my last name and share my home with you permanently. You've already got my heart."

"Then, ask me."

Chance was confused. "Ask you what?"

"Ask me to marry you."

"Now?"

Regina smiled. "Yes, now." She held out her left hand.

This wasn't how he envisioned his proposal. He planned on a nice dinner under romantic candlelight with soft music when she was in a happier place. Her being naked and wrapped in a blanket after a suicide attempt wasn't his idea of romance, but he would do anything for this woman.

Chance got down on one knee and held her left hand in his. "Regina, will you do me honor of being my wife? Will you allow me to wake up next to you each day and make love to you each night? I want our babies to have your smile and gorgeous eyes. I want you to take me shopping and throw out my old clothes. I want you to—"

Regina kissed him. "Enough! Yes, I'll marry you. I'm sorry I tried to leave you and thank you for showing me that I do have something to live for. I love you, too."

"Don't ever do that again."

"Okay, I promise. You know you have to get me a ring, right?"

Chance began laughing. Regina was going to be fine, but he wasn't going in to the shop today. He was staying there with his girlfriend to make sure she understood that he was willing to do whatever it took to make everything all right.

Chapter Sixty-Four

Wedding Bells Are Ringing

Weeks passed and it was now November. Love was thick within the air for the Purdue women, but so was hatred. Since the day they found out about Leslie and Antonio's betrayal, neither Regina nor Shelia had set foot back in Grandma Grace's house. Especially, after they heard that Antonio had moved in. They paid Ms. Pearl to pack up all Regina's personal items and sent a courier over to retrieve them. Leslie called and texted them both repeatedly, but they refused to answer or respond.

Leslie and Antonio were planning a grand Christmas Eve wedding. The two attention whores planned to flaunt their so-called love for all to see in front of more than three hundred guests. They even worked out a lucrative deal with a reality show production company to film it and pictures had already been shopped around to several publications to bring in additional money. They had already received a sizeable deposit, which they spent. They would receive the balance once the show aired.

Both Regina and Sheila received a wedding invitation, but neither of them bothered to respond. Nor did Sheila and Regina invite Leslie to theirs. Sheila and DaQuan opted to go to the justice of the peace the day before Thanksgiving. They already had a family and saw no need for a fancy wedding. They had wasted too many years apart from each other and wanted to be together as man and wife as soon as possible. The decision to wait until they were married to consummate their union made them want to hurry things along as well. The nuptials were performed in Judge Martin Blackwell's quarters with Regina, Aunt Teresa, Chance and Xavier present. Sheila wore a simple, but elegant white, lace, mermaid dress and a veil. She even wore Grandma Grace's pearl necklace and her mother's earrings. DaQuan wore the same charcoal suit he wore to his grandmother's birthday party with an ivory tie and handkerchief. Sheila thought he looked better in it now than he did then. They were going to make Regina's wedding a part of their honeymoon.

Chance and Regina opted for a destination wedding. They wanted to be away from prying eyes and gossip. Unlike Leslie, Regina wanted a simple ceremony on the white beaches of Jamaica. Only about thirty people, mostly close friends and family attended,, but that was more than enough for the bride and groom. Sheila was the Matron of Honor. Chance's brother, Chadwick, was the best man and Xavier served as the ring bearer. Regina walked down the aisle barefoot in a light blue sundress that stopped just above the knee. White and blue roses with baby's breath adorned her hair. Teresa's husband, Zachery, gave her away. Regina walked down the aisle smiling at the man who vowed to make her forget Antonio ever existed. Since the day she said she would marry him, he had been making good on his promise. Once she shifted her focus off the people who hurt her and onto she and Chance's life together, her happiness returned. She felt so much better. She looked forward to being Mrs. Chandler and birthing little Chandler babies who would have impeccable style and learn how to fix cars just like Chance's father taught him.

Chance wore a linen shirt and slacks and no shoes as well. He looked like the happiest man in the world. A tear slid from his eye as he watched Regina slowly make her way down the aisle and when she reached him and smiled he was overcome with emotion. She was the most beautiful creature he had ever seen and she was all his.

"Excuse me, Pastor," he said. "This may be breaking tradition but I can't help myself." Chance then pulled her to him and kissed Regina passionately as the guests and the pastor hired to perform the ceremony erupted in laughter. When he finished, Regina could hardly stop laughing herself. "I love you, woman."

"I love you too," she said between giggles.

Regina hoped he never stopped being impulsive when it came to their love or lost his desire for her. He was a good man and she was one blessed woman. She had a surprise for him, though. Chance still had no idea she would become a multi-millionaire once they were married. After dealing with Antonio, she wanted to make sure that Chance's love for her was pure. He assumed she had money because she was a Purdue, but he had no idea how much. Regina never told him. When he found out she wasn't the maid's daughter, he and asked why she couldn't afford to pay for the repairs on her car. She simply told him that her Grandmother's money was tied up in court and it could take years to settle the matter. He assured her that he had plenty of money and they would both be fine. They were going to be more than fine and part of her wedding gift to her new husband was a massive contribution to the expansion of his business.

Chapter Sixty-Five

Leslie

Leslie was miserable without her cousin and sister. She never really had girlfriends. Most of her so-called friends hung with her because she was a Purdue. She tried to replace them with Audrey and Karen, but it wasn't the same. All they wanted to do was party and shop. Having a steady boyfriend for the first time in years was cool, but she and Antonio were moving so fast. He moved in the mansion two weeks after Regina moved out. Being able to make love without having to sneak around was nice, but Antonio had a lot of character flaws that she never noticed before. He was moody, rude, and messy.

She also found the tattoo of Regina's name on his chest more disturbing than ever. She made him wear a shirt at all times. The only place he could be without one was the shower and she refused to take one with him until it was removed or covered up. By the third week in the house, he had a crucifix and flowers tattooed over it. That helped, but Regina knew that under all that artistry was her older sister's name. To make matters worse, he proposed to her with the same ring he gave Regina. When she told him that was inappropriate, he said he didn't see anything wrong with it. Leslie refused to wear it. Instead, she wore her mother's wedding ring. She found it in her grandmother's jewelry box after she died.

They were now the talk of the town. Everyone seemed to know what they had done and when she and Antonio tried to go to events like normal couples, she saw people whispering about them. Regina's friends gave her the evil eye. Soon the party girl no longer wanted to party. She spent a lot of time at home, but so did Antonio. He had no plans of getting a job since he was marrying a Purdue. She tried to tell him that was her money and he would still have to work, but he laughed and said the only person that he was going to work for was himself. He wanted them to open up their own financial services firm. Since they weren't married yet Regina hadn't received a dime, but somehow Antonio had already gone out and purchased a new Corvette. On top of that, he was a slob. She tried to make him understand that Ms. Pearl came and cleaned because she wanted to not because she had to and he was abusing her kindness by being so nasty. He didn't care. He told her to hire someone.

Leslie was sure she liked Antonio a lot, but she was not fond of his obsession with her family's money. The only problem was if she didn't marry him she wouldn't get any of it. She was in quite a predicament and she had no one to talk to about it since Regina and Sheila had basically disowned her.

She never meant to hurt her sister, but since Regina didn't want Antonio, why couldn't she have him? In a few weeks, hundreds of people would be all over the grounds of the mansion for a winter wonderland wedding that she had paid for by maxing out her dead grandmother's credit cards. She figured they hadn't realized she was dead since they were still sending bills to the house.

Leslie had no one to turn to other than Aunt Teresa. She still had to approve her marriage so she could get her money. "I might as well get this over with," she said and made the call. She wasn't looking forward to this meeting at all.

An hour later, Leslie and her aunt sat in a coffee shop. Teresa listened while sipping her latte. When Leslie finished updating her on her recent activities and explaining her side of what happened between her and Antonio, Teresa told her exactly what she thought.

"I'm not much for judging others, but you done messed up. I advise you not to marry this young man. It sounds to me like he only wants you for your money. Not to mention the fact that you are missing all the ingredients that make a good marriage."

"What are those things? I'm sure we have some of them," said Leslie.

"Love, honesty, trust, selflessness. The desire to make the other person happy and the willingness to do those things. Marriage isn't about you. Marriage is about loving someone so much that one of your greatest joys is to be good to them. I haven't heard you say one thing about what Antonio sows into your life other than good sex. It sounds like all he does is take.

"I'm only supposed to approve marriages where love is involved. However, if this is the bed you want to lie in I'm going to let you. I hope you know what you're doing. I fear you're going to learn the hard way that money can't buy happiness. You're even willing to lose the only immediate family you have left to get it. I must say that I'm disappointed in you, Leslie. I expected more, but I wish you two the best."

"Thank you, Aunt Teresa. At this point, my inheritance and Antonio are the only things I have."

"No, baby. You have me. If you stop this now, you can salvage what's left of your dignity and self-respect and probably your family."

Leslie laughed. "What good are those things if I'm broke?"

Teresa shook her head. "I'm praying for you, girl."

Chapter Sixty-Six

Sheila

Sheila and DaQuan stood in the bathroom looking at one another. After a wonderful honeymoon in Jamaica, they were settling nicely into married life.

"What does it say?" he asked. Today he was wearing an Incredible Hulk T-shirt.

"I can't look. I'm scared. You look."

"Okay, but I'm not touching it because you peed on it."

Sheila hit him in the chest. "Shut up and look."

DaQuan moved closer to the white stick sitting on the vanity and said, "Aww, man. Babe, I'm sorry to have to tell you—" He picked Sheila up and spun her around. "My baby is gonna have another one of my babies! He set her down then bent down and kissed her stomach.

"Oh God, thank you! And thank Grandma Grace for knowing what I needed when I didn't," she said.

"Amen to that," said DaQuan. "I love you, Mrs. Reynolds."

"I love you, too, Mr. Reynolds."

Xavier burst into the bathroom. "Mommy and Daddy, what are you doing? I heard you screaming."

"We're just talking, baby, are you okay?" said Shelia.

"Yes, ma'am. I'm great. I like being a family."

DaQuan kissed his son and then kissed his mother. "I do, too, son. And guess what? We're going to be an even bigger family because you're getting a little brother or sister."

"Yay!" Xavier shouted and began doing a little dance around the bathroom. They all laughed.

Sheila no longer cared about revenge. She was just happy that Vivian and Max were no longer in her life. A trial had been set for them and she was confident that justice would prevail. What a mighty God she served. His plan was much better than the one she tried to put in place for herself.

Chapter Sixty-Seven

Regina

It was Christmas Eve and the day of Leslie's wedding. Regina had a sick feeling in the pit of her stomach. It had been there all day. Her sister and her ex-boyfriend were about to get married. She spent the last two months hating them both. It was time to let it go, but she didn't know how. She drove to the cemetery where the family crypt was housed. Her grandparents, her parents, and Shelia's parents were all there as well as several other family members that had gone before them. It was unseasonably warm for December, but still cold inside the stone structure. She sat in the middle of the floor and had a long talk with her ancestors. She told them how much she missed them and how hard it had been for her without them. She told them about Chance and how good life was with him. She told how Sheila and DaQuan got back together and she had never seen her cousin so radiant as she was on her wedding day. She cried while sharing how her sister and Antonio had broken her heart, but it was Chance who helped her put the pieces back together and start a new life that didn't feel empty without them in it. Regina allowed her tears to help purge her of hatred. She wanted to get it all out. Those would be the last tears she shed over the pain Leslie and Antonio caused her. When Regina left the cemetery, she felt better and lighter because the heaviness in her heart was gone. She pulled out her cell phone and sent her sister a one-word message: Congratulations!

Chapter Sixty-Eight

Leslie

Leslie looked at the sea of guests at her wedding. This wedding was going to be the talk of the town for years to come. She and Antonio made sure the guest list was full of the who's who in the city. The reality show film crew was there. She knew that most of the people there came to be nosey and hoped to be on television, but she didn't care. This union was the type of scandal everyone loved. Leslie and Antonio were truly cut from the same cloth and they were going to make as much money together as they possibly could.

Leslie stood at the end of a red velvet aisle waiting to walk down and stand beside her husband-to-be. There were no groomsmen and no bridesmaids. The two people she would want in her wedding refused to speak to her so she opted to have no one. Her dress looked like a costume out of a Disney movie. It was white with a long flared skirt. Mink fur lined the collar, sleeves, and the hem. Sequins and jewels were sewn into the fabric so that she sparkled at every turn. Her hair was swept up to accentuate her long neck and atop her head set a crown with diamonds, rubies, sapphires and other jewels. She was magically breathtaking. Antonio stood giddily next to Bishop Proctor looking like a little kid who was about to get permission to open his Christmas presents early. He looked handsome in a black tuxedo with tails and a red bow tie. Everyone stood as a full orchestra played the wedding song and Leslie made her way down the aisle. Once she reached the two of them, Bishop began speaking.

"Dearly beloved, we are gathered her today…"

"Excuse me, Bishop, I hate to interrupt this ceremony, but the bride and groom are under arrest," said the booming voice behind them.

All of the guests collectively gasped.

"I'm Detective Johnson. Regina Watson-Purdue and Antonio Dockers you are both under arrest for identity theft and forgery. We received an anonymous tip that you two were both using the deceased Grace Purdue's credit cards to make purchases. Corvettes, this wedding, your honeymoon. You guys had a ball, didn't you?"

Antonio looked like someone let the air out of his balloon. "Detective, can we please do this after the ceremony? I'm getting married. If we're going to go to jail, let us go as husband and wife. I love this woman and don't want to wait another day to marry her. It's Christmas and marrying her would be the best present a man could dream of."

The officer was not moved. "No can do. You are both going to jail single. Maybe if you can make bail you can go to the courthouse, but I doubt it. It's the holidays and the courts are shut down. Officers take them away."

"You can't do this!" screamed Leslie. "I'm a Purdue. Do you know who my grandmother was? She made a sizable donation to the force every year. I'm going to sue your entire police department. This is a violation of my civil rights. I demand that you let me get married!"

The detective laughed and then nodded at the officers standing behind him. Two uniformed officers put handcuffs on them both and read them their Miranda

Rights. It was all caught on film, courtesy of the reality show TV crew.

The detective was right. They couldn't get a bond hearing until after the holidays. Leslie was finally seen by a judge on January 5. Her bond was set at $500,000 because the courts thought she was a flight risk. She had no money and sat in jail another ten days before someone came to her rescue. When she was released, she took a cab to the mansion and attempted to enter the gates. Armed security informed her that Sheila had gone to court to have her banned from the property lest she tried to sell items in the house for cash. Her things had been placed in storage. He gave her the address and a key to the storage unit. She was now not only broke, but homeless, too.

Leslie tried to call Antonio, but his phone was disconnected and she had no idea where he was. She hadn't heard from him since they were arrested. Leslie had never felt so alone in her life. She got back in her cab and instead of going to get her things, she went to the crypt where her family was buried. It was January and it felt like it. It was thirty degrees outside, but the icy wind made it feel more like twenty. The crypt's concrete floor was cold and hard, but she didn't care. As far as she was concerned, she was the walking dead and the cemetery was exactly where she belonged. Leslie missed her parents and grandparents so much. While in jail, with no one to come save her, she realized the magnitude of what she'd done. When she needed her family the most they were nowhere around, but she couldn't blame them. She had done this to herself with selfish greed. She had no idea what to do next so she laid there and wept until she fell asleep.

Leslie awoke to find Aunt Teresa standing over her. Her fingers and toes were frozen and she couldn't feel her face.

"Get up, girl, before you die of hypothermia. No use crying over spilled milk. Come on, let's get you home and cleaned up. Then we can figure out what to do with the rest of your life."

"Home? What home? Haven't you heard? I've been kicked out of the mansion. I'm homeless."

"Mine, girl. I have a room all fixed up for you. Grace would never forgive me if I left you out in the cold. She'd probably come back to haunt me. That woman loved you more than you'll ever know. She just wanted you to get yourself together and become the kind of woman she raised you to be. Somehow, you started to believe that what's between your legs is more valuable than what's between your ears. I'm gon' put you on the right path if it's the last thing I do. Now, get up!"

Leslie picked herself up off the concrete floor and followed Teresa to her car.

"Aunt Teresa, have you heard from Antonio? Technically, I am still his fiancée and would like to reach out to him," she said.

"Yeah, some rich old woman from out of state posted his bond. He came by the mansion, got his stuff, and left town with her. Bastard didn't even try to get you out of jail. So much for loyalty."

"That sounds like something he would do. Thanks for bailing me out."

"I didn't bail you out. I let you stay there so you wouldn't get yourself in more trouble by marrying that bastard. No amount of money is worth that."

"If you didn't bail me out, then who did?"

"He did." Teresa nodded her head toward the black SUV that was sitting in front of her aunt's white Lexus. Standing next to the car, in a leather trench coat lined with lamb's wool and dark sunglasses, was a man who looked like….but it couldn't be.

He opened his arms and said, "Hey, baby. Remember me?"

"Thaddeus!" Leslie ran to him, jumped up, and wrapped her legs around him. She squeezed him with all her might. She had to make sure it was him. It felt like him. She planted kisses all over his face and neck. She had never been happier to see anyone in her entire life.

When she was satisfied that it was him she said, "But how?"

"I told you, baby. Ain't but one quick way out the dope game and that's death. I faked my own death so I could give you the life you wanted. I didn't know you'd find a replacement for me so soon though," T-Money said, looking at her angrily.

"Thaddeus, that was about survival. I was trying to get my money. He didn't mean anything to me. I want you! Please forgive me. He ain't got nothing on you. You faked your death for me? That's so romantic!" They both laughed.

"I did it for us. People would have tried to use you to hurt me and I couldn't let anything happen to you. So I did what I thought needed to be done. You still got the code to my safe?"

Leslie looked confused for a moment and then remembered the cryptic text he sent the day he supposedly died. "Yeah. It's in my phone. Why did you send it to me if you were still alive?"

"Because I was afraid I'd forget it. I had to destroy my phone and computer and leave town quickly. I've been in the islands biding my time and waiting for the right moment to come get my girl. I got millions in that safe, baby. You don't need your grandmother's money. We're going to be fine."

Leslie kissed him again. "This is so hard to believe. If you're not dead then who did your family bury?"

T-Money laughed. "I dunno. Whoever the mortician I paid decided to bury. Money can get you a lot of things, even a corpse."

"I see. I've got a couple more questions. What about Chareese and the baby?

"That baby ain't mine. I never went raw in that chick. She was bangin' Slick, too, and thought I didn't know. As soon as I was buried, and she found out my family didn't have any money, she told him the baby was his. He'll take care of it along with the other five kids he got." T-Money laughed again.

"So that was you who saved my life at the house?"

"Yup. A couple of my street soldiers thought they were going to come in my home, steal my things and abuse my girl. Naw, I wasn't having it. After I knew you were safe, I left the city, but I'm back now. You ready to get out of here? This place ain't been good to you. Let me take you away and we can start over."

"Why not? Everybody here hates me anyway."

"Not everybody. Your Aunt Teresa over there seems to think pretty highly of you." He opened the door of the truck for Leslie to get in.

"Wait." Leslie ran to Aunt Teresa and gave her a hug. Teresa hugged her tight and kissed her forehead.

"Aunt Teresa, you knew?"

"No, but Thad came to me after you got locked up and he couldn't find you. I've known him since he was a skinny teenager. I busted him for selling weed in school. No matter how hard I tried I never could get him to get out those streets…until now."

"Oh, thank you, Aunt Teresa! You have literally changed my life."

Teresa usually wore a steel exterior, but somehow this wild child pulled at her heart. That's why she made sure that Leslie was arrested before she could marry Antonio. When he was released, she threatened to make his life miserable the rest of his days if he didn't cease all contact with her niece and leave town. Antonio was smart enough to know not to mess with a mad cop and reunited with the rich client he stole the ring from; he had no problem being her boy toy if it kept him safe and rolling in dough.

"I promised my sister I'd look out for you. You're not like the other girls. You crave a different kind of life and I think you and Thad would be good for each other. I'm sure you will be able to work things out with Regina and Shelia in time, but until then, go live your life and be happy. Just call and check in with me every now and then."

"I will. I love you and thank you!"

"I love you, too, but don't thank me. Thank God. He's the one that's kept you in spite of all the wrong you've done. He's a God of second chances. Don't waste yours. Now, go before somebody recognizes Thad and I have to bust a cap in 'em."

"Yes, ma'am!" Leslie said and then got in the car with T-Money to begin their brand new life.

About the Author

After embracing careers as a radio talk show host, marketing and media professional, and voice over artist, Jae Henderson decided to add inspirational author to her roles. She first displayed her witty way with words and keen insight into the human emotion through her inspirational romance trilogy: *Someday*, *Someday, Too*, and *Forever and a Day*. Her other releases are *Things Every Good Woman Should Know, Volume 1 and 2* and *Where Do We Go From Here*, which she co-authored with Mario D. King. Her next book, *Husband Wanted*, was released in June of 2016. Jae's entertaining tales about the astounding power of love and God's ability to care for us in the midst of life's storms have been warmly received by readers.

Jae Henderson is a graduate of The University of Memphis where she earned a BA in Communications and an MA in English. She is the former host and producer of *On Point*, a once popular radio talk show geared toward youth and young adults. Other accomplishments include serving as a contributing writer for the award-winning, syndicated *Tom Joyner Morning Show* as well as co-hosting the blog talk show *Spiritually Speaking*.

Jae is also a successful voice over artist. Her signature voice has been heard in hundreds of commercials for companies such as McDonald's, Regions Bank, and Kroger. She's even done a couple of cartoons. Jae also uses her oratory skills as an engaging effective speaker, who enjoys motivating others to live their best life. When Jae isn't writing, speaking, or volunteering, she works as a public relations/media specialist. She currently resides in her hometown of Memphis, TN.

Stay Connected

Websites

www.jaehendersonauthor.com
www.imagoodwoman.com

Facebook Fan Page
www.facebook.com/imagoodwoman

Twitter
www.twitter.com/jae_henderson

YouTube
www.youtube.com/jaehenderson

Instagram
www.instagram.com/jaehendersonauthor

Email
Imagoodwoman2@yahoo.com

Book Clubs
For book club discussion questions visit, www.jaehendersonauthor.com

If you enjoyed this book, please leave a review on the Amazon.com, Barnesandnoble.com or Goodreads.com.

Made in the USA
Columbia, SC
22 March 2025